CLASSIC WEL
SHORT STORIES

CLASSIC WELSH SHORT STORIES

Selected by

GWYN JONES
and
ISLWYN FFOWC ELIS

Oxford
OXFORD UNIVERSITY PRESS
1992

PR
8966
.E5
C6
1992

Oxford University Press, Walton Street, Oxford OX2 6DP

Oxford New York Toronto
Delhi Bombay Calcutta Madras Karachi
Petaling Jaya Singapore Hong Kong Tokyo
Nairobi Dar es Salaam Cape Town
Melbourne Auckland

and associated companies in
Berlin Ibadan

Oxford is a trade mark of Oxford University Press

Selection and Introduction © Oxford University Press 1971

First published 1971 as Twenty-Five Welsh Short Stories
Reissued with the title Classic Welsh Short Stories *1992*

All rights reserved. No part of this publication may be reproduced, stored in a retrieval system, or transmitted, in any form or by any means, electronic, mechanical, photocopying, recording, or otherwise, without the prior permission of Oxford University Press

This book is sold subject to the condition that it shall not, by way of trade or otherwise, be lent, re-sold, hired out or otherwise circulated without the publisher's prior consent in any form of binding or cover other than that in which it is published and without a similar condition including this condition being imposed on the subsequent purchaser

British Library Cataloguing in Publication Data
Data available
ISBN 0-19-282940-8

Library of Congress Cataloging in Publication Data
Twenty-five Welsh stories.
Classic Welsh short stories / selected by Gwyn Jones and Islwyn Ffowc Elis; with an introduction by Gwyn Jones.
p. cm.
Originally published as: Twenty-five Welsh stories. 1971.
Stories translated from Welsh and originally written in English.
1. Short stories, English—Welsh authors. 2. Short stories, Welsh—Translations into English. 3. Wales—Fiction. I. Jones, Gwyn, 1907– . II. Elis, Islwyn Ffowc. III. Title.
823'.01089429—dc20 PR8966.E5T9 1992 91-30330

Printed in Great Britain by
Biddles Ltd.
Guildford and King's Lynn

Contents

CONCORDIA UNIVERSITY LIBRARY
2811 NE HOLMAN ST.
PORTLAND, OR 97211-6099

Acknowledgements

The editors express thanks to all the authors and translators whose work appears in this volume. They are particularly indebted to the Welsh Arts Council for providing them with seven translations of stories written in the Welsh language. For permission to use copyright material they are grateful to the following:

David Alexander for 'Hangman's Assistant', from *The Welsh Review*, 1946

The publisher and Mrs. W. Elwyn Jones for E. Tegla Davies, 'Samuel Jones's Harvest Thanksgiving' (Cwrdd Diolchgarwch Samuel Jones yr Hendre), from *Y Llwybr Arian* (Hughes a'i Fab, 1934); English translation by Dafydd Jenkins

Rhys Davies for 'Canute', from his *Collected Stories* (Heinemann, 1955)

The editor of *Taliesin* and Islwyn Ffowc Elis for 'Song of a Pole' (Y Polyn), from *Taliesin*, 1967; English translation by the author

Mr. Nicholas Sandys for Caradoc Evans, 'Joseph's House', from *My Neighbours* (Melrose, 1919)

George Ewart Evans for 'Let Dogs Delight', from *Welsh Short Stories* (Penguin, 1941)

Miss Cassandra Williams and David Higham Associates for Margiad Evans, 'A Party for the Nightingale', from *The Welsh Review*, 1948

Sian Evans for 'Davis'

The publisher and David Higham Associates for Geraint Goodwin, 'The White Farm', from *The White Farm* (Cape, 1937)

Richard Hughes for 'A Moment of Time', from *A Moment of Time* (Chatto & Windus, 1926)

The publisher and Bobi Jones for 'The Last Ditch' (Y Ffos Olaf), from *Storïau '70* (Gwasg Gomer, 1969); English translation by Elizabeth Edwards

The publisher and Glyn Jones for 'It's Not by his Beak You Can Judge a Woodcock', from his *Selected Short Stories* (Dent, 1971), © Glyn Jones 1971

Gwyn Jones for 'The Pit', from *The Buttercup Field* (Penmark Press, 1945)

The publisher and Harri Pritchard Jones for 'The Miracle' (Y Wyrth), from *Troeon* (Llyfrau'r Dryw, 1966); English translation by the author

Mrs. Idwal Jones for Idwal Jones, 'China Boy', from *China Boy* (Primavera Press, Los Angeles, Calif., 1936)

The publisher and John Gwilym Jones for 'The Wedding' (Y Briodas), from *Y Goeden Eirin* (Gwasg Gee, 1946); English translation by Islwyn Ffowc Elis

R. Gerallt Jones for 'The Letter' (Y Llythyr), from *Gwared y Gwirion* (Cyhoeddiadau Modern, 1966); English translation by the author

The publisher and Mrs. Alun Lewis for Alun Lewis, 'Ward "O" 3 (b)', from *In the Green Tree* (George Allen & Unwin, 1946)

David Monger for 'The Man Who Lost His Boswell', from *The Welsh Review*, 1948

The publisher and Eigra Lewis Roberts for 'Deprivation' (Y Golled), from *Storïau'r Dydd* (Gwasg Gomer, 1968); English translation by Enid R. Morgan

The publisher and Kate Roberts for 'Cats at an Auction' (Cathod Mewn Ocsiwn), from *Hyn o Fyd* (Gwasg Gee, 1964); English translation by Wyn Griffith

The publisher and the Trustees for the Copyrights of the late Dylan Thomas for Dylan Thomas, 'The Dress', from *The Map of Love* (Dent, 1939)

Gwyn Thomas for 'O Brother Man', from *Gazooka* (Gollancz, 1957)

The publisher for D. J. Williams, 'A Good Year' (Blwyddyn Lwyddiannus), from *Storïau'r Tir Glas* (Gwasg Gomer, 1936); English translation by Wyn Griffith

Mrs. Islwyn Williams for Islwyn Williams, 'Adjudication' (Y Feirniadaeth), from *The Welsh Review*, 1946; English translation by the author

Introduction

This is the fifth anthology of Welsh short stories to appear in the English language, and the first with any real claim to be true to its title or representative of its subject. This is because it is concerned with short-story writing in the two languages used by the people of Wales and their authors, namely Welsh, *Cymraeg* (here offered in translation), and English, *Saesneg*; whereas earlier collections, for a variety of reasons, most of them sound and all of them inescapable, in large measure confined themselves to the work of Welsh writers in English.

The first of them in point of time was the Faber collection of 1937, which in its shortcomings as in its merits faithfully limned what must nowadays be called the then-state of the subject. It had no named editor, and achieved the hits and misses and somewhat haphazard excellence to be expected from the labours of an advisory board. Among the hits can be counted Margiad Evans's short novel and minor classic, *Country Dance,* Dylan Thomas's magnificent 'The Orchards', one of Caradoc Evans's more brilliantly dismaying pieces, 'The Way of the Earth', and a fine story called 'The Conquered', by Dorothy Edwards, whom I remember having seen in the late twenties swanning along a College corridor at Cardiff in a broad-brimmed black hat, grass-green costume, the longest ear-rings this side of Tiger Bay, and a cigarette-holder whose fifteen inches of elephant ivory ensured that you got more of the smoke than the smoker. She was my first visible author, and I beheld her with awe. A year or two later, not at all the enamelled symbol of sophistication my Valley eyes took her to be, she ended a life that had grown intolerable to her on the railway line south of Caerphilly.

It was for this same collection that I wrote my own first short story, 'Shacki Thomas', straight from the heart and the Sirhowy Valley, at the invitation, I suspect, of my Dolgellau-born friend Wyn Griffith, and not uninfluenced in a phrase or two by my Merthyr-born friend Glyn Jones, whose *Blue Bed* that same year was a new wing on the rapidly rising Anglo-Welsh literary movement. This, too, was the only collection of the five to contain a story by our best-known gentlewoman forerunner, Allen Raine, which tempts me to two generalizations. Altogether the volume contained eight stories written by women, and of women in the Welsh short story it may conservatively be said that never since have they had it so good. With a couple of distinguished exceptions in both Welsh and English the genre has tended to be a masculine affair. Also, recalling Allen Raine, who was before my time, Herbert M. Vaughan, whom I know best as a book-collector, and Blanche Devereux whom neither I nor anyone else seems to know at all, one realizes that Welsh writers are rarely seen to advantage in an assured middle-class milieu, or since so few of them belong there, in an assumed middle-class posture. Some of our literary virtues, and no doubt various of our deficiencies, stem from the almost complete absence in Wales over a long period of an artistically creative gentry or an aristocracy inclined to patronage. Both matter and manner in the literature of our two languages have been affected by the incompleteness of our social spectrum. Finally, of the twenty-six stories in this first Faber anthology only four were translations from Welsh, three from the hand of Wyn Griffith, the other undertaken by Dafydd Jenkins. Their authors were Kate Roberts and D. J. Williams, E. Tegla Davies and Richard Hughes Williams.

Next came the Penguin volume of 1940–41 (it was quickly reprinted in wartime, and bibliographical details vary from edition to edition). It seems to me now, as its editor, that it did best with Tegla Davies's unrelenting-God-of-the-Old-Testament-put-that-in-your-black-pipe-and-smoke-it thanksgiving story, which surely could have come from nowhere but Welsh-speaking Wales in the afternoon of its Nonconformity, and with the new talents of George Ewart Evans, Alun Lewis, and A. Edward Richards; but that I chose poorly from Arthur Machen, who already looked decisively of another age, and from Dylan Thomas too. (Though in his case I seem to recall a not untypical entanglement in the tripwires of communication, followed by a scurrying change more respectful of the copyright laws.) Of the sixteen stories four were translations from Welsh, and I think W. J. Gruffydd squared off the quartet because one murky morning I incautiously asked him whether Welsh-speaking Wales had a fourth practitioner as good as Kate Roberts, D. J. Williams, and Tegla, and he assured me that she had. I would certainly have included Margiad Evans if space had run to it, or Gruffydd had not come up with his three aces and a joker.

Space ran to it fifteen years later, in 1956, when I came again to edit a volume of Welsh short stories, in the World's Classics series of the Oxford University Press. Things had moved on since 1937 and 1940–41. In the thirties and forties there had taken place an unprecedented expansion, indeed an explosion, of writing among the English-speaking majority of Welshmen. A mere dozen years saw the first books of Idris Davies, Margiad Evans, Geraint Goodwin, Wyn Griffith, Emyr Humphreys, David Jones, Glyn Jones, Gwyn Jones, Jack Jones, Alun Lewis, Richard Llewellyn, Dylan Thomas, Gwyn Thomas, R. S. Thomas, Vernon Watkins, and the appearance of two literary journals friendly to the new kind of story, *Wales* and the *Welsh Review*. These had been briefly preceded by the first books of Rhys Davies and Richard Hughes, and these in their turn by Arthur Machen, Edward Thomas, W. H. Davies, Caradoc Evans, and Huw Menai. These are not the whole of the story, nor were they all part of the story, but that the twenty-five years from 1930 to 1955 were climacteric for this branch of letters in Wales appears even more obvious now than it did then. Happy the editor who could choose from their riches. What resulted was a volume of twenty-six stories by eighteen authors, of which only four were translations from Welsh, for in that particular the restriction of choice stayed as severe as ever. For the record these authors were Kate Roberts, D. J. Williams, and Islwyn Williams. In all other respects it was a personal selection, not aiming to be safe, sound, and inoffensive, because the Anglo-Welsh short story didn't come to flower because its authors were these things, but because their world was filled with animals and sunshine, fields and sea, girls, leaves, and the smells of summer, the obsessive realities of youth, love, pain, grief, and death. Two world wars, the great Depression, embattled ideologies, industrial strife and social struggle, the decline of Nonconformity and the seedtime of idealism in secondary education, national stirrings and the company of one's kind, the contrast between the womblike warmth of patria, valley, village, and the huge, exciting, and desperate world outside—to be young, and Welsh, and an author was to be born each day over again, and one would not have exchanged this impassioned experience of region, hope, newness, and self-fulfilment for any other concatenation of time, place, and fortune in the world's history.

Maybe too during these prolific decades the Welsh (by which for the moment I unashamedly mean the Anglo-Welsh) short story took on a shape and style that later writers are finding it hard to fight clear of. So many of its practitioners were individuals to their toe-ends, both in style and subject matter, Caradoc Evans (he was still writing), Rhys Davies, Glyn Jones, Alun Lewis, Gwyn Thomas, and Dylan Thomas among them, but a family resemblance is unmistakable: lyrical, humorous, sardonic, genial, sensual, tragical–comical–industrial–pastoral, and all of them men for whom the visible world exists. Even their faults were the faults of life and feeling.

In 1959 Faber re-issued their *Welsh Short Stories* in so radically revised an edition that it must be thought of as a new and separate work. This time it had an editor, and a good one too, George Ewart Evans. Fresh from *Ask the Fellows Who Cut the Hay*, he put a sharp scythe to the tired grass of 1937. Fifteen authors died on a sigh, and of the eleven that kept breathing only six were represented by the same story. Of the twenty-five stories only three are in translation, this time by Kate Roberts, D. J. Williams, and Islwyn Ffowc Elis. The editor's selection took account of the developments and changes in the Anglo-Welsh short story since the early forties; he displayed many new names to his readers, including those of Henry Mansel, William Glynne-Jones, John Wright, and Dilys Rowe; and he wrote a powerful and informative introduction to help his readers see the Welsh short story in the light of old tradition and new history.

But where was the Welsh-language story all this while? The space given to Welsh-language authors in all four anthologies was patently unjust. Not from malice, and not from deliberate neglect. But for lack of opportunity. The number of stories translated from Welsh into English, though heavily outnumbering traffic in the opposite direction, was all too few. Kate Roberts had contributed to the *Welsh Review* as early as March 1939, and to *Life and Letters* a little later, and in 1946 the Penmark Press published twelve of her stories under the title *A Summer Day*. But what was this in an area of Welsh writing where the English reader is at best inadequately catered for or, more often, not catered for at all? It has been a main concern of the present volume to redress, so far as lay in the editors' power, this long-recognized imbalance. Even so, little could have been done without the help of the Welsh Arts Council. As part of its programme of making literature in the Welsh language available to the English-reading public, the Council generously made provision for the translation of some twenty stories, and gave us our choice of them. In the event, and through nobody's fault, our choice was not so wide. Not all our horses could be brought under starter's orders; of those that were not all finished the course; and of those that finished not all were placed. We have therefore settled for fifteen Anglo-Welsh (i.e. English-language) and ten Welsh (i.e. Welsh-language) stories, because this conforms to the realities of the material available to us.

We have also, on a further impulse to justice, set up a small pavilion for our countrymen in exile, and peopled it with Idwal Jones, a Welsh-speaking son of Merioneth who departed by way of cowpunching, journalism, films, and gastronomy, and other exotic trades to California, where he wrote fine stories about the white and yellow aboriginals of those parts. He was a good friend of our Welsh literary journals, and has left a good Welsh thumbprint on page 155 of 'China Boy'. Of the World's Classics volume I said, in its Introduction, that its stories were all by Welshmen and about Welshmen, but quite apart from 'China Boy' that is not the case here. They are all by Welshmen, or Welshwomen, true; but they are about what they are about, and set where they are set. A Welsh soldier-poet in India (Alun Lewis), a Welsh scholar-poet in

Canada (Bobi Jones), a Welsh doctor in Dublin (Harri Pritchard Jones), a Welshwoman in Herefordshire (Margiad Evans was part-Welsh, -English, -Swedish), and another Welsh doctor in Boswell-land (David Monger)—after all, who expects Wales to play all her rugby matches on Cardiff Arms Park?

The literary, as opposed to the personal, relationships of the two groups of Welsh writers have not been without strain and misunderstanding. Writing in different languages, often in different parts of the country, out of different assumptions (sometimes even of what a short story is, or, strange to relate, what a 'Welsh' short story should be), and with different audiences in view, it would be surprising if none among them had ever animadverted over-warmly, or with excessive chill, upon another. Language is the strongest emotive issue in Wales today, and in any case his language is as determining for a writer as his sex. Inevitably those who write in Welsh feel a responsibility not only for our native and ancient tongue, for which we all honour them, but for aspects of Welsh life, thought, and tradition which just as inevitably are less compelling for those whose life, thought, and tradition have been, in differing measure, differently moulded. The results are all-pervasive, and rightly so, and for the most part translation cannot blur them. Few readers, I think, even without an editorial indication, would doubt that at least seven of our Welsh-language stories bear the evidence of their Welsh-language origin. Whether the same deduction would be drawn from a parallel volume in which the Welsh stories appeared in the original and the Anglo-Welsh were translated into Welsh (the suggestion comes in a letter from Richard Hughes), who can say?

Two characteristics of the Welsh-language stories are as apparent as they are expected. They are least so (I offer a personal opinion) in a slice-of-life story like 'The Miracle' and the special case of Islwyn Williams who wrote Swansea-Valley Welsh and English with equal facility, translated himself both ways, and always gives the impression of an original, whichever his language. But native Welsh writers in general convey the feeling of 'Welsh Wales' and its way, or ways, of life with altogether more assurance than those who do not fully belong to it can hope to do. 'A Good Year' and 'Cats at an Auction' could not have come from an Anglo-Welsh hand, and I don't think I am inspired to this conclusion by a knowledge that they did not so come. Second, a high proportion of native Welsh writers express directly or indirectly a political consciousness and sense of national purpose which are rarely found in the work of their differently committed and differently orientated brothers of the other tongue. Thus it seems to me that no Anglo-Welsh author could have written 'The Last Ditch', because in so doing he would condemn himself out of hand for using the English language, and while there are a few dedicated souls who make a deliberate choice of the language in which they write creatively, the vast majority have this chosen for them, not through original sin or primal virtue, but by history, geography, and the accidents of birth and upbringing. Which raises a number of issues not requiring an answer here. Save to remind anyone in danger of forgetting it that 'Anglo-Welsh' is a literary not a racist term, used more in Wales than outside to denote the literature produced by those of our fellow-countrymen whose creative language is English. The authors of Anglo-Welsh literature are Welshmen and Welshwomen, as are the authors of Welsh literature.

Like the Anglo-Welsh short story, the Welsh-language story is written by individuals, and these are as various as individual human beings ought to be. H. E. Bates in an appreciative but searching review of Kate Roberts's *A Summer Day* said that her stories belonged to 'the literature of still waters'—which proverbially run deep. He saw her too as one of those rare artists who know their limits and within them achieve a full and perfect range. In this anthology Eigra Lewis Roberts's 'Deprivation' is another story of still waters, conveying the minuscule enormities of quiet lives in quiet places, quietly observed and quietly recorded. Somewhere a great fish may be fanning his tail; we suspect it, but we shall never know, for he will never break surface. 'A Good Year' and John Gwilym Jones's 'The Wedding' are the masculine counterparts of these feminine achievements, richer-textured, warmer-hued, with a fuller rhythm, and more joyfully redolent of soil, people, feasts, and ceremonies. What all four have in common is composure and decorum, and these, it appears to me, are qualities evident in the classical Welsh short story (that is the pattern of story established by the masters) to an extent neither inherent in, nor much sought by, the Anglo-Welsh, who so frequently reach for a heightened subject matter, a highly-wrought diction, and a high-powered narrative convention. When the reader reads and ponders 'Cats at an Auction', 'A Good Year', 'Samuel Jones's Harvest Thanksgiving', and 'The Wedding' on the one hand, and 'Canute', 'O Brother Man', 'The Dress', 'Ward "O" 3(b)', and Glyn Jones's 'Woodcock' on the other, he may, or may not, feel with me that there are distinctive differences between the two groups, of method, means, and intention, that these differences are probably inalienable, and that we should all be thanking our stars that this is the case.

However, while it is unlikely that either of the present editors will be buried on a Welsh Boot Hill under the blameless inscription, 'Died, an innocent bystander', it is not in our mind to display two rival coteries or draw up two opposing armies, and praise one at the expense of the other or neither at the expense of both. We have therefore not attempted to group, much less segregate, on any principle whatsoever. Once chosen, as we believe, on merit, we have let our twenty-five fellow-countrymen and women find their own places in their own book and speak in such order as each reader may determine for himself. Some of them, by a good omen, will for the first time be speaking to each other. Still better, for the first time ranged side by side, they will all, Welsh-language and English-language authors, be speaking with their several voices to Wales and the world.

GWYN JONES

July 1970

RHYS DAVIES

Canute

As the great Saturday grew nearer most men asked each other: 'Going up for the International?' You had the impression that the place would be denuded of its entire male population, as in some archaic tribal war. Of course a few women too intended taking advantage, for other purposes, of the cheap excursion trains, though these hardy souls were not treated seriously but rather as intruders in an entirely masculine rite. It was to be the England versus Wales battle, the object now under dispute being a stitched leather egg containing an air-inflated bladder.

The special trains began to leave round about Friday midnight, and thereafter, all through the night and until Saturday noon, these quaking, immensely long vehicles feverishly rushed back and forth between Wales and London. In black mining valleys, on rustic heights, in market towns and calm villages, myriads of house doors opened during the course of the night and a man issued from an oblong of yellow light, a railway ticket replacing the old spear.

The contingent from Pleasant Row, a respectable road of houses leading up to a three-shafted colliery, came out from their dwellings into the gas-lit winter midnight more or less simultaneously. Wives stood in worried farewells in the doorways. Their men were setting out in the dead of night to an alien land, far away from this safe valley where little Twlldu nestled about its colliery and usually minded its own business.

'Now be careful you don't lose your head, Rowland!' fretted his wife on their doorstep. 'You take things quiet and behave yourself. Remember your trouble.' The 'trouble' was a hernia, the result of Rowland rescuing his neighbour Dicky Corner House from a fall of roof in the pit.

Rowland, grunting a repudiation of this anxiety, scuttled after a group of men in caps. 'Jawl,' shouted one, 'is that the whistle of the 'scursion train? Come on!' Out of the corner house ran Dicky, tying a white muffler round his neck. Weighted though they all were with bottles for the long journey they shot forward dramatically, though the train was still well up the long valley.

The night was clear and crisp. Thousands of stars briskly gazed down, sleepless as the excited eyes of the excursion hordes thronging all the valley's little stations. Stopping every few minutes, the train slid past mines deserted by their workers and rows of houses where mostly only women and children remained. It was already full when it stopped at Twlldu, and before it left, the smallest men were lying in the luggage-racks and sitting on the floor, placing their bottles safe. Some notorious passengers, clubbing together, had brought crates of flagons.

Dicky Corner House, who was squat and sturdy, kept close to Rowland, offering him cigarettes, or a swig of his bottle and a beef sandwich. Ever since Rowland had rescued him he had felt bound to him in some way, especially as Rowland, who was not a hefty chap, had that hernia as a result. But Rowland felt no particular interest in Dicky; he had only done his duty by him in the pit. 'Got my own bottle and sandwiches,' he grunted. And 'No, I am not feeling a draught.' The train rocked and groaned through the historic night. Some parts of it howled with song; in other parts bets were laid, cards played, and tales told of former Internationals.

Somewhere, perhaps guarded by armed warriors, the sacred egg lay waiting for the morrow. In its worship these myriads had left home and loved ones to brave the dangers of a foreign city. Situated in a grimy parish of that city and going by the name of Paddington, the railway terminus began to receive the first drafts at about 4 a.m. Their arrival was welcomed by their own shouts, whistles, and cries. From one compartment next to the Pleasant Row contingent a man had to be dragged out with his legs trailing limply behind him.

'Darro,' Rowland mumbled with some severity, 'he's started early. Disgrace! Gives the 'scursionists a bad name.'

'Hi,' Dicky Corner House tried to hail a scurrying porter, 'where's the nearest public house in London?'

'Pubs in London opened already then?' asked Shoni Matt in wonder and respect, gazing at 4.30 on the station clock.

'Don't be daft, mun,' Ivor snarled, surly from lack of sleep. 'We got about seven hours to wait on our behinds.'

A pitchy black shrouded the great station. Many braved the strange dark and wandered out into it. But in warily peering groups. A watery dawn found their numbers increased in the main thoroughfares; early workers saw them reconnoitring like tribal invaders sniffing out a strange land.

'Well, well,' said Rowland at ten o'clock, following his nose up the length of Nelson's column, 'how did they get that man up there? And what for?'

'A fancy kind of chimney-stack it is,' Dicky declared. 'A big bakehouse is under us.' He asked yet another policeman—the fourth—what time the public houses opened, but the answer was the same.

'Now Dicky,' said Rowland, in a severe canting voice like a preacher, 'you go on behaving like that and very sorry I'll be that I rescued you that time.... We have come here,' he added austerely, 'to see the International, not to drink. Plenty of beer in Wales.'

'I'm cold,' bleated Shoni Matt; 'I'm hungry; I'm sleepy.'

'Let's go in by there,' said Gwyn Short Leg, and they all entered the National Gallery, seeing that Admission was Free.

It was the Velasquez *Venus* that arrested their full attention. 'The artist,' observed Emlyn Chrysanthemums—he was called that because he was a prize-grower of them in a home-made glass-house—'was clever to make her turn her back on us. A bloke that knew what was tidy.'

'Still,' said Rowland, 'he ought to have thrown a towel or something across her, just by here——'

'Looking so alive it is,' Ivor breathed in admiration, 'you could smack it, just there——'

An attendant said: 'Do not touch the paintings.'

'What's the time?' Dicky Corner House asked the attendant. 'Are they open yet?'

'A disgrace he is,' said Rowland sharply as the contingent went out. 'He ought to have stayed home.'

By then the streets were still more crowded with gazing strangers. Scotland had sent tam o'shantered men, the North and Midlands their crowds of tall and short men in caps, bowlers, with umbrellas and striped scarves, concertinas and whistles. There were ghostly-looking men who looked as if they had just risen from hospital beds; others were unshaven and still bore the aspect of running late for the train. Many women accompanied the English contingents, for the Englishman never escapes this. By noon the invaders seemed to have taken possession of the metropolis and, scenting their powerful majority, they became noisy and obstreperous, unlike the first furtive groups who had arrived before dawn. And for a short while a million beer-taps flowed ceaselessly. But few of the visitors loitered to drink overmuch before the match. The evening was to come, when one could sit back released from the tremendous event.

At 2.30, into a grey misty field surrounded by huge walls of buzzing insects stickily massed together, fifteen red beetles and fifteen white beetles ambled forward on springy legs. To a great cry the sacred egg appeared. A whistle blew. The beetles wove a sharp pattern of movement, pursuing the egg with swift bounds and brisk dance-figures. Sometimes they became knotted over it as though in prayer. They worshipped the egg and yet they did not want it. As if it contained the secret of happiness, they pursued it, got it, and then threw it away. The sticky imprisoning walls heaved and roared; myriads of pin-point faces passed through agonies of horror and ecstacies of bliss. And from a great quantity of these faces came frenzied cries and urgings in a strange primitive language that no doubt gave added strength to the fifteen beetles who understood that language. It was not only the thirty below the walls who fought the battle.

The big clock's pallid face, which said it was a quarter to midnight, stared over the station like an amazed moon. Directly under it was a group of women who had arranged to meet their International men there for the journey back. They looked worried and frightened.

And well they might. For surely they were standing in a gigantic hospital-base adjacent to a bloody battlefield where a crushing defeat had been sustained. On the platforms casualties lay groaning or silently dazed; benches were packed with huddled men, limbs twitching, heads laid on neighbour's shoulders or clasped in hands between knees. Trolleys were heaped with what looked like the dead. Now and again an ambulance train crawled out packed to the doors. But still more men kept staggering into the station from the maw of an underground cavern and from the black foggy streets. Most of them looked exhausted, if not positively wounded, as from tremendous strife.

But not all of them. Despite groans of the incapacitated, grunting heaves of the sick, long solemn stares of the bemused helplessly waiting for some ministering angel to conduct them to a train, there was a singing. Valiant groups of men put their heads doggedly together and burst into heroic song. They belonged to a race that, whatever the cause, never ceases to sing, and those competent to judge declare this singing something to be greatly admired. Tonight, in this melancholy place at the low hour of midnight, these melodious cries made the spirit of man seem undefeated. Stricken figures on floors, benches, and trolleys stirred a little, and far-gone faces flickered into momentary awareness. Others who still retained their faculties sufficiently to recognize home acquaintances shouted, embraced, hit each other, made excited turkey-cock inquiries as to the activities of the evening.

A youngish woman with parcels picked a zig-zag way to under the clock and greeted another woman. 'Seen my Glynne, have you?' she asked anxiously; 'I've been out to Cricklewood with my auntie.... Who won the match?' she asked, glancing about her in fear.

'You can tell by the state of them, can't you!' frowned the other.

Another woman, with a heave of hostility, said: 'Though even if Wales had lost they'd drink just the same, to drown the disappointment, the old beasts.... Look out!' The women scattered hastily from a figure who became detached from a knot of swaying men, made a blind plunge in their direction, and was sick.

'Where's the porters?' wailed one woman. 'There's no porters to be seen anywhere; they've all run home.... Serve us right, we shouldn't have come with the men's 'scursion.... I'm feeling ill, nowhere to sit, only men everywhere.'

Cap pushed back from his blue-marked miner's face, Matt Griffiths of Gelli bellowed a way up No. 1 platform. He was gallantly pulling a trolley heaped with bodies like immense dead cods. 'Where's the backwards 'scursion train for Gelli?' he shouted. 'Out of the way there! We got to go on the night-shift tomorrow.'

'The wonder is,' said a woman, fretful, 'that they can find their way to the station at all. But, there, they're like dogs pointing their snouts towards home.'

Two theological students, solemn-clothed as crows, passed under the clock. They were in fierce converse and gesticulated dangerously with their flappy umbrellas. Yet they seemed oblivious of the carnal scenes around them; no doubt they were occupied with some knotty Biblical matter. The huddled women looked at them with relief; here was safety. 'We'd better get in the same compartment as them,' one of them said to her friend; 'come on, Gwen, let's follow them. I expect they've been up for a conference or an exam.' Soon the two young preachers-to-be were being followed by quite a band of women though they remained unconscious of this flattering retinue.

'That reverse pass of Williams!' one of the students suddenly burst out, unable to contain himself and prancing forward in intoxicated delight. 'All the matches I've been to I've never seen anything like it! Makes you want to grab someone and dance ring-a-ring o'roses.'

Elsewhere an entwined group of young men sang 'Mochyn Du' with an orderly sweetness in striking contrast to their mien; a flavour of pure green hills and neat little farmhouses was in their song about a black pig. On adjacent platforms other groups in that victorious concourse sang 'Sospan Fach' and even a hymn. As someone said: If you shut your eyes you could fancy yourself in an eisteddfod.

But in the gentlemen's convenience under No. 1 platform no one would have fancied this. There an unusual thing had occurred—the drains had clogged. Men kept descending the flight of steps only to find a sheet of water flooding the floor to a depth of several inches. They had to make do with standing on the bottom steps, behind them an impatient block of others dangerously swaying.

And this was not all. Far within the deserted convenience one man was marooned over that sheet of water. He sat on the shoe-shine throne which, resting on its dais, was raised safely—up to the present—above the water. With head lolling on his shoulder he sat fast asleep, at peace, comfortable in the full-sized armchair. Astonished remarks from the steps failed to reach him.

'Darro me,' exclaimed one man with a stare of respect across the waters, 'how did he get there? No sign of a boat.'

'Hoy, bachgen,' another bawled over, 'what train you want to catch? You can't stay there all night.'

'Who does he think he is,' someone else exclaimed in an English voice—'King Canute?'

The figure did not hear, though the head dreamily lolled forward an inch. Impatient men waiting on the crowded steps bawled to those in front to hurry up and make room. Soon the rumour that King Canute was sitting below passed among a lot of people on No. 1 platform. It was not long before someone—Sam Recitations it was, the smoking concert elocutionist—arrived at the bottom step and recognized that the figure enthroned above the water was not King Canute at all.

'I'm hanged if it isn't Rowland from Pleasant Row!' he blew in astonishment. 'That's where he's got! ... Rowland,' his chest swelled as in a recitation, 'wake up, mun, wake up! Train is due out in ten minutes. Number two platform....'

Rowland did not hear even this well-known Twlldu voice. Sam, himself not in full possession of his faculties, gazed stupidly at the sheet of water. It looked deep; up to your calves. A chap would have soaking wet socks and shoes all the way back to Wales. And he was appearing at a club concert on Tuesday, reciting four ballads; couldn't afford to catch a cold. Suddenly he pushed his way through the exclaiming mob behind him, hastened recklessly through the platform mobs, reached No. 2 platform and began searching for the Pleasant Row contingent.

They were sitting against a kiosk plunged in torpid thought. Sam had to shake two or three of them. 'I've seen him!' he rolled. 'Your Rowland! He isn't lost—he's down in the men's place under Number One, and can't budge him. People calling him King Canute——'

They had lost him round about nine o'clock in crowded Trafalgar Square. There the visiting mob had got so obstreperous that, as someone related later at a club in Twlldu, four roaring lions had been let loose and stood lashing their tails in fury against these invaders whose nation had won the match ... and someone else said that for the first time in his life he had seen a policeman who wore spectacles. While singing was going on and two or three cases of assault brewing, Rowland had vanished. From time to time the others had missed him, and Dicky Corner House asked many policemen if they had seen Rowland of Twlldu.

Sam Recitations kept on urging them now. 'King Canute?' repeated Shoni Matt in a stupor. 'You shut up, Sam,' he added crossly; 'no time for recitations now.'

'He's down in the Gents under Number One,' Sam howled despairingly. 'English strangers poking fun at him and water rising up! He'll be drowned same as when the Cambrian pit was flooded!' He beat his chest as if he was giving a ballad in a concert. 'Ten minutes and the train will be in! And poor Rowland sitting helpless and the water rising round him like on the sands of Dee!'

Far off a whistle blew. Someone nearby was singing 'Cwm Rhondda' in a bass that must have won medals in its time. They shook themselves up from the platform, staring penetratingly at Sam who was repeating information with wild emphasis. Six of them, all from Pleasant Row. Awareness seemed to flood them simultaneously, for suddenly they all surged away.

By dint of pushing and threatening cries they got down all together to the lower steps of the convenience. Rowland had not moved in the shoeshine throne. Still his head lolled in slumber as if he was sitting cosy by his fireside at home after a heavy shift in the pit, while the waters lapped the dais and a yellow light beat down on the isolated figure indifferent to its danger. They stared fearfully at the sheet of water.

'Shocking it is,' said Gwyn Short Leg, scandalized. 'All the Railway Company gone home, have they, and left the place like this?'

'In London too!' criticized Ivor, gazing below him in owlish distaste.

Then in one accord they bellowed: 'Hoy, Rowland, hoy!'

He did not stir. Not an eyelid. It was then that Shoni Matt turned to Dicky Corner House and just looked him, like a judge. His gaze asked—'Whose life had been saved by Rowland when that bit of roof had fallen in the pit?' Dicky, though he shivered, understood the long solemn look. 'Time to pay back now, Dicky bach,' the look added soberly.

Whimpering, Dicky tried to reach his shoe laces, on the crowded steps. But the others urged excitedly 'No time to take your shoes off. Hark, the train's coming in! Go on, boy. No swimming to do.'

Dicky, with a sudden dramatic cry, leapt into the water, foolishly splashing it up all round his legs. A pit-butty needed to be rescued! And with oblivious steps, encouraged by the applause of the others, he plunged across to the throne. He stepped on the dais and, being hefty, lifted Rowland across his shoulders without much bother. He staggered a bit as he stepped off the dais into the cruelly wet water.

'Careful now,' shouted Emlyn Chrysanthemums; 'don't drop him into the champagne.'

It was an heroic act that afterwards, in the club evenings, took precedence over tales of far more difficult rescues in the pits. Dicky reached the willing arms of the others without mishap. They took Rowland and bore him by his four limbs up the steps, down the platform, and up the other, just as the incoming train was coming to a frightened standstill. After a battle they got into a compartment. Dicky took off his shoes, hung up his socks over the edge of the rack and wiped his feet and calves in the white muffler that had crossed his throat.

'Wet feet bad for the chest,' he said fussily.

All the returning trains reached the arms of Wales safely, and she folded the passengers into her fragrant breast with a pleased sigh of 'Well done, my sons.' The victory over her ancient enemy—it was 6 points to 3—was a matter of great Sunday celebration when the men's clubs opened in the evening, these having a seven-day licence, whereas the ordinary public-houses, owing to the need to appease old dim gods, were not allowed to open on Sundays.

The members of the Pleasant Row contingent, like most others, stayed in bed all the morning. When they got up they related to their wives and children many of the sights and marvels of London. But some weeks had passed before Rowland's wife, a tidy woman who starched her aprons and was a great chapel-goer, said to him in perplexity: 'Why is it people are calling you Rowland Canute now?'

Only that evening, Gwyn Short Leg, stumping to the door on his way to the club, had bawled innocently into the passage: 'Coming down, Rowland Canute?' Up to lately Rowland had been one of those who, because he seemed to have no peculiarity, had never earned a nickname.

'Oh,' Rowland told his wife, vaguely offhand, 'some fancy name or other it is they've begun calling me.'

'But a reason there must be for it,' she said inquisitively. 'Canute! Wasn't that some old king who sat on his throne beside the sea and dared the tide to come over him? . . . A funny name to call you.'

'What you got in that oven for my supper?' he asked, scowling at the news in the evening paper.

She knew better than to proceed with the matter just then. But of course she did not let it rest. It was the wife of Emlyn Chrysanthemums living three doors up who, in the deprecating way of women versus the ways of men, told her the reason. There are nicknames which are earned respectably and naturally, and indeed such nicknames are essential to identify persons in a land where there are only twenty or so proper baptized names for everybody. But, on hearing how Rowland earned Canute, his wife pursed in her lips like a pale tulip, opening them hours later to shout as Rowland tramped in from the pit:

'Ah, Canute is it! . . . Sitting there in that London place,' she screamed, 'and all those men——' She whipped about like a hailstorm. 'You think I'm going to stay in Twlldu to be called Mrs. Rowland Canute, do you! We'll have to move from here—you begin looking for work in one of the other valleys at once.'

And such a dance she led him that in a couple of months they had left Pleasant Row. Rowland got taken on at the Powell pit in the Cwm Mardy valley, several stout mountains lying between that and Twlldu.

Yet give a dog a bad name, says the proverb, and it will stick. Who would have thought that Sam Recitations, growing in fame, would visit a club in far-away Cwm Mardy to give selections from his repertoire at a smoking concert? And almost the first man he saw when he entered the bar-room was Rowland. 'Why now,' his voice rolled in delight, 'if it isn't Rowland Canute! Ha, ha——' And, not noticing Rowland's dropped jaw of dismay, he turned and told all the clustering men what had happened under Paddington platform that time after the famous International—just as the history of the rescue had been told in all the clubs in the valley away over the mountains.

JOHN GWILYM JONES

The Wedding

Translated from the Welsh by Islwyn Ffowc Elis

'*We are met together in the presence of God for the purpose of uniting these two persons...*'

I am, like the marriage service, dignified enough, simple and unassuming enough, but painfully formal. Speaking it so often has made it as mechanical to me as my prayers and the burial service. I can easily say one thing with my voice while thinking of something quite different. In an unguarded moment I could speak of these persons here present putting on immortality. Many a time I have wondered what would happen if, instead of asking 'So-and-so, wilt thou have this man to be thy wedded husband?' I asked, 'So-and-so, wilt thou have so-and-so's heart?' and she sang, 'I will without dela-a-ay! My heart's belonged to Hywel for many a da-a-ay!' In these rash moments I feel like a giddy girl. But so things are, and so they will be.

And so I am, and so I shall be now. I am deep in the rut, and think of everything in terms of a preface and three heads. Soon I shall give advice to these two persons. I shall preface my remarks with the marriage at Cana of Galilee and the Lord Jesus's interest in the small joys of the children of men. I shall speak in the first place of the need to bear the one with the other in the wedded life; secondly, of the opportunities for enrichment, the one in the other, in the wedded life; and thirdly and lastly of the propriety of giving pride of place to God, the Great Reality, in the wedded life. From now on I must, like the ploughshare, be content in the furrow. Only the crude, superficial experiences common to thousands will come my way. I hear the high wind and the heavy rain. I see the most prominent hilltops and the wide rivers. Gone is the morning of my life with its breezes and daisies. Come is the heavy afternoon with its dog daisies. I have formed a thick skin to take the insult here, the censure there. I have learned to count ten before answering back. I come and go between the bickering of elders and the death sighs of the faithful. I have lost all poise in trying to balance the factions. Like Pavlov's dogs I react instinctively, unconsciously, to specific sounds at specific moments. 'Earth to earth, ashes to ashes,' says my voice, and my face unknown to me forms the tearful expression expected of it. 'I baptize thee, Peris Wyn,' says my voice, and my face involuntarily melts into a smile. 'This is my body, This is my blood,' says my voice, and I am clothed from head to foot in the essential, traditional gravity.

Yet, when John Llywelyn's letter came ... 'It is you who christened us both and received us both into membership, and we would like you to marry us ...' I could not help being proud. I felt that my life had not been entirely in vain. Weaned from the ambitions of youth, from its visions and hopes and joys, I grew into the tepid, monotonous ordinariness of a good minister of Jesus Christ and contented myself with my lot. This is my cross, but under its weight I have felt as much earthly happiness as is possible and fair to the likes of me. I have been faithful over a few things, and I know I shall enter fully some day into the joy of my Lord.

'Who presents this woman to be married?'

'I present her.' And good riddance to her. I step forward, squaring my shoulders lest that wife of mine or my brother Wil or any of the family whose company we requested the pleasure of here think that I care a damn for any of them. Tonight I shall go to Davy John's shop and I shall say, 'Two ounces of shag, Davy John.' 'Two ounces?' he'll say, stressing the word 'two' like a reciter. 'Yes, two,' I shall say, my stress as good as his, throwing down my money like a lord at the races. And next week I'll buy three ounces. The butter and the tea and the sugar will last longer with one mouth less to feed. The week after I'll get myself a new pair of boots. Come the end of the month I'll go to town to G.G.'s to be measured for a suit with a stripe in it. 'What d'you think of this one?' I'll say, off-hand like, to my brother Wil. In less than a year I'll be offering my tobacco tin to Jones, the quarry steward. 'Have a pipeful, Mr. Jones?' 'I don't smoke shag.' 'Neither do I...'

'Catrin, where's my stud?' 'How should I know? Where did you put it?' 'If Lizzie Mary were here she wouldn't take long to find her father's stud...' 'This rice pudding isn't as good as usual.' 'Isn't it?' 'Too watery by far.' 'I haven't made any for years. Lizzie Mary always made it...' 'Catrin, did you bring *Y Faner*?' 'Drat, I forgot.' 'Lizzie Mary never forgot her father's paper on a Wednesday night...' Well, as Twm-Yes-and-No always says in the Literary Society, there's so much to be said for one side and the other that I can't decide. I think I'll abstain from voting.

'John Llywelyn Evans, wilt thou have this woman to be thy wedded wife?'

'I will.' The organ pipes are neatly arranged according to size, those at both ends looking so tall and thick because those in the centre are so small. It is a comparative matter. And somewhere in the middle there are two, of which I cannot tell with certainty which is the taller. I know that if Mr. Lewis struck the sounds that emerge from them there would be at least half a tone between them, and then my ear would catch the difference.

I should like to be a critic able to list the books of the ages in order of merit. That, of course, is impossible. It would not be difficult to choose the books at both ends. My large pipes would be the Bible and the *Mabinogi*. 'Yes,' my critics would say, 'we agree that the Bible should be at one end, but why the *Mabinogi*? Have you never heard of Euripides and Tacitus and Shakespeare and Cervantes and Dante and Balzac and Tolstoy and Goethe and...?' 'Yes, of course, I have heard of them all, but I am a Welshman.' 'Ah,' they say, like schoolmasters, 'but literature is above nationality. You must not think within the confines of your own land; you must reach out, spread your wings, and see an author and book in their proper place in the growth of the literature of the whole wide world; you must acquire a classical mind and learn to compare and contrast and see how much one author learned from those who went before him. And then decide whether he added to the riches or merely lived off the riches of his forebears. A good critic must know whence came a lyric and a novel. They are not things made of nothing, hovering in air, unconnected as gossamer. That is sheer romanticism, criticism that is nothing but personal taste, a whim.'

I know that all their arguing has a cruel logic. But for me there is no argument wrought in the minds of men that can topple the *Mabinogi* from its pedestal. Myfanwy and Ceridwen and Eluned have more beautiful names that Lizzie Mary. Miss Davies at the County School probably knows more about cookery than Lizzie Mary. Jane Tŷ Gwyn has a sweeter temper and Megan Tŷ Capel lives nearer the mark. Lizzie Mary's mind is made of English penny dreadfuls and newspaper headlines and Hollywood movies: I'll admit it. She has very little idea of politics or literature, and Reaction and Revolt in the one as in the other mean nothing to her. But she's my sweetheart, and that's all that matters. Will I take this woman to be my wedded wife? I wi-i-ill without dela-a-ay! My hea-a-art's belonged to Lizzie for many a da-a-ay! You'd be frightened out of your wits if I sang like that, wouldn't you, the Reverend Edward Jones? You'd be surprised at how near I am to doing it. There's Lizzie Mary handing her bouquet to her sister Gwen, and Robin fumbling with finger and thumb in his waistcoat pocket for the ring. He is very fond of the *Mabinogi* too. Poor Robin!

'Lizzie Mary Jones, wilt thou have this man to be thy wedded husband?'

'I will.' There: I have spoken the words simply, coolly, feeling nothing more than the reasonable excitement of any bride. This is not how I imagined my wedding. There was a time when I saw myself as the young man's fancy. I wandered with him through the white wheat and sauntered along the paths of the sheep till we reached the green blade of grass. But at last, after many tribulations, after bearing the cruelty of father and mother, after writing with blood from my own arm, I was forced to stand beside Maddocks in church, wretched as a faded lily. Behind me sat my proud family; beside me, haughtily, Maddocks was marrying my body while outside, somewhere, breaking his heart, was Wil. Don't break your heart, Wil. Soon the Maid of Cefn Ydfa will lie still in her grave and Wales will be singing your idyll . . .

There was a time when I imagined myself saying 'I will', trembling with a consuming passion. Beside me stood a powerful he-man, a man among men, not unlike Clarke Gable in *I Adored Her*. He had one of those haggard attractive faces with wavy, brilliantined hair and a cheeky little twist to the corner of his mouth. I felt exhilarated at having humiliated him and bewitched him into saying 'I will' with such humble gratitude; yet the touch of his hand on mine as he placed the ring made me flesh, every inch of me. I stood there brazen, abstractions like morality and chastity and temperance having ceased to be, even quite tangible things like my father's frown and my mother's smack and the tongue of Betsan Jones next door having become as nothing in the world to me...

Another time I would marry above my station. Behind me would sit my mother. 'A Triplex grate, wooden bedsteads, a three-piece suite and a carpet,' she would say to herself. 'I'm taking a fortnight's holiday this year,' my father would say to the quarry steward, 'to stay with my daughter at Bumford Hall.' 'I'm off to Paris,' my sister Gwen would say. 'To Paris?' 'Yes, with Lady Elizabeth.' 'Lady Elizabeth?' 'My sister, Lady Elizabeth Bumford, you know...' But here's what happens. I am marrying one of my own kind, not forced and not feeling anything other than the ordinary thrill of any girl on her wedding day. I say 'I will' quite simply, seemingly unconcerned, perfectly satisfied and perfectly happy because I know I am doing the right and the wise thing to do.

'Then let the man place the ring on the fourth finger of the woman's left hand.'

There's the ring on her finger. Now I am a man who covets his neighbour's wife, a fornicator in my mind, a victim of unease and the weariness of things half done, a soul without a body. For me there will be bouts of lust without the forgiveness that follows lusting with another, and afterwards the drowsy torpor in loneliness. And pain and guilt the next morning, because I can never free myself from the chains of the Ten Commandments or the bonds of the thousand and one commandments of my home. Thou shalt not commit adultery, thou shalt not bring false evidence, thou shalt not play cards on Sunday, thou shalt not put a shilling on a horse, thou shalt not imbibe strong drink. I do all these things, gnawed by the traditional guilt of a child of the *seiat*. I am robbed of the delight of sin and of the short-sightedness that sees only the single isolated act.

Last night I tossed and turned for hours. Tonight it will be worse. To tame myself I stretch and tauten every muscle. I wind myself into a ball, my arms tight around my legs, my chin on my knees. I beat the pillows with the monotonous rhythm of a piston. I tire of this and turn, suddenly furious. I turn again. Again and again I turn. And all this time the thing will be working its way through my mind, creeping and wallowing there like a frog in slime ... But at this moment I am perfectly happy; indeed, better than happy. I can observe myself last night and tonight and every night without emotion, without prejudice, and see the abomination, not because the Old Testament and my mother have taught me so, but because I have experienced a mystical uplift, a purification. My mind has been cleansed, and in this brief cleanliness I can observe myself last night and tonight as a stranger. I am more critical, I see more clearly the futility and the waste of energy. But they are the futility and the waste of energy of another man—not mine. Bred within me is the integrity of a good critic, who sees faults without prejudice and notes them without malice. They are not my faults, therefore I am not obliged to make resolutions. It is not for me to smother the lust of another man who lived last night and will live again tonight.

I wonder if it is by giving us this glimpse of the old man and making us feel the strangeness of him that Jesus Christ forgives our sins? This joy is well known to me. Always, it is something from without that forces it upon me: poetry, a good sermon, a Bach fugue, a clear argument, pictures, acting, a high mass I heard once.

And today, the marriage covenant in accordance with the holy ordinance of God. By my side, John Llywelyn shivering as he used to do after a cold dip in Llyn Hafod Ifan, when we are all pain without but warm with joy and life within. Gwen, the sounds of the service giving her drowsy eyes the happy look of the young when they contemplate their end. I can imagine her composing a sonnet: 'When my frail corpse is lowered to the grave...' Old Edward Jones with his honest intonation turning this ring, and I do solemnly declare, and so that you may stand before God when the secrets of all hearts are revealed, into pure worship. In the fine breeze of this sanctification I can look at Lizzie Mary without coveting her, and feel her closeness without lewd thoughts. This is the purification, the beauty absolute. It gives me forgivingness (don't ever mention those ten pounds again, Evan Hughes), and jocularity (you fell, did you, Huw *bach,* come here, let me pick you up), and humility (I am not worthy), and a bit of boasting too (I can do all things).

'Inasmuch as John Llywelyn Evans and Lizzie Mary Jones have made a covenant together in marriage . . .'

Today I am seventeen. I stand in the big pew in Penuel dressed in blue silk beside Lizzie Mary, my sister, who looks surprisingly self-possessed in white. I am very, very happy. Yesterday I was in school listening to Miss Rees's usual drivel. Her questions are as inevitable as the sore on her lip. That sore is her souvenir of the Great War. It was in that war that she lost her sweetheart. Which mutation follows *yn*? Why is *eu gilydd* incorrect? What is an anchoress? Where is Sarras? Who was Moradrins? Spinsterish, barren trivialities like herself. But I won't think about her and her type. I shall think about the adventurous things and the beautiful things in my life, such as learning for the first time the difference between the male and the female of the white campion; the breeze that cools the scent of the gorse; wetting my feet in Cae Doctor river and having my feet wet all day without catching cold; finding the nest of a hen that lays out; being ill and having neighbours bring me calves' foot jelly; closing my eyes and wondering who will cry for me when I'm dead. Lizzie Mary's wedding day will be among them. Some day little Gwenhwyfar will sit on my lap and ask, 'Mam, what were the nicest things that happened to you?' And I shall say, 'Well . . . finding a double-yolk egg . . . and your Aunt Lizzie Mary's wedding day . . . and . . .'

But what did I say? Little Gwenhwyfar? Mam? Today Lizzie Mary is consecrating herself to be a mother. In our family tree her name will be coupled with John Llywelyn's. I wouldn't like to be like Queen Anne alone in her family tree. Although she too probably had a sore on her lip . . . I am the Holy Grail. I am the sacred vessel preserved by Joseph of Arimathaea. Here I stand, in the court of Pelleas, grandfather of Galahad, in all the glory of my holiness, pure, intact, like the Virgin Mary, incorruptible, immaculate. Who comes now on a pilgrimage from Arthur's court in Camelot? Who is this with the golden spur on his right foot? Burt? Lionel? Percival? Galahad? Come, my Galahad! Come, predestined seeker of the Holy Cup. Delay with hermits along the untrodden paths of dark forests, but come! Tarry awhile with sweet maidens in wooded vales, but come! Deliver monks from the excommunicate bodies in their sacred burial grounds, but come! Slay your ten knights and slay your forty, but come! Be sad at the burial of Percival's sister, but come! Come, and I shall nourish thee with my spiritual food, I shall show thee my secrets, I shall anoint thee king of my realm. Come! Come!

'And now the Reverend Arthur Davies will read a portion of the Scriptures.'

'The Lord is my shepherd, I shall not want ...' This is my first church, and my first wedding since I was inducted here, but I was not asked to officiate. I realize, of course, that memories and affection bind John Llywelyn and Lizzie Mary to their old minister, but for the life of me I cannot help being offended. These things always happen to me. I have always come second. To mother, I come second because my brother Robin smiles more readily and sees more quickly his chance to do a good turn. I was always second in my class at County School simply because Bobi Tan y Wern had more ability. It was second class honours, second section, that I got at College, and it was only after Rolant had turned down this church that it was offered to me. No one is ever unjust to me. That's the trouble. If there were injustice it would all be so much easier to bear. Always there are ample and adequate reasons why I should be set aside, and I can see them and admit the fairness of them. Something always stands between me and fulfilment. I begin everything I do knowing full well that my success will be only middling, and therefore I cannot throw myself body and soul into anything. One part of me does what it ought to do, while the other just wanders.

I want to consecrate myself wholeheartedly to my work ... to penetrate into the mystical awareness like Saint John of the Cross and Saint Teresa and Ann Griffiths. Gwen Jones is a pretty little piece. Really to know the love which casteth out fear. I wonder how old she is. That my soul might die unto itself to live in God. She's not too young. To walk in the light that makes the miraculous birth and the resurrection as natural as the drawing of breath. There's passion in those sultry eyes. To swoon in the heavenly bliss. Those full lips and young breasts. Green pastures. Under a hedge ... Oh Lord, why must I be plagued with this eternal duality? Why must I be this hybrid of holiness and lust? Why can't I be either all body or all soul? Why cannot my passions run loose, free of the preventive power of Thy breath of life? Why cannot my soul leap and dance free of the fetters of lust? Why can't I be a body–soul and soul–body, inseparable as a compound word? The one to make mild the other, the other to enliven the one? So that in following Thee I shall possess Gwen and in desiring Gwen be in love with Thee? Such a thing is possible. I will make it possible ... but who am I to will anything? I too shall set out, like Percival, on my adventure. I shall wander through the woods where birds sing. I shall fight with the serpent and see the ship of white samite. I shall speak with the man who bears the name of Jesus Christ on his crown, and lose blood from a wound in my thigh. I shall arrive at the court of Pelleas and my eyes shall behold the glory of the Sacred Cup. But it is Galahad who will see his adventure completed; Galahad, the predestined seeker, who will find his Holy Grail.

'*And now may the grace of the Lord Jesus Christ and the love of God and the fellowship of the Holy Ghost be with you now and evermore. Amen.*'

KATE ROBERTS

Cats at an Auction

Translated from the Welsh by Wyn Griffith

Elen sat in her parlour, undecided whether or not to go to the auction. By now, she had lost all interest in the corner cupboard. She had been looking for one for some years, but her failure had weakened her desire. When she heard that there was one among the late Mrs. Hughes's furniture, something of the craving came back to her. And yet, as she looked round at things in her own room, thinking of it brought little pleasure to her mind. Too like having a child when the other children were grown up, and the corner cupboard would only remind you of a strange growth on the trunk of a tree. She had polished her own furniture for years until it shone like silk, and rumour had it that Mrs. Hughes was not house-proud. If that were true, it would make the corner cupboard still more of an unexpected child. But sometimes you grow fonder of it than of the others. Yes, she would go to the auction.

And now, she began to look at her furniture from the other side of the grave, as it were. Some day all her things would be scattered: the dresser here, the chest there, the oak table somewhere else: orphans separated and adopted by different families, and by then her own furniture would be in no better state than Mrs. Hughes's. However, that was a glimpse from beyond the grave, she remembered, and of no importance. The pang that the thought brought with it soon vanished. It didn't matter a pin today to Mrs. Hughes what state her furniture was in. By the evening it would be thrown here and there like the mats under the feet of a dog in a hurry.

Yes, she would certainly go. Still, she sat on, waiting, and she began to think about Mrs. Hughes. She didn't know her too well, although they both went to the same chapel. The dead woman—a widow—was one of a group of women who always spoke English although their Welsh was much better, busy with sales of work, preparing food for the monthly meetings and supper for the Literary Society, doing all the things that Elen never did. Elen always thought of her as one of a bunch, with nothing special to distinguish her from the rest of the sixty-year-old ladies. In fact, what difference there was served only to make her less conspicuous, to merge her with the rest and make her disappear into it. The others were well-dressed, colourful, had their hair waved, used lipstick, trying to improve upon nature. Mrs. Hughes and her clothes lacked colour, dressed always in pepper and salt, and her hair, beginning to turn grey, blended with her clothes like a brook running into a river. Everything about her looked poorer than it really was. No one could tell when she got new clothes, for they were always the same colour.

She had plenty of money, so they said. Rumour had it that she was mean, and that her house was untidy if not worse, in spite of the fact that she could well afford to pay for help to keep it in good shape. She need never have died, they said. She was found dead in bed one morning when someone broke into the house because she hadn't been seen for some days and there were several milk bottles outside the door. If she had sent for the doctor in time, they said, she would have been alive today, for there was nothing much wrong with her. And then, of course, they began to invent reasons for her not calling her friends in, or the doctor, although she had a telephone in the house. She didn't want anybody to see what state the house was in, for there were signs that she had got up once or twice to prepare a meal. However, Elen thought that it wasn't her business to act the detective. Her concern was to buy the corner cupboard, if she so decided. Yes, if. She realized that the woman's sudden death was really responsible for her own hesitation about owning the cupboard now. What if she also? . . . She felt depressed. But she'd go, nevertheless. She'd see people, see a bit of life. An auction was part of life, even an auction of a dead woman's belongings. Life was like that, the living buying the effects of the dead, living a little longer. Now she would see her friend Marged who went to every auction, without any intention of buying anything, merely to see people in a new environment, different from the sermon, the play, or a concert. People were different at an auction, Marged said.

She made for the room where the furniture was—the sitting-room, she supposed. The corner cupboard was there in its place. A really good one, and something could be made of it when it had been cleaned. But more than that would have to be done to the room. The wallpaper was old, stained by the rain, damp marks all over it, like a map of Anglesey over the fire place, and of the Mediterranean towns under the windows. Tiles from the hearth missing, gaps like teeth fallen out of a denture. On coming in, she noticed that the curtains seemed all right from the outside, but from inside she saw that they looked like network, rotten, and about to fall down. She wouldn't have been surprised to see them fall gently as the dew, untouched, as if some spirit had let go of them. The dust of years had hardened at the edge of the skirting board, like a strand of pack-thread.

The buyers came in from the other rooms. Elen saw a chair and sat on it. A young woman was already sitting on a chair, as if she had been nailed to it, looking at no one. Newly married, by the look of her, neat in her grey skirt and up to her thin red lips. There were scores like her in the town: her hair done in the latest style, short at the back, a mound of it in front, making her look like a scrawny hen. On Elen's left there was a small step-ladder, a man of sixty sitting on it, with bifocal spectacles, and every time someone came in, he looked through the bottom half of the lenses. Soon, Marged came in and sat between Elen and the young wife.

'Are you going to buy anything?'

'I don't know, I might. The corner cupboard.'

The young wife turned her head slightly, and then back again. Her foot tapped the floor nervously and she turned her ring round her finger.

'Things are going well here, in spite of the look of them,' said Marged. Four women came in, friends of Mrs Hughes, and sat on a bench near by. The oldest of them, Mrs. Jones, was her greatest friend, and they went together on holiday each year. 'I never thought,' she said, 'that the house was in such a state. No wonder she never asked me in.'

'No,' said one of the others, 'she preferred other people's houses.'

'Cheaper, too.'

'Listen,' said Marged.

'Who could help it?' answered Elen.

Mrs. Jones turned her head up and looked at the walls and the ceiling as if she was scanning the sky and counting the stars. 'When I die,' she said, 'my house won't be in the state this is in.' The man looked at her through the lower half of his spectacles and grunted a scornful 'Humph.' Elen felt as if someone had put a cold poultice over her heart, a wave of disgust came over her.

'Judas,' said Marged, her teeth clenched. 'The bitch.'

'Hush,' said Elen.

At that moment, Mrs. Hughes meant something more to her than the late Mrs. Hughes. She came back to life, one of the bunch of women about the chapel, looking at them, smiling, enjoying herself in their company at someone else's auction. And then she dropped out of the bunch like a wheat sheaf falling out of a stook.

More people came in, and the young wife looked more and more nervous. Voices from the back, one louder than the rest, voice and accent of a country woman. 'Don't forget, she was a kind old thing, a smile for everybody no matter who they were. Not much in her head, but she was good to her friends and very loyal. She and her husband were very happy together.'

The auctioneer came in, and the young wife began to bite her lip. The corner cupboard was put up first.

'Three pounds,' said the little man on the steps, as if he were glad to get it off his chest.

'Three pounds five,' said the young wife quietly, moving her head so that the mound of hair moved forward as if she were a ram about to charge the auctioneer.

'Three ten,' said Elen brightly, to her own surprise.

'Three twelve six,' said the man.

'Three fifteen,' said Elen boldly.

'Four,' from the young wife.

'Four ten,' said Elen.

'Whew,' said the little man, and gave up bidding.

'Five,' the young wife said, fiercely.

'Five guineas,' said Elen.

Mrs. Jones leant forward to look at her, and it dawned on Elen that she would like to have that cupboard, not merely to add to her furniture, but as a memento of that colourless old lady, so that she could say to her, 'I bought this at your auction because I was sorry your friends had left you.' 'Five pounds ten,' said the young wife.

Elen was on the point of raising the bid by five shillings when the young wife, her head on one side, gave her such a look of appeal, just as some dogs do when someone whistles near them. Elen was defeated, and the auctioneer knocked down the cupboard to the young wife for five pounds ten. She went straight out without looking at anybody.

Elen was not interested in the rest of the furniture, but she stayed where she was, and began to meditate. On the floor, just near her, there was an old worn carpet, folded anyhow. She looked at the folds, and soon they began to take shape as a nose, mouth, forehead, and ears. They turned into a corpse lying in a grave, putty-coloured, indifferent to all criticism, the body of a woman unconnected with all that was being sold in her house today, separated from her friends. For a long time she kept looking at the face, expecting the features to change, something of a smile to appear because she had thought kindly of her. But there was no sign of it. And then a man came in, heavy booted. He trod on the carpet and the features vanished. He had walked upon the dead woman's face, in her coffin.

They finished selling the contents of the room, and before the man came down from his seat on the steps, a bright cheerful woman came up to him.

'Well, dear, did you get it?'

'No. What chance has a man got against these damned determined women?'

'None at all. That's why I sent you. Come home, dear. I've got salmon for tea.'

'Much better. You don't want a corner cupboard to keep a tin of salmon.'

The two went out happily, and the steps were moved to another room.

'I'm going home,' said Elen to her friend.

'Why? Come to the other room to see what's there.'

'I've seen and heard too much already.'

'You're disappointed because you didn't get the corner cupboard.'

'No, I'm not . . . it's gone to someone just setting up house.'

'Selfish little creature.'

'Of course. Everybody's selfish at an auction.'

They moved into the next room where a lot of odds and ends were to be sold: old ornaments, pictures, bedlinen that had never been unpacked, sheets and blankets, the edges soiled. Stocks of underwear that had never been opened.

'What possessed the woman?' asked Marged.

'Why couldn't she have had some pleasure out of wearing them?'

'Perhaps she meant to, some day.'

Mrs. Hughes's friends joined them. 'She had clothes enough to change them a bit oftener,' said Mrs. Jones.

'Hush,' said one of the others. 'That's her brother over there.'

'Why shouldn't he hear? He's another of the same kidney or he'd have taken these things away instead of letting them be auctioned.'

Marged insisted on staying to the end and going all through the house to look. Elen went to the sitting-room where the corner cupboard had been, but someone had taken it away. The chairs had gone, too, and there was nothing left but the carpet folded in the middle of the floor. She looked again for the face she had seen in it and gradually it came back. There was Mrs. Hughes's face looking at the empty room, as unconcerned as before, but this time as if she had gained the victory over everybody, her mouth more firmly closed. Elen moved across to the window and looked again at the carpet. The afternoon sun shone through the window upon the floor. Some day, she thought, the room could be made to look cheerful again. She looked again at the carpet: the face had changed, the mouth was smiling.

Marged came in and caught her staring. 'What's the matter

with you? Are you ill? You're as white as a sheet. Come home and have a cup of tea with me. I've been all over the house, there's nothing left except a piece of soap in the bathroom.'

As they went out through the hall, Mrs. Hughes's brother was talking to some of his sister's friends. 'A very good sale,' he said. 'Everything sold, and at a good price.'

Elen turned to look back at the house. The curtains were still up, and the house looked just as it did when Mrs. Hughes was there. Only those who had been inside would know how false the picture was, an empty shell.

'Why are you so quiet?' asked Marged over her tea cup.

'Just thinking.'

'Of what?'

'Mrs. Hughes.'

'Nonsense—she doesn't exist any more.'

'I don't know. I found her very much alive this afternoon, more so than she ever was in her life.'

'You didn't think much of her when she was alive.'

'No. People have to die before we get to know them.'

'Well, she'd be alive today if she hadn't been so stingy. She had money enough to pay for help.'

'Life had grown too much for her.'

'Even if it did, there was no need for it to happen.'

'We don't know. We don't know what's the first thing to give way inside us.'

'She could have spent her money. Just see how her brother and his wife will squander it.'

'Very likely. But we don't know what little thing will begin to fail in us, beginning to get so heedless even to spend money. She did spend money on some things.'

'Yes, that was very strange.'

'We'll never know what began to fester inside her and to drain away her energy. I don't think it was the fear of anyone seeing her house. The woman in her had been defeated.'

'You are too kind to her.'

'We ought to be kind to the dead.'

'Perhaps you're right. But I can't see why we should be depressed because of Mrs. Hughes.'

'We are made of the same stuff.'

'Well, we are alive today. Drink your tea and have another piece of bread and butter.'

John, Marged's husband, came home from work.

'What kind of a sale was it? Did you buy anything, Elen?'

'No.'

'She let the corner cupboard go to a slip of a young girl, newly married.'

'You've got plenty of furniture, and some day your own things will go to auction.'

Elen left them. The two would go on discussing her behind her back, Marged as heedless as the corpse she first saw in the carpet, revelling in telling John all about the sale. To Marged this was just a sale like any other sale, somewhere to see people, not to get to know them, dead or alive.

When she got home, she sat in her sitting-room and looked affectionately at her furniture. The pieces all belonged to each other and made an entity and so they should remain. It wouldn't be John, Marged's husband, who'd have the say about her furniture. She would write to her solicitor to change her will: her furniture was to be kept together in store until it rotted and fell to bits like Mrs. Hughes's curtains.

GEORGE EWART EVANS

Let Dogs Delight

The first time anyone heard about him was when young Danny Lewis came home from the mountain and said he'd been bitten by a big brown fox that could run as fast as a train.

The kids had been up on the breast of Gilfach-y-Rhyd, playing Indians among the rocks. Danny had jumped down from a big boulder nearly on top of this fox. Curled up it was, asleep in the sun. It took one bite at him and was away along the path towards Craig-yr-Hesg, as quick as a moment.

There was no mistake about the bite—the teeth had gone right into the kid's forearm—but down in Pontygwaith they were not too sure about the fox. They hadn't seen a fox around the Gilfach in years; not since Jenkins the Farm had taken to shooting them.

It was Wil Hughes Flagons who really noticed him first. Just below Craig-yr-Hesg Farm there's a fairly level shelf of ground bitten into the side of the mountain. Wil Flagons was up there one Sunday morning sitting against a rock. He had his greyhound bitch, the famous Tonypandy Annie, with him, and while he was nearly dozing off after reading the newspaper, the bitch suddenly tugged at the lead and started barking and kicking up no end of a shindy. Flagons looked up and saw what was worrying her.

About two hundred yards away was a big brown greyhound, poking around among the rocks. When the dog heard Annie barking, he turned round sharply, cocking up his head, like a gossip. And what a head! It was as smooth-lined and well-cut as a snake's. The dog held it high, but as soon as he saw Flagons, down it went and he was off towards Craig-yr-Hesg, up past the quarry on to the moorland.

One glance at the dog in action and Wil Flagons knew he was a right 'un. The dog moved like a champion, taking the rocks and the sheep-wall like a bird; like a fairy; like no milgi that's been in this valley.

A quarter of an hour later the bitch spotted the dog again, right up on top, on the moorland. He was basking quiet in the sun. Flagons stopped, slipped the lead off her collar, and said to her very gentle, like he did before races: 'After him, gel!'

When the dog saw the famous Annie blazing towards him, he just cocked up his head and looked interested. But just as he got up to meet her, he saw Flagons standing with the lead in his hand, away in the background. Without as much as a sniff for Annie, the dog turned, and was off in the opposite direction like the wind. And Annie, thinking it was all a bit of sport, went full pelt after him.

Now Wil Flagons has got a few middling words handy when he's surprised. He must have used them all when he saw what happened to his famous Annie when she went after the big greyhound. He couldn't believe his eyes. The dog was leaving her standing, and before they were half-way across the bit of moorland he was as distant from Annie as a rich relation. Tonypandy Annie, mind you, who was meeting all comers and was live fire on the skin of the bookmakers.

Flagons really thought he had the nystagmus when he saw it. He went home after he'd collected the bitch, and he got so worried, trying to think whose dog it was, he couldn't get to sleep. He thought once it may be Twm Aberdare's dog that had got loose; but Twm's dog couldn't raise a gallop, leave alone make Annie look like a lap-dog. He had to give it up and he dropped off to sleep dreaming he was riding down to the sea on the back of the big greyhound.

Next day he went round all the pubs in Pontygwaith asking questions; but when he started to talk about the dog in the mountain the blokes didn't take him serious, thinking he was on the cadge for a pint; so he was none the wiser at the end of it.

But after a week or two, one thing was sure: the greyhound was as wild as the bracken. No one came to claim him, though even if they did they couldn't get within a quarter of a mile of him to catch him. As soon as he saw anyone coming he'd look furtive over his shoulder and slink away into the thick ferns, as smooth as a fox.

He must have hated humans like poison. He wouldn't wait for the sight nor the smell of them. The last one he came up against must have treated him like nothing you'd care to tell about. The dog had been beaten till there was no trust left in him. Wil Flagons could see that plain enough, but he couldn't forget how quick the dog was and he would have given one of his eyes to catch him.

Whenever he got a chance he used to be up on the mountain, watching the dog move about. One evening he borrowed a spying glass and went looking for him special. He found him, as usual, up by the Big Rock, and he spent half an hour watching him, sizing him up; his shoulders and the strong curve of his body. Suddenly it struck him that the dog was wearing a collar. Then it came to him in a flash. He shut up his spying-glass and off he went for home, with Tonypandy Annie trotting along behind. Catch him? 'I'll catch him,' said Flagons, 'and then for some fun, Annie gel.'

First he looked up Dai Banana, who lived next-but-two, and asked him for a loan of his terrier. Now Dai Banana was proud of the terrier, which was a champion ratter, notwithstanding he had about four breeds of dog in him, and Dai wouldn't hear about lending him to Flagons until he knew what all the fun was going to be about. So he had to let Dai into his secret.

Now it was his idea to train Annie to grab the wild dog by the collar when they were playing together on the mountain. Then Annie would hold him until they came up to get him proper. After a few grunts and grumbles, Dai Banana agreed to lend his terrier for Annie to practise on, on condition, of course, that Flagons would pass on a handful or two of the clover when the wild one would be winning all the races he was talking about.

So the both of them started to train the bitch to do the collaring act. And that was the easiest part of the business; for Annie was as knowing as they make 'em. Flagons had nursed her like a baby and she knew the lift of his little finger. She went at it, natural as walking, and Dai Banana's terrier had a rough time at the rehearsals; though show fight he did at first and raised hell till they calmed him.

Well it all went on fine, and after a week Flagons thought Annie knew enough to have a cut at the wild greyhound. So he and Banana took her up the Gilfach one evening just before dusk and hid with her behind the sheep-wall.

After a bit the greyhound came down and Annie acted her part as cunning as a monkey. The wild one seemed proper tamed at the sight of her. He pranced around, rubbing his flank against her and raising his head, really friendly. Then Annie, quick as lightning, turned and did her act; did it to perfection. She got his collar all right; there was no mistake about that; but then—well, Annie herself didn't know what happened just then. No sooner had the dog felt the pull on his collar after the quick turn of the bitch than he stiffened his neck, and with a sharp twist of his head and his shoulders he sent Annie and the collar flying, ten yards away, into the bracken; and before you could say Jawl the dog was a brown bullet streaking across the moorland. Annie, with tail between her legs, and looking like nobody's bitch at all, brought the broken collar back and dropped it near Flagon's feet. He found the name of a bloke—a bad number from the next valley—written plain upon the brass part of it.

Well, if it had been anyone else bar Wil Flagons he'd have left the dog quiet on the mountain after this bit of business, but being Flagons you couldn't expect him to put all his hopes in his Annie after he'd seen the wild one's paces. One thing the wild life had done to the dog for sure; it had made him yards faster than any Mick of a milgi Flagons had ever seen come after a live hare or a rabbit-skin.

Anyhow, the greyhound was on the mountain for another month, with Flagons tickling his brains to think out another scheme to nab him; and when the winter was coming on and there was less chance of him picking anything up about, the women in Top-Row—the houses that have crawled half-way up the side of the mountain—were putting bones and scraps outside their back-door in the evening. The greyhound would come down regular after dark to collect them.

Now Flagon's house was in the Top-Row, just handy; so it was natural he got the idea of putting bones and scraps of meat just inside of the gate at the top of the garden, and trying to nab the dog when he came inside to get them.

For a week Flagons was lurking about the top of his garden after dark, with enough bones to start a factory. But he never got his hand near the wild greyhound. He saw him one night, though the dog was away before he could make one step towards him.

But Flagons was a trier, and especially where he could smell out a bit of money; he'd as much patience as a blind spider then. So, although he had failed twice to get the dog, he made up his mind to have another shot at him; three tries for a Taffy, Annie fach, he said one afternoon as he brought the bitch down from a canter on the mountain: We'll catch him this time. He had one more trick left in his bag; Tonypandy Annie herself; an old one, maybe, but the very last.

About this time Annie was not saying no to a bit of courting, and he was sure that if he tied her up inside the shed, with the door open, she would bring the dog, if he was within five miles of Top-Row and had any blood in him at all.

And, fair-play to Annie, fetch him she did. On the second night, Flagons, keeping watch alongside a bottle of something, saw the wild dog slink into the shed. It was him right enough; he saw him plain in the bit of light he'd left shine on purpose through the back kitchen window. Annie's come-hither had brought him.

Now, although he was aching to run up to the shed, Flagons had enough sense to keep to his hiding place for that night, because he knew he'd have to go slow and be middling cunning to shut the door on the right side of the greyhound. So he waited and saw him slide out silent like a shadow on the mountain.

Next day he made a sort of contraption on the door of the shed, with a cord leading down to his hiding place, so that when he pulled the cord the door would shut with a bang, and stay shut. Proper handy with his wits was Wil Flagons when something pricked him enough to use them.

Waiting that night for the dog to come down, he was as excited as the time his Annie won the Hundred Pounds and Silver Challenge Bowl. He'd made sure of him this time, and before the dog did actually come through the gate Flagons had spent at least a couple of hundred of the winnings.

The dog came through the gate the same as the night before; very slow and wary; but as soon as he was through he slid into the shed, quick, without a glance to the side of him.

Flagons held his breath and Annie stopped short in her whimpering. The dog was inside. He waited for a few moments to make sure, then he pulled the cord, and the door of the shed shut with a bang. Then there was a snarl and a loud barking.

As he ran up the path, lighting his torch as he went, Flagons could see his picture in the papers, holding the dog. The Year's Champion: Beat All Comers ... He slipped inside the shed. There was Annie in one corner, real frightened, wishing, no doubt, she was somebody else; opposite was the wild greyhound, staring at Flagons enough to burn him. But he made no move to get the dog; he just knelt down and started talking.

Now they say that Wil Flagons had such a way with dogs that he could put his hand out to the fiercest after a bit of talking; and he'd won a few bets over this and never once been bitten. But the more he talked this time the more the wild dog blazed hate and his soft words snarling back at him. And when at last he did stretch his hand out, very gentle, the dog sprang, and with a savage snap at his hand jumped clean over his shoulder. Bang went the dog against the door, and down came the contraption, and he was clear away on to the mountain.

It all came out down in the surgery the next morning, when Wil had three stitches in the back of his hand, and a bit of strong advice from the old doctor.

Well, weighing everything up, it wasn't surprising that Wil went bitter against the wild greyhound; it was only natural. He swore something horrible when anyone mentioned him after that. The dog, he said, was a wrong 'un, with no more worth in him than his looks.

But one morning a few weeks later he rolled into the bar of the Ffynon; proper up in the air with excitement; Annie was going to have pups; he knew it all along; it didn't matter a button that he hadn't caught the wild greyhound; it didn't matter he had gone to all that trouble; had a gammy hand and lost three weeks' work in the bargain; Annie was going to have pups and the wild dog was the father of them; and if the pups didn't turn out to be the fastest things on four legs he'd swear he'd go in for rabbit-breeding.

Proper elated was Wil before the bitch had her pups. He had a good few names, like Brown Streak and Treharris Trailer, stored up ready, and even started to build a place to keep them. But one morning he woke up to find the famous Annie mothering the queerest set of mongrels that had ever been together in a sugar-box. There was a bit of Dai Banana's terrier in just every one of them.

Only one man ever mentioned the wild greyhound to Wil Flagons after that; and he was a johnny from away, and since nobody had ever told him, he couldn't know any better.

DYLAN THOMAS

The Dress

They had followed him for two days over the length of the country, but he had lost them at the foot of the hills, and, hidden in a golden bush, had heard them shouting as they stumbled down the valley. Behind a tree on the ridge of the hills he had peeped down on to the fields where they hurried about like dogs, where they poked the hedges with their sticks and set up a faint howling as a mist came suddenly from the spring sky and hid them from his eyes. But the mist was a mother to him, putting a coat around his shoulders where the shirt was torn and the blood dry on his blades. The mist made him warm; he had the food and the drink of the mist on his lips; and he smiled through her mantle like a cat. He worked away from the valleywards side of the hill into the denser trees that might lead him to light and fire and a basin of soup. He thought of the coals that might be hissing in the grate, and of the young mother standing alone. He thought of her hair. Such a nest it would make for his hands. He ran through the trees, and found himself on a narrow road. Which way should he walk; towards or away from the moon? The mist had made a secret of the position of the moon, but, in a corner of the sky, where the mist had fallen apart, he could see the angles of the stars. He walked towards the north where the stars were, mumbling a song with no tune, hearing his feet suck in and out of the spongy earth.

Now there was time to collect his thoughts, but no sooner had he started to set them in order than an owl made a cry in the trees that hung over the road, and he stopped and winked up at her, finding a mutual melancholy in her sounds. Soon she would swoop and fasten on a mouse. He saw her for a moment as she sat screeching on her bough. Then, frightened of her, he hurried on, and had not gone more than a few yards into the darkness when, with a fresh cry, she flew away. Pity the hare, he thought, for the weasel will drink her. The road sloped to the stars, and the trees and the valley and the memory of the guns faded behind.

He heard footsteps. An old man, radiant with rain, stepped out of the mist.

Good night, sir, said the old man.

No night for the son of woman, said the madman.

The old man whistled, and hurried, half running, in the direction of the roadside trees.

Let the hounds know, the madman chuckled as he climbed up the hill, Let the hounds know. And, crafty as a fox, he doubled back to where the misty road branched off three ways. Hell on the stars, he said, and walked towards the dark.

The world was a ball under his feet; it kicked as he ran; it dropped; up came the trees. In the distance a poacher's dog yelled at the trap on its foot, and he heard it and ran the faster, thinking the enemy was on his heels. Duck, boys, duck, he called out, but with the voice of one who might have pointed to a fallen star.

Remembering of a sudden that he had not slept since the escape, he left off running. Now the waters of the rain, too tired to strike the earth, broke up as they fell and blew about in the wind like the sandman's grains. If he met sleep, sleep would be a girl. For the last two nights, while walking or running over the empty county, he had dreamed of their meeting. Lie down, she would say, and would give him her dress to lie on, stretching herself out by his side. Even as he had dreamed, and the twigs under his running feet had made a noise like the rustle of her dress, the enemy had shouted in the fields. He had run on and on, leaving sleep farther behind him. Sometimes there was a sun, a moon, and sometimes under a black sky he had tossed and thrown the wind before he could be off.

Where is Jack? they asked in the gardens of the place he had left. Up on the hills with a butcher's knife, they said, smiling. But the knife was gone, thrown at a tree and quivering there still.

There was no heat in his head. He ran on and on, howling for sleep.

And she, alone in the house, was sewing her new dress. It was a bright country dress with flowers on the bodice. Only a few more stitches were needed before it would be ready to wear. It would lie neat on her shoulders, and two of the flowers would be growing out of her breasts.

When she walked with her husband on Sunday mornings over the fields and down into the village, the boys would smile at her behind their hands, and the shaping of the dress round her belly would set all the widow women talking. She slipped into her new dress, and, looking into the mirror over the fireplace, saw that it was prettier than she had imagined. It made her face paler and her long hair darker. She had cut it low.

A dog out in the night lifted its head up and howled. She turned away hurriedly from her reflection, and pulled the curtains closer.

Out in the night they were searching for a madman. He had green eyes, they said, and had married a lady. They said he had cut off her lips because she smiled at men. They took him away, but he stole a knife from the kitchen and slashed his keeper and broke out into the wild valleys.

From afar he saw the light in the house, and stumbled up to the edge of the garden. He felt, he did not see, the little fence around it. The rusting wire scraped on his hands, and the wet, abominable grass crept over his knees. And once he was through the fence, the hosts of the garden came rushing to meet him, the flower-headed, and the bodying frosts. He had torn his fingers while the old wounds were still wet. Like a man of blood he came out of the enemy's darkness on to the steps. He said in a whisper, Let them not shoot me. And he opened the door.

She was in the middle of the room. Her hair had fallen untidily, and three of the buttons at the neck of her dress were undone. What made the dog howl as it did? Frightened of the howling, and thinking of the tales she had heard, she rocked in her chair. What became of the woman? she wondered as she rocked. She could not think of a woman without any lips. What became of women without any lips? she wondered.

The door made no noise. He stepped into the room, trying to smile, and, holding out his hands.

Oh, you've come back, she said.

Then she turned in her chair and saw him. There was blood even by his green eyes. She put her fingers to her mouth. Not shoot, he said.

But the moving of her arm drew the neck of her dress apart, and he stared in wonder at her wide, white forehead, her frightened eyes and mouth, and down on to the flowers on her dress. With the moving of her arm, her dress danced in the light. She sat before him, covered in flowers. Sleep, said the madman. And, kneeling down, he put his bewildered head upon her lap.

GWYN THOMAS

O Brother Man

'You will know,' said Mr. Rawlins at the beginning of his civic morality talk to the assembled prefects on Friday morning, 'that no one has done more to tackle the practical assessment of juvenile delinquency than myself. Theorizing about the thing is easy enough. Colleagues of mine in this very school are good at it. They talk gibly about the wartime blackout, broken homes, unbalanced curricula, ill-functioning hormones, and the rest, but do they ever venture into the front line of this battle? They do not.'

Mr. Rawlins paused. His normally restless face was whipped into stillness by bitter thoughts.

'You will remember a boy of this school, Chaplin Everest. I can speak freely about him now because I have arranged to have this boy placed on a farm many miles from here and if he has not, by now, rustled all the livestock, burned the cornfields, and poisoned the farmer, he will stay there and keep the hair of myself and his neighbours on this side of total greyness for another year or so.

'Everest started off at a brisk rate at the age of ten. Department stores were his meat. He one day looted the outfitting department of one such store. Just loaded the clothes on to his person and then asked the manager for a drink to refresh him when he was nearly fainting from the heat of this enormous cocoon of raincoats he had on. On another occasion Everest stole a gramophone record and he took it back because there was a scratch on one side and a ruse by the tenor to dodge a top note on the other. He would lift a pen and then create an uproar demanding a finer or thicker nib whatever his fancy might be. Since Everest was never known to do any writing this gesture can be taken as a piece of sheer virtuosity. A queerly vocal and, in a sense, responsible kleptomaniac, that was Everest.

'You know the value I set on music as a means of diverting criminal impulses. I thought this would work with Everest. I offered him a place as a violinist in the small orchestra that plays in the Junior Assembly. While there he made some of the sharpest moves in the history of any musical group. He undid the strap of and removed the watch of that very sensitive and self-absorbed flautist, Walter Fawcett, when Fawcett was half-way through the descant of "Angels of Jesus, Angels of Light", a first-rate hymn whose libretto I had urged Everest to read beforehand so that he could get the full flavour. And within three weeks of Everest rubbing in his first bit of resin the music stands of the entire band were found in a second-hand shop, and a chemist informed that Everest had slipped into his shop and taken some first-aid material to apply to his legs which had been abraded by the stolen metal on his way down to the town. At that period Everest was working part-time with a draper and when the draper found things getting a little bare around the walls he made a search of Everest's home. Everest's bedroom was found to have a stock of haberdashery that ran Austin Reed a hot second. The draper did not know whether to take Everest to court or trundle his counter to Everest's bedroom and start afresh from there.

'I was on the point of giving up hope and breaking Everest's violin over his head when we found him one morning sitting in a corner of the orchestra almost out of sight behind a wall of brass. He had found a euphonium and in the course of that morning's hymn, a simple one admittedly, he managed to strike a series of tremendous and relevant notes on this instrument. Some of these notes were of excessive volume and sea captains in the roads off Cardiff wired in to ask what we could see that they couldn't. Everest assured me that he had come quite fairly by the euphonium. His father, he said, had bought it out of the product of an insurance policy on an uncle, a chapel-goer, who had been worried into the grave by Everest's conduct.

'Everest seemed reformed. Looking back at it now, I am prepared to explain this by the heaviness of the instrument. Anything that hinders movement makes for virtue.

'Now you may think the thing could have ended there. The town well rid of a delinquent and Everest blowing himself into a torpor of righteous conformity.' Mr. Rawlins sighed and stared at a far corner of the sports field, where the boys dressed in white were jumping over each other. 'Life will at times wear a look of idiot tranquillity. Be sure that at just such moments the monstrous ironies which are shortly going to batter you flat are dusting each other's truncheons and urging each other courteously to take the first whack.

'In the second month of Everest's serving as euphonium player this town was made a borough. The prospective mayor, having made the switch from a short chain to a long chain and rattling both with what I thought a certain ostentation, made his first mayoral procession through the town. He considered that the parade had a quiet, sour look and matters were made worse having groups of Dissenters on the flank, fanatical lovers of a drab, civilian status who went up and down the procession making crude, flatfooted remarks about the mayor's chain. The mayor demanded more colour, body, tone, a blare and a blaze of municipal pomp that would shame or silence the critics.

'The word went out that the two military bands the town had once had were to be revived. They were called the Institute band and the Legion band. The Legion band got restarted promptly because they had a licensed club and that could feed them with funds for new instruments and uniforms. But things were more laggard with the Institute band and no move was made to reopen their old band club-house on that waste patch near the gasworks.

'While the old members of the Institute band were being encouraged to limber up for a march back into history, Everest came up to me one morning and said: "Please, sir, you know my uncle? He's not dead."

'The statement meant nothing to me. That was the way with Everest. He would state something and you would have to tramp through a thousand feet of tangential facts and fictions to reach the point from which he was actually speaking. Besides, that morning I was confused, not at my quickest. I had found a whole row of boys in the hall fitting grossly secular words to that splendid hymn "Bread of Heaven". I was in no mood for Everest and at the back of my mind I felt that there were drunken, un-Welsh overtones about some of the notes produced by Everest on that euphonium which had encouraged the tap-room humour of those interpolations. "In general terms, Everest," I said, "I am glad your uncle is not dead. But what is this to me? I do not wish to appear callous, but do I know him?" "You remember, sir," Everest said very earnestly as if reproving me for the shortness of my tone, "you remember the uncle who died and left the insurance and my father bought my euphonium?" "Oh yes, Everest, of course. The insured chapel-goer. Let his life and the fruit of his prudence be a lesson to you. What about him now, Everest?" "Well, sir, he isn't dead." "You mean . . .?" "Yes, sir. There was no insurance. My father didn't buy the euphonium. I stole it."

'This was too much for me. To hear "Bread of Heaven" and that tortuous confession from Everest on one morning was going too far. Two nights before, I had seen a film at the Y.M.C.A., specially screened for youth-leaders, in which the priest in charge of a camp for delinquent boys had shaken one of the less regenerate boys like a rat. The priest himself had made that point. "I am shaking you," he shouted in his rage, "like a rat because you are a rat." That, I thought, was the line with Everest. I grabbed him by the tie and started to shake, trying rather foolishly as I see now to explain to him that I had seen a priest do this in the Y.M.C.A. Everest's movements were quick and hardly perceptible. I found myself shaking the tie like a kind of lasso, but Everest himself was now standing, patient and cool, about six feet away. The Headmaster came in that moment. Try explaining to anyone why you should be waving a noosed tie at a boy who just stands there looking tolerantly at you.

'I visited the home of Everest that evening. A broken and demoralized home. The father, a peering and thoughtful man, had a long record of dishonesty and had been to gaol. His life and personality were of the most shuffling and indeterminate sort. The mother had vanished, perplexed and tired, years before. As soon as I stepped through the door father and son got down to it and made me a meal of excellent fish and chips. It was good to see them fend so well for themselves. On his second chip Everest owned up to having broken into the bandhouse near the gasworks and taken the euphonium. "The back window of that bandhouse is very easy," he said in the sort of slow cold voice that should be reserved for science. The father cried a little as if this sort of roguery had never come within his experience, but it might, too, have been the very strong vinegar of which the father had poured a good half-bottle over his chips.

'I consoled the father and said: "It'll be all right. The boy will take it back and all will be forgotten. Any day now the Institute band will be returning to the old bandhouse to dust off their instruments and it is important that the euphonium be there waiting for them." I turned around to repeat this to Everest but he had slipped out of the kitchen. I went outside the kitchen door and shouted around for him. No trace.

'I told Mr. Everest that he himself would have to take the euphonium back. He lifted up his wet face from his chips, then hobbled around the table and put his hand on my shoulder. I had not noticed the hobble before. When frying the fish he had seemed pretty spry when moving out of the range of flying fat but now he had one of the most pronounced limps I had seen. I felt the night filling up with vast deceptions. Everest had probably left the kitchen in that covert way at some signal from his father. I tried to make my face as hard as I could.

'Then Mr. Everest started to talk. He explained that if he had only been in a fair state of health he would have been down to the bandhouse to replace the instrument while the chips had been on so that we could have had our meal without any taint of fear or guilt in the air. But he told some tale of having fallen over a fellow-prisoner who had dropped in a faint in the exercise yard of the prison while some brutal overseer had been making them run at top speed. Mr. Everest had been in a condition since then which made it impossible for him to get into any building through the window, however much he would like to do so and once or twice he had so liked. "Anyhow, not with a euphonium," he said. "That's a very hampering article, the euphonium." Then he put his face very close to mine. He said: "Mr. Rawlins, two things will keep me out of gaol in the future. The first is the terrible pain I get whenever I cock my leg, which is bad for burgling because it makes me give out a terrible groan." He cocked his leg suddenly and scared the wits out of me with the groan he gave. "And the second thing is the wonderful friendship you've shown my son."

"And I knew at once that he wanted me to set the seal on that friendship by transporting that piece of brass back to the bandhouse. Normally I would have told Everest to get back on the hinge and start finding his son or carrying the thing himself. But I had been touched by the fine meal that had been prepared for me by those two lonely and desperate beings, even though I wondered who in that neighbourhood might still be looking for the three thick cutlets we had enjoyed. Besides, I felt like some scratch of dangerous action to ease the itch of embarrassment I had felt when the Headmaster had come into the hall that morning and found me apparently trying to snare Everest back into his own tie. "You're a scholar," said Mr. Everest. "You can do it. And remember what my boy said about that window in the back of the bandhouse." I listened and as my fingers drummed on the table I realized more clearly than ever that morally that family could not have been better named. High, remote, and glacial.

'He handed me the euphonium. "After this," he said, "the boy will be able to consider himself as much your son as my son." And the way we smiled at each other we must both have been made a little drunk by all that vinegar and emotional excitement. Then he added that I had better leave by the back way. By now I was entering into the spirit of the thing and I asked Mr. Everest whether it wouldn't be better to have some cover for the euphonium like a shawl or a mac. My panic made the thing seem larger as Mr. Everest stood ready to slip it to me. I thought we should be lucky to get it through the kitchen door to start with. Mr. Everest was against any covering. He said that that kind of camouflage would only make it worse. "Draws attention," he said. He gave a bang on the metal. "Best be brazen," he said and laughed.

'He wished me luck and I started up the garden path. I was nervous as a kitten, stealthy as a cat, using only the tips of my toes and holding the euphonium lightly in my arms ready to toss it instantly into a bush if challenged. As I fumbled with the latch of the door that led into the back-lane I swore I saw the face of the boy Chaplin staring at me from behind a rose bush. The face was grave, quite unselfish, and I had the feeling that if it were really Everest he was wishing me well.

'I reached the bandhouse in the shadow of the high wall that surrounds the gasworks. There is a greasiness in the shadows in that part of the town and the smell of gas which is perpetual near that wall did not take long to skim away all the resolve and high spirits that had come so oddly upon me in the Everests' kitchen. For a very small fee I would have returned to the safety of my sitting-room and thrown the euphonium over the gasworks wall, there to puzzle the people who run this undertaking. But I thought of Everest, of how much more likeable and stable the boy had been since playing at the morning services. I owed it to him now to see that he would not be saddled with another stretch under the probation officer or in a reform school for an offence which was not, in a fundamental sense, immoral. How, I asked myself, and no question has ever rung out with such sonority at such a small distance from a gasworks, how does the law stand on thefts committed to procure the means of salvation?

'I found the window mentioned by Everest. The window was shaky to the touch but awkwardly far from the ground. The same man had designed the Institute bandhouse as had designed the Institute and he was far gone in Gothic. Even without the euphonium the entry would have taken a lot of deftness. The only thing was to get the window open, balance on the sill and lift the euphonium in after me.

'I got the window up and hoisted myself on to the sill. I found myself sitting squarely on one of the longest and most penetrating fitments ever used in the building of a window frame. That and the feeling of terror which had come upon me from the moment I had set my hand upon the sill had done something to shrink my legs, and the euphonium on the ground outside looked as far away as if it were at the bottom of a cliff.

'Then I heard a good deal of noise from a public house about three hundred yards away. It was a place called The White Rock because it was traditionally the place where that legendary harpist Dafydd took his last careful look at Mynydd Coch and gave up the ghost and harping with one angry kick at the strings. A considerable group of men were leaving The White Rock and they sounded happy about something. They were happy, as I found when their voices grew nearer and the gist of their talk grew plain. They had not only taken drink but had, just a few minutes before, in the long room of The White Rock, decided to reform the Institute band without delay and were at that very moment on their way to the bandhouse to lubricate and polish their instruments. I could hear the louder of them declare that they would soon be shaming and outblowing the Legion band. "That lot!" I heard one of them say. It was the voice of their euphonium player, Nathaniel Roscoe, a man barbarous in his devotion to noise. "They've never risen a cultural notch above Sousa and that selection from Chu Chin Chow where my cousin Reynold Roscoe makes a special effect in the Cobbler's Song by tramping up and down the stage looking pensive, humming very low and using a hammer."

'I heard them rattle the door in front of me as they inserted the key. For all my patiently laboured gentleness I could at that moment have killed Everest and I could also have spared a side-blow for Nathaniel Roscoe but I instantly prayed to God to forgive me that thought and to help hoist me off that prong or catch on which I was impaled. One day I will ask the boys in the bandhouse about the shape and function of it. No doubt it is connected with the strange inner lore of bandmanship.

'By an act of sweating fury I lifted my body off the sill and fell to the ground outside. I pulled the window down just as the front door was thrown open. I heard the roaring voice of Roscoe say a second before the window closed to: "Hullo, these Legion boys have been here."

'I gathered the euphonium into my arms and bolted. I am not sure why I did that. Probably some foolish fear of fingerprints planted in me by my recent traffic with the Everests. It would have taken an hour to wipe that instrument clean at all thoroughly. I ran at full speed through the lane that ran parallel to the main street of the town that debouches into the square.

'My movements were crouched and erratic with panic and strain and every ten seconds or so I heard the metal of the euphonium strike hard against the asphalt as if trying to brake me. I heard the sound of a brass band playing but my time sense had been disordered by shortness of breath and I supposed that the Institute band, in the few seconds since I had started my run with the euphonium, had grouped around their conductor and launched into a tune. I tried to check my run to think more carefully about this point but my fears were making fools of all my limbs and before I knew it I was in the main street at the very moment when the Legion band, in their civilian suits and making a rehearsal march, swung past the opening of the lane through which I had been making my way from the bandhouse. Few people had spotted me. Thoughts fell like bolts in my mind. With a brass band coming up the street, what is the public to think of a euphonium player who darts away from them at right angles? I pulled my hat as low as I could over my eyes and fell in as a kind of extra in one of the band's back rows where the instruments seemed roughly of the size and shape of the one I was carrying. I put the mouthpiece of the instrument to my mouth, imitating the angle most general among my neighbours, but fortunately produced no note that might have proved my lack of right to be there. My posture must have been overdone because I was told sullenly by one of the drummers to go back to the orthodox hold and keep in step.

'As we approached a zone of clear light I saw the Headmaster of my school come out of one of the local vestries. I held the euphonium up high enough to hide my face and just as I was doing this and trying at the same time to pull my hat down even lower, that brusque drummer who had cautioned me before, that ex-wrestler Noah Finney, banged at my euphonium with his drumstick and said that he was beginning to suspect that I had been sent by the Institute band to break up the harmony and the order of march. He also leaned forward and pulled at my hat, saying that any sort of pressure on the brow was the worst thing out for a euphonium player. I fled up the very next opening. I heard the kettle-drummer, that timid semi-invalid Benjamin Boon, say to Noah Finney that if he had known that things were going to be so jumpy on the march he would never have joined except for sit-down performances.

'I found my way back to the Everest home. Father and son were in the kitchen prepared to start on another considerable meal.

Not one of them asked why I was back or what had happened. The boy took the euphonium from me and played what I took to be some sort of rogue's grace over the food. He said the instrument did not seem to have taken any harm from its jaunt. The father invited me to help them in putting away the very oily dish of chees and onion. I said nothing. I shook their hands to compliment them on being on point duty at what was without question one of the busiest and brassiest sections of the life force. I put my fingers briefly into the hot cheese to get some warmth and confidence back into my body. Then I left.

'The next day I was busy. I bought a new euphonium and caused it to be delivered anonymously to the door of the Institute bandhouse. The boy Everest joined the band the next day and he and Nathaniel Roscoe made a good pair but I think there is an essential nihilism in Roscoe, a baritone in light opera as well as a euphonium player, which did not help Everest solve any of his later moral equations.

'And there was another thing. I was pretty certain that the Headmaster had spotted me as I walked on the flank of the Legion band despite that last desperate tug at my hat, which had left little more than an inch of my face in view. My flannel trousers had been freshly washed and were excessively light and easily recognized, and the Headmaster had a naturally downcast glance which made him good at trousers. I remembered that his father, years before, had written a history of all the chapels between Cross Hands and Seven Sisters. These had been issued in a de luxe leather-bound edition at a high price and at a time when the market for leather-bound books about chapels anywhere had dropped down dead. I paid the full price for this work and asked the Headmaster to accept the collection on behalf of the school. He did that and I do not think his opinion of me improved much even then.

'All that expenditure was not without its bitter little echoes in my private chambers. At the time I was becoming friendly with a charming and dignified lady of this town. I had the intention of subsidizing a trip to the National Museum for about twenty members of the Sunday School in which she was interested. These were children from a rough quarter and had maximum need of some cooling thoughts about the past. I had made the promise to my friend. Then Everest, the great gutter of hopes, had come along and that was that.

'Behind every piece of virtue on this earth there is a legion of aching hearts and empty pockets. Somebody has paid. I know.'

R. GERALLT JONES

The Letter

Translated from the Welsh by the author

'Remember to write.' Clic-di-clac, clic-di-clac, clic-di-clac. The train's clattering wheels jangle mam's words in my mind as I sit in the corner and stare unseeing at the rain rushing by.

'Remember to write.'

I'm looking out of the dirty carriage window. The sea flows past in a hurry to get back to Pwllheli, to Llŷn, to Nain, and to Nefyn. God, I'd give a thousand pounds, two thousand, two thousand and dad's Morris car and the cricket book with Don Bradman's picture, to be playing football in Nefyn instead of going away to school. To be able to turn in my own time on Pwllheli platform after seeing someone else off to school, to walk through the wooden barrier, wait for as long as I like near the Wyman's bookstall and see the counter-full of sweets, to buy a *Hotspur* and the *Sporting Record*, and then to saunter out into the lovely rain. I'd stand then in the middle of Station Square and start getting really wet, and I'd look up and down Pen Cob like an old farmer before deciding which way to go. Then I'd turn to the left, in no hurry, and wander slowly towards the bridge. I'd stand there for hours and hours in the rain, watching the swans. Old snobs, swans are, pretending they don't know anyone's looking at them. Down there they go swimming round and round like lunatics for ages, their little black feet pumping like train's wheels underneath them. Like a train. Clic-di-clac, clic-di-clac; remember to write. 'Dear Mam, I don't like school. Please can I come home. At once. Yours in brief . . .'

But it will be ten weeks before I can walk Pen Cob again. Ten weeks. How long is ten weeks? It's almost as long as from this very second to the end of the world, from today to that time Nain talks about when a drunken man kicked the policeman's hat in Llanllyfni fair, it's like as-it-was-in-the-beginning-is-now'n-for-ever-shall-be-world-without-end-amen. Nobody can see to the far end of ten weeks. It's altogether too long for anyone to think about. I grab my *Hotspur* and try to read about Cannonball Kidd, who can score a goal from halfway against the best goalie in the world. But it's no use. I can't get interested even in Cannonball Kidd. I can feel a great empty hole in my belly, and I stare out through the window without seeing anything but the drizzle on Pwllheli station. 'Dear Mam. Here's the letter. I've got a pain in my belly. Oh, please can I come home...'

I was sitting on the parapet on my bridge when Math came to tell me that I too was going away to school. I didn't understand what that meant to begin with. The bridge wasn't an ordinary bridge then, of course, it was a captain's bridge. My ship was on its way to India and China to see all the treasures of Peru and the little yellow children it talks about in the hymn. When Math rushed pell-mell down past the mill and shouted that he had important news for me, I slunk off to hide on the stone ledge that ran underneath the bridge just above water level, and stayed there still as the stone itself without daring to swallow or to release just one simple tiny breath until I was almost bursting...

'Hey, Johnny, I've got big news!'

No answer from me. I move carefully along the ledge, and find a place to sit, then settle down quietly, quietly, with the soles of my feet just tickling the water. I can trail the bottoms of my shoes in the water fine without wetting my feet at all; or only a little bit sometimes. Math changed his tune.

'Captain, sir, I have an important message for the fleet, sir!'

Huh, I say to myself, does he think I was born yesterday? And I sit back in the shadow of the parapet and dream that I'm living in a cave without anyone knowing I'm there, and the whole world far far away.

'Oh, Johnny, come on, I've got something terribly important to tell you.'

What does he have to say, I ponder. Perhaps it isn't bad news after all. Perhaps we'll go for a trip to Pwllheli after lunch. Or farther still. To Bangor to watch the football? What if I miss a trip to Bangor to watch the football?

'All right, kid, if you want to play silly buggers, you won't find out then. Not until you have to.'

I hear Math making a decision, starting off up the hill again. Then I get up suddenly and run along the edge; I don't want to be left alone underneath the bridge; everything is cold and nasty, and the big stones drip green and wet.

'Hello! Math, hello there! Math!'

'Come out of it, you little monkey, so that I can tell you.'

And after I'd climbed, dirty and bedraggled, up the wall and sat beside him on top, I heard the story. I didn't understand at all. Math had been away at school a long time, but that was different. Math was fifteen and a stranger. He didn't really belong in our house.

And now I was going as well. No more walking between the hedges to school. What did 'away' mean? Was it farther than Pwllheli? Perhaps it was as far as Bangor. Math said that the name of the place was Shwsbri, but that meant nothing. It sounded a bit like strawberries, and strawberries could be found in Llaniestyn, if only in Mr. Barret's garden. Would it be possible to fish in the pond after being 'away', or to sit on the bridge, or to go to Felin Eithin shop to buy fresh bread and eat all the crust on the way home? Could I play trains in the front room? Clic-di-clac, clic-di-clac. Oh, Mam, I don't want to go to Shwsbri. 'Dear Mam. I don't know where I'll be when you receive this letter. I have jumped off the train. I am going to India because I don't want to go to Shwsbri away to school. Yours truly ...'

I fling down the *Hotspur*, stare indignantly at Criccieth station outside, and attack my meat sandwich. It must be hours and hours since I had breakfast.

At Dovey Junction, when I have more or less forgotten the end-product of the journey, and am poking around the platform happily enough, what do I see in the middle of a crowd of people at the far end of the station but a school cap. Exactly the same colour as the sparkling new cap which is safely tucked away in my own pocket. I stand stock still. Then I creep back step by step round the corner to the gents. I stand there for a minute, my heart pumping away and my breath catching in my throat. Another boy going to the same place! Who is he? He looks incredibly clever and beautiful in his cap. I peer around the corner of the gents to look at him. He is standing still in the middle of the platform, with a new, leather case by his side. And what is he doing? Reading a newspaper! The only one I have ever seen reading a newspaper is my father. And my father is old. Do boys read newspapers in Shwsbri? Dear God, what sort of place am I going to?

When the Shwsbri train comes in, I jump smartly into an empty compartment near the back. Please God, I say, don't send that boy into this compartment. But I know perfectly well that it is no good. He arrives soon enough, swaggering his way down the corridor, cap over one ear. And in he comes. After flinging his bag up on the rack overhead and settling himself in a corner, he gives me the once-over, like a farmer at the stock-market.

'I see we're going to the same place,' he says off-handedly, pointing at the corner of my new cap that's peeping stupidly out of my coat pocket.

'I goin' to Shwsbri,' I volunteer.

'Yes, old son, we're all going there on this train,' he says, 'but you and I are going to the same school.'

'Oh. Yes.' There are too many English words chasing each other across his lips for me to follow properly. I can do nothing but sit and stare stupidly at his middle. Oh, Mam, I don't want to go away to old school, where they talk funny and boys with newspapers and no damn anybody speaking Welsh. Diawl, diawl, diawl, I say, leaning heavily on my lonely obscenity, I don't want to go to old school.

'I s'pose you're a new boy,' he offers, after a dreadful, long pause.

'Yes.'

'Mm. Well, you ought to be wearing your cap, you know. It's an offence not to wear your cap.'

'Oh.' I grab my black and yellow cap and stick it on my head. 'Offence?'

'Offence. Crime. Breaking the rules. What's the matter, don't you understand English?'

But the question does not require an answer, and he snuggles up behind his papers and comics to chew sweets and whistle tunelessly from time to time to show that he remembers I'm here. In Welshpool, three others descend on us, everyone laughing madly, thumping backs, pumping hands, and speaking a totally incomprehensible language, with words like 'swishing' and 'brekker' and 'footer' and 'prep'. After they've had their fill of taking each other's caps and kicking each other and flinging cases back and forth, someone notices me.

'What's this, Podge, freshie?'

'Yes,' says the veteran. 'Welshie as well. Can't understand a word of English.'

'Good God.' He gets up and stands in front of me and stares into my face. I can see the blackspots in the end of his nose. By this time, everyone is listening intently. He holds his face within three inches of mine. If I was brave, I would knock his teeth down his throat. If I was like Math or the Saint. But I'm not.

'Welshie are you? Welsh? Welsh?'

'Yes,' I say sadly, 'I am from Pen Llŷn.'

Everyone starts hooting with laughter, rolling around on their seats. The questioner tries again.

'Going to Priestley School are you? School? School?'

'Yes.'

He turns triumphantly to the others.

'Bloody hell, fellers, we'll have some fun with this when we get there. All it can say is yes.'

And everyone starts rolling with laughter once again. I push myself far back into my corner for the remainder of the journey, feel the damn silly wetness in my eyes, and try to think about Cannonball Kidd, about caravans, about Barmouth, about anything but about Mam and Pen Llŷn this morning. Cli-di-clac, clic-di-clac. 'Remember to write a letter.' Clic-di-clac, remember to write.

When the train reaches Shwsbri station, they all forget about me soon enough, and the whole gang rushes out on to the platform, their bags flying in all directions, caps shining new in the rain, everyone talking. On the platform, standing stiff as a poker, there's an ugly woman in a feathered hat, her lips one grim line, and a thin black walking stick in her hand. As each one of them sees her, he stops dead, pulls his cap straight, hauls trousers up, tries to get everything back into line.

'Well.' She looks at them as though she suddenly smells something unpleasant. 'Isn't there anyone else with you?'

Then she sees me standing in the carriage door, cap in hand, and my tie round the back of my neck.

'Oh.' With a come-and-gone smile flashing across her white teeth. 'Here he is. Are you Jones?'

'Yes, missus. My name is Joni Jones.'

'I see. Well, from now on you'll be Jones. Jones J. We don't use names like Johnnie at school, do we? And nice little boys don't say missus, Jones. My name is Miss Darby. Now boys, let's be on our way. We'll all be ready for our tea, I have no doubt.'

And off she goes along the platform, her stick clicking up and down, and her bottom waddling regularly from side to side like a duck's. And everyone follows her quiet as mice, and me following everyone else like Mrs. Jones the Post's little terrier dog.

I don't remember much about the next two days, thank God, only an occasional minute here and there. But I know very well that it's all far worse than any nightmare I've ever had about the place before I got here. And I had plenty of those. Everyone in this Priestley looks old and very experienced and talks a mouthful of English. The teachers have never heard of Wales, I don't think, and the cabbage is tough as string and black and green like watercress, and the bed is hard as sleeping on the floor, and the headmaster teaches something called Latin in a room with iron bars across the windows. Every night before going to bed I go to the lavatory to cry quietly and then go back to that old cold barn where everyone is pretending to sleep, and waiting to bait the Welshie.

On Sunday, we are all gathered together in the Latin room with a piece of paper and a small square envelope each, and the head tells us to write a letter home to say we are all right, have arrived safe and have had enough to eat. Well, I grab my brand new fountain-pen, and start to write my letter.

Dear Mum and Dad,

I hope you are O.K. like me. I have arrived safe. The food is quite good and the school is quite nice. I am looking forward to the holidays. Remember me to Spot and to Llyn y Felin.

This in brief,

JONI.

RICHARD HUGHES

A Moment of Time

'*That* was the end of the world,' he said, and sighed. 'It's all gone—finished.'

'I had not noticed it,' said I.

The eyes that regarded me were flecked with brown in the iris.

'No? No; perhaps some wouldn't. But there is no more Space, no Time, no Matter.'

'But there is,' said I. 'I can see a sunset in the sky, and there is a smoky mist in the hollows.'

'There is not,' said he.

'And I can hear that lame mare nicker.'

'You cannot,' said he.

'And the bank soaks through my breeches.'

'It does not,' said he.

'But today is Friday.'

'It is not,' said he.

'Yet you are still biting your black finger-nail.'

'I am not,' said he.

'And talking to me.'

'I am not,' said he.' How could I be talking to you? The world is ended.'

'Then what is it I am seeing? Am I like a man struck blind who carries under his lids what he last set eyes on?'

'All your senses are clean cut off you like limbs, and you have only the illusion of them, as men do who have lost a leg or an arm.'

At that I was dismayed, because I have always taken a great delight in my senses. Then a little, melancholy, wandering smell wisped down the road: partly bitter, from the scent of a horse in it and some new whitewash.

'I don't believe you!' I cried suddenly.

'You do not,' said he, 'for you are destroyed too.'

'Will! Ynysfor!' I cried, in sudden panic, using his Bardic name. 'Ynysfor! If it's all Illusion, are you also destroyed? What are you, Will?'

'I AM *not*.'

'You deny that you exist, then?'

'I do not deny it: for if I do not exist, how can I deny?'

Then that many-coloured goat from Hafod Uchaf got up-wind from me. I could see him, and the wind brought him, and his small feet clicked on the rock. Somewhere very high up the lambs were yelling because of the frost between their two toes. Steadily the tide of mist rose, while the sun went down in a glory of cloudlets like little green fish-scales.

'I don't believe you!' I cried again. 'It's real, I tell you; *real*.'

'Have you never said to yourself in a dream, "Now I really am awake"?'

'Yes. But why should I dream all this?'

'Why are dreams ever dreamt?'

'They say, to save the mind from some shock too terrible for it.'

'And what shock could be more terrible than the ending of all things? The heavens are rolled up as a scroll: in the twinkling of an eye the earth, and all that in it is, consumed as with fire. What shock could be more violent than that?'

My hair tingled on to its ends with horror. 'I will not dream!' I cried. 'If I am a naked soul lost in the Absolute, at least I will know it! I dare not love Dream with the love I have given to the real world; I will count three, and wake! One—two——'

'You cannot,' said Ynysfor.

'Three!' So I opened my eyes. Darkness was quietly settling down among the hills, where the voices of plovers floated. Then I lay down on my face, and rubbed it in the wet grit of the road.

'I *will* wake up!' I cried.

'You will dream that your forehead is all bloody,' said Will. 'But how will that wake you? If there is no more Time, there is no Future: therefore you can never wake.'

I wiped the misty glass of my watch with my thumb.

'It is ten minutes since you told me that the world was ended.'

'The action of a dream may cover many weeks, and yet the dream itself only last a few seconds.'

'How long am I, then, dreaming this?'

'One moment of time—the moment of the world's ending.'

'And how long will the action of the dream last?'

'For ever. If there is no time, Eternity coincides with a moment. You can never cease dreaming.'

'But if I suffer Illusion, I exist: if I dream, I am. I cannot be cheated into a belief that I exist.'

'Suppose that you exist....'

'Then *you*: have pou no existence outside my dream?'

'If I have, it is in utter isolation. There is no more Space, therefore there can be no proximity, no communication, only utter isolation. For no soul can any other soul exist. If I do exist, in this isolation, how can I say "yes"? The communicative *me* you only dream.'

The moisture from the mist collected on my hair, and two drops rolled over the dried blood on my cheek.

'What you have been saying is a pack of paradox,' said I. 'Nothing can both be and not-be.'

'On the contrary, it is on the exact balance of Being and Not-being that existence depends. I will show it. All things—all Time, all Space, all Mind—*perish*. If Time could survive the destruction of Mind, then it would be possible for the act of destruction to become complete, then would Mind *have perished*: but because Time cannot survive it, the existence of all minds must hang for ever poised on a moment, the moment of their destruction, dreaming that Time and Space still are, exactly balanced in an eternal dead-lock between Being and Not-being. That is the infinite Dead-lock, causing the infinite, convincing Dream of men: and so an Illusion of Time, of Space, of Self, as still existent, arises.'

'In fact, the end of the world has made no difference whatever to anything,' said I. 'Since it is impossible to know that it has ended, everything goes on exactly as before. I might prove conclusively in some paper that the world had ended, and myself and that paper with it three issues before.'

'It makes absolutely no difference to you,' said Ynysfor, 'since you can't believe it.'

'Man! Man!' I cried, suddenly raging. 'What do you want to *make* me believe it for? If you know it is ended, why can't you keep silent?'

'It is the truth.'

'But you will never convince anyone.'

'Never.'

'But if we shall never know, it makes very little difference whether it be true or false.'

'No, no: perhaps not; to you.'

The scratches on my face were smarting. 'Not *now*,' I said.

'Now?' He played with the word, as if to remind me that it was meaningless.

Then a young girl trotted by on a grey mare, nervous of the lurking night. I stood up, and fitted my pipe to my teeth.

'I must get on with my dream,' I said; and left him.

ISLWYN FFOWC ELIS

Song of a Pole

Translated from the Welsh by the author

On a moonlit night a man can love a telegraph pole. Especially a new one, rising nuptially from the stones of the hedge amid a row of old and blackened ones.

'What does a telegraph pole mean?' asked Wil, eyeing this one along its luminous height. 'I'll tell you. An organ.'

He pressed his ear against the wood and closed his eyes. I too was listening to the chord in the wood and the windy moon fluting in the wires when Wil said again,

'Men are very foolish to worry about bread and brass. This toils not, it spins not, and yet it can sing like faith.'

'It'll rot,' I said.

Wil opened his eyes and filled them with the slender white temple.

'I'm a priest now,' he intoned. 'I always wanted to be a priest. Why, you say, you who are one of the dumb ones of this world? I'll tell you why. To fail in an impossible job. That's the only failure with a shine to it. The only failure worthy of a chair poem or a crown ode.'

'You can't sit in a crown or wear a chair on your head,' said I.

But Wil had swallowed this priest idea.

'To try and interpret the thought that isn't thought,' he confided to the pole. 'To preach the truth that's not like anything that's true.'

'Come home, it's nearly Christmas,' said I, being one of the dumb ones of this world.

'Aye,' continued the priest, 'to be drops to the rain and rays to the sun and a miraculous birth to that which cannot be born. If I knew what's inside this singing tower I could awaken the world.'

I couldn't let Wil have the beautiful pole all to himself, so I sat with my legs astride it and peered up its length. The moment was fortunate, for now the moon was right atop of it.

'With this gimlet,' I said, 'I'm boring right into the light.'

'Don't put it out!' Wil was angry. 'There are men like you who creep around playing with the switches of the world, darkening it room by room, collecting darknesses as Bryn *bach* Hyfrydle collects stamps. And men like me have to rush around on your heels putting back the light.'

But he was giving up being a priest now and turning into a poet.

'Yes,' he said.

'Yes what?'

'There *is* dignity and stateliness and unsullied self-respect in telegraph poles.'

I spotted the quotation and said knowledgeably, 'Sir Thomas Parry-Williams.'

This discussion was strangled at birth because now Wil got seized with his conviction.

'Jos,' he said, moonlight welling up in his eyes, 'we must move this unsullied pole.'

'Move it? Where on earth to?'

'To the top of Y Foel. Did you ever have the feeling that there was one thing in life that you couldn't live unless you did it? Something that made you sweat and blush only to think about it?'

'Little Olwen School House long ago.'

'Something, my very clever chap, that scattered the bundle of prejudices you were wrapped in with your swaddling clothes and gave you a brand new bundle instead?'

'Only a purple moon——' I tried to quote Hedd Wyn.

'That something for me, Josi, is this pole. This, to me, is the revelation, the crack in the shell, the splitting, saving catharsis. God, I'm good tonight. Tonight, I know what it is to *live*.'

'One dazzling moment, when our clay——' I tried to quote Cynan.

'But.' Wil knelt before the pole. 'Revelation is no use, Jos *bach,* without a tongue, and feet, and hands. Understand, and you must speak. Know, and you must do.'

It was clear now that Wil was pure purpose. He talked new, looked new, was new from head to foot. At that moment I could have followed him to the end of the earth and over the edge. He was *mein Führer.* I saw his dirty oilskin and manured trousers in the fulling-mill of the moon, transformed in the light that is less than light. Wil was going to do. But do what?

'I've just told you, worm. Move this pole to the top of Y Foel.'

'Why?'

He spun round, grabbed my coat lapels and shook me fiercely.

'"Why" is a dirty word. D'you get that? Don't ever ask it again.'

Wil was right, Wil was always right. We settled down to our plan.

Next morning Wil and I, Jos, stood beside the pole, each with his spade. The pole was smaller and greyer in the larger light of the sun, the countryside welling up, green, around it. But Wil had sufficient faith for two. His love for the pole had not waned.

By eleven the hole about the foot of the pole was a cube yard. Harri Postman slipped off his bike to meddle.

'Got a new job, boys?'

'Yes,' said Wil. 'Are you a fair climber?'

'The best in these parts,' bragged Harri.

'Stop lying, you bloody licker of stamps.' Wil dug more fiercely. Postman looked menacing.

'Listen, Red Wil. I was climbing telegraph poles before you could climb out of your pram. And I'd be at it today if that baby-oil doctor hadn't said my heart was wobbly and I'd better keep my feet nearer the ground.' Harri looked longingly towards the wires above. 'There's where my heart is still,' he said thickly. 'I've put more pots on poles than you've eaten peas.'

'You couldn't do it today,' growled Wil into the hole beneath him. 'Your head's gone lighter. You'd have a fit.'

'D'you want me to show you?' Harri barked, his face aflame.

Wil offered him a big pair of pliers.

'We want the wires cut. This pole's going.'

Postman's hand stopped within a hair's breadth of the pliers.

'Union,' he muttered.

'I'll take care of the union,' said Wil.

'Right.' Postman spat on his palms, grabbed the pliers, and was up the pole spikes like a squirrel. The clipping of the wires sang in my ears and I watched them swanlaking on the breeze down, down to the morning grass.

While Harri was up on the pole Hughes the surveyor's new car slid to a stop alongside. He stepped out of the car, closed the door with a sweet click, drew a tiny cigar from its cellophane cell and lit it.

'I didn't hear anything about this, William.'

'No, Mr. Hughes. Would you mind giving us your opinion on this hole? You're an authority on holes.'

'At once.'

Hughes stepped to the edge of the hole, knelt on his handkerchief, and held a two-foot rule between finger and thumb against the bared soil.

'The hole's not bad, *as* a hole,' he said. 'But this side will fall in unless you prop a stake or two against it.'

'What sort of stakes, Mr. Hughes? The job's new to us.'

'Oh, I'll show you.'

The surveyor vanished, but reappeared almost immediately with two fresh stakes.

'From Twm Ifans's hedge,' he said crisply. 'If you take them back as soon as you've finished he won't notice. He's a cross enough old twit, it's right we should use him whenever we can.'

The stakes were propped against the naked earth. Hughes and Harri Postman were in no hurry. Both stayed to watch, Harri to help half-heartedly, Hughes to offer advice and to mumble astonishment at the imbecility of the Post Office removing a good new pole which had just been set up.

When the pole began to sway, a motorcycle stopped on the road, bearing Griffiths the policeman. As soon as Wil saw the long blue body screwing round to stare at us, he stuck his shoulder against the pole and cried out loud:

'Help! It's falling on me!'

The long blue body leapt off its bike and rushed to grip the pole with both hands.

'Thanks, officer!' cried Wil. 'Thank heaven you were here. If it hadn't been for you, God only knows——'

'That's all right, my boy,' said the officer, forgetting in a moment of fulfilment that Wil was several years his senior. 'I would be doing less than my duty if I stood aside and watched you cracking your collar-bone.'

Twm Ifans too appeared at that moment, his face ribbed red with hate towards human kind.

'What's this infernal row, you tea-break layabouts? You've only just been here putting up that nuisance——!'

He shut up when he saw the officer.

'Give help, Twm Ifans,' said Wil. 'We're moving this out of your way.'

'If that's so...' Twm grumbled, his face already less red and ribbed, 'if I'm to be rid of those cursed wires from my field...'

He too put his shoulder to the pole.

The only others who stopped on the road that morning were two Englishmen in a Jaguar on their way to the head of the valley for a day's fishing. Thinking that someone had been hurt, as true Englishmen they stepped out to offer help. Wil took good care to accept.

When the pole finally lay graciously alongside the road, its fat wires plucked from its body and uprooted from Twm Ifan's field, Wil turned to address his little congregation. Tears rolled down his cheeks. I knew he was overcome by his love for that pole.

'Friends,' he began throatily, 'have you ever thought what an honest thing a bit of wood can be? Even in its paint and spikes it can be nothing but itself. The only thing that can change it is our imagination. What will you make of it? Whatever is missing in your life, make it that. This, Harri Postman, is the job you lost, that your life's not the same without it. This, Hughes, is the wife you thought you were marrying. This, Griffiths, is the sergeant's stripes which have evaded you time and again since you came here. This, Twm Ifans, is the kind mother you never knew. And this, gentlemen of the Jag., is the unhurried, unthrombotic country life you've escaped to these mountains today to find. Doesn't it deserve a better place than this? Don't you feel compelled, each and every one of you, to *do* something to it?'

It's difficult to explain what happened next. In fact, nothing. Perhaps, if that sack of a cloud had not parked its black self across the sun, or that little razor of a breeze had not nicked our necks, then Wil could have . . . what?

All I know is this: one minute, everyone was listening to Wil, eyes and mouths wide open: Harri Postman, Hughes the surveyor, Griffiths the policeman, the gentlemen of the Jag., even Twm Ifans . . . and myself, for sure. Each one of us in sweet paralysis, with dreams ascending in the empty wind where the pole had been. Nothing existed in the whole wide world except Wil's voice . . . and Wil's voice . . . and Wil's voice . . .

But the next thing I saw was Griffiths the policeman turning, with a slow dawning of doubt, to Hughes the surveyor to mumble, 'Is this . . . well, is this *regular*, Hughes?'

'Regular?' Suddenly disturbed, Hughes scratched in his pocket for his tin of tiny cigars. 'Well, dash it . . . I suppose so . . . Well, dash it, I wonder?'

The long blue one regarded the dead pole lying beneath the hedge and drew a deep official breath.

'Perhaps we'd better . . . telephone, Hughes.'

'Telephone, Griffiths?'

'The appropriate authorities. The Post Office.'

'Oh, yes . . . the Post Office.'

Out of the corner of my eye I saw Harri's bike disappear like the shadow of a dream round the leafy bend. Bearing Harri, of course.

Then, Twm Ifans exploded.

'I knew it!' he snarled through the remains of his yellow false teeth. 'I knew there was some damned hanky-panky going on here. I knew that you bloody bureaucrats couldn't make up your minds about any single bloody thing. Is that cursed pole to *be* here or isn't it? Eh? Are those grisly wires going back again into my best field? Well? Answer me, you onions. Hughes? Griffiths?'

'There'll probably be an inquiry,' said Griffiths.

'Inquiry! Great Lord——'

'Now, Twm Ifans. That's bad language, that is. I can book you for that on the spot.'

This cooled Twm's burning rage somewhat. But he grumbled, 'I can book my own stakes, at any rate.'

He tugged both stakes from the hole. The side collapsed and half filled the pit with earth. To complete his protest Twm spat abundantly into what remained of the pit and stumped away, a stake under each arm, out of the sight of bureaucracy.

The two Englishmen were still there, staring in cold amazement at the embryo revolution. But they did not stay long. The one with the billowing moustache turned to his clean-shaven friend and pronounced, 'Damn funny business, this.'

When both had settled down in the Jaguar, the moustache reappeared for one last look.

'Damn funny altogether.'

And away they went, the tips of their fishing rods, ready for action, waving out of the open windows.

There remained Griffiths the policeman wetting the point of his pencil, Hughes the surveyor intemperately wetting the tip of his cigar, myself wetting no matter what, and Wil.

The court was merciful. So, at least, people said. Two pounds each with costs, and an order that Wil should see a specialist to have his head searched. The erudite man pronounced that there was indeed a touch of schizophrenia or paranoia or megalomania or one of the lengthy words so soothing to the civilized mind.

I need hardly say that the pole is back in its place, properly dressed, its wires once again rooted in Twm Ifans's earth. His face and his Welsh are more colourful than ever.

But on many a fine night, when the sky is clear and the moon is full or nearly, Wil and I go and caress the pole. I sit with my legs astride it and peer up its luminous length till the moon is right atop of it and feel that I have married the light. Wil begins to dream aloud and I fall again into that sweet paralysis.

After all, one white morning he very nearly persuaded his fellow-men to plant a telegraph pole where a telegraph pole was never ordained by civilization to be. Had he succeeded, Griffiths might have been a happier man, Hughes a stronger, Harri Postman a healthier, Twin Ifans a kindlier, and the gentlemen of the Jag. might have accepted the marvel as Englishmen can accept marvels when they must.

And why should we not dream? As Wil said one night, leaning on the pole that was rejected by men:

'You see, Josi, any creep of a bureaucrat can beat us, and any circus that calls itself a law court can empty our pockets. But glory be to the Great Creator of this piece of wood when it was a living thing, they can't buy our dreams.'

DAVID ALEXANDER

Hangman's Assistant

The under-manager looked up from his writing as they entered the office. He was a tall haggard-faced man.

'I'm expecting a hangman here this morning. I want you and Dai to give him a hand.'

'A hangman!' Twm Pant was taken by surprise. He saw that Dai was messing about with his pipe. That was Dai all over. A sly one, and yet...

'That's right, a hangman.' The under-manager was annoyed, 'They're going to hang Ianto Lewis in the stables.'

Twm became cautious. If this was a leg pull ... But he noticed that even Dai was beginning to show some interest.

'Wait a bit—what do they want to hang Ianto for?' Twm was watching the under-manager's face. A quick darting look at Dai's face convinced him that there was nothing between them.

'Oh, I don't know—something he did about twenty years ago. They just found out about it.'

'Oh no—not me.' Twm had just realized that the under-manager was serious. He had nothing against Ianto Lewis. A bit of a waster perhaps: getting drunk and always changing his lodgings. Besides, hanging a man wasn't in his grade. He was a labourer, and they couldn't force him to do it. Not that he liked Ianto any more than somebody else, but when it came to a point of hanging him...

'You can count me out. I'll have nothing to do with it.'

The under-manager was furious. Twn knew he was going to choke. A bit of a fool, that's how Twm described him. Hanging on to his job just because he was under-manager when he was full of silicosis. They waited for the bout of coughing to pass. His face became purple, then blue, and finally settled back to its normal grey. He expectorated into the open fireplace.

'You'll carry out my order or go home.'

'Are you sending me home?' Twm was on his mettle.

'I'm asking you to give this hangman a hand to hang Ianto Lewis.'

'And you know you can't force me to do it. Light pick and shovel work, that's what my certificate says. I've got silicosis, and hanging a man is outside my grade. I'll make a case out of this; I'll take it to the lodge committee.'

'Oh, one of the clever ones are you? All right, I won't ask you to hang anybody. Now let's see. Light pick and shovel work you said. Down by the weighbridge you'll find a tram with a barrel in it. A barrel full of something interesting. It will be a nice bit of light shovel work. You'll unload it.'

'I'll do that before I hang anybody.' Twm left the office, and Dai turned to follow him.

'Hey, Dai Herbert, where do you think you're going?'

Dai stopped. The under-manager looked at him sourly. The simulated innocence on Dai's face merely served to increase his irritation.

'You go and give this hangman a hand to hang that swine of a Ianto.'

Twm had emptied the barrel. That barrel had puzzled him. Where had the stuff come from? He went into the empty sawmills. The barrel wasn't the only thing that worried Twm. There was that silly business about Ianto Lewis. It was queer, too, that apart from Dai Herbert and the under-manager he had seen no one on the surface that morning. Perhaps it was Sunday morning. He tried to think back to the day before; the day he and Dai had gone off early. It was no good, he couldn't think what day it was. He couldn't even remember getting up that morning. His mind groped helplessly about as it did on those mornings when he sometimes woke and couldn't remember what day it was. But this morning there was no sudden flash of recollection when the succession of days, ceasing to crowd his mind, fell into their proper order. His brain continued to grope in a mist of doubt. He would ask Dai—casually, so as not to show that he had been thinking too hard about it.

Then coming down the track from the powder magazine he saw a man with a limp. That was what Twm had thought at first. When he looked closer he saw that the man walked one foot on the rail sleeper and the other in the holes worn between them by the pounding of the horses' feet. He walked as if he had one short leg, swaying from side to side like a rocking ship. He carried a noosed rope in his right hand. This must be the hangman; so it was true after all. As the man drew near Twm realized that he was looking at him through the sawmill window. The track came down to the corner of the sawmill before swerving into the main tramline, and as the man approached Twm withdrew a little from the window. It seemed as if the hangman had been waiting for him to do this, for he suddenly changed into a huge, yellow, tiger-like cat, and sprang on to an upturned tram outside the window. It glared in with burning eyes at the frightened Twm, and he had time for one cold spasm of fear before the cat was a man again, walking away towards the pumphouse where Ianto Lewis was held a prisoner. From the way his shoulders shook Twm knew that he was laughing.

Twm stood watching for a long time. They would be taking Ianto into the stables to hang him. It was a long time before he saw them coming out of the pumphouse. Ianto Lewis was in the middle, the hangman on one side, and a man dressed as a prison warder on the other. Following close behind and towering above the trio came the huge bulk of Dai Herbert. Dai's right hand was resting on Ianto's shoulder. How Twm hated him at that moment! That hand was somehow typical of all that he feared was true of Dai. A gesture empty of use and significant only in so far as it betrayed Dai's absence of spirit.

He watched the procession march around the dung-heap and into the stables. There followed a long still silence. He felt he would know the moment Ianto Lewis died. He would know because he had the terrible feeling that it was he who was hanging Ianto in his mind. The whole fantastic situation belonged to him; he felt a depressing responsibility for what was taking place. But everything happened without the consent of his will. He could not will for himself the knowledge of what day it was.

A soft thud told him that Ianto Lewis was hanged.

Dai Herbert came into the sawmill. His face was flushed, and he looked excited.

'What day is it?' Twm could restrain himself no longer. Everything was out of hand. Dai's face warned him that he was going too far. He saw the excitement die out and a bewilderment grow in its place. He turned away from Dai towards the window.

'So they hanged poor old Ianto.' Dai did not see Twm's wistful eyes. Twm was glad of that: he didn't want Dai to know how much the question cost him.

'Aye—poor old bugger, he's dead enough by now. You should have seen him. His head rolling on his shoulder, and his tongue hanging out—— Aye, that much.' Dai measured the length of Ianto's hanging tongue on his arm.

Dai went towards the weighbridge with his hands in his pockets. Twm watched his bulk receding. He felt very sad: he would never be able to laugh with Dai Herbert again.

Ianto Lewis walked out of the stables as if nothing had happened. He lifted his trousers as was his habit, put a match to his clay pipe, and walked slowly out of sight towards the tip. Dai Herbert had his back towards the stables and did not see him. Twm was about to hail him when the hangman and the warder came out of the stables full of excitement. They saw Dai and the hangman waved his arms.

'There he is—there he is!'

Dai saw them and gave a sudden shout of fear. He turned and started running down the valley. He blundered down along the black edge of the tip. The two ran swiftly after him, the hangman swinging the noosed rope above his head. Dai reached the young alder trees and tore his way through them. Above the crash of the branches rose Dai's screams—high and piercing, like a frightened woman's. Twm watched the plunging trio until they passed into a grove of green oaks far down the valley. He saw them emerge on the other side, closer together as if they were about to catch the fleeing Dai. Then they became merged into the grey-black mass of a slag heap beyond the trees.

ISLWYN WILLIAMS

Adjudication

Translated from the Welsh by the author

For the first time that afternoon he felt an involuntary tremor passing through his whole body, a kind of hot trembling in the pit of his stomach, a quick, almost imperceptible jerk of his legs and shoulders. The palms of his hands and the hollows under his eyes were moist too. *Diawch,* better watch his hands or he'd be marking his collar.

The hall was filling up. It was getting warmer there now; the choirs and the parties were arriving, that's what it was. It would be packed out in half an hour. Still, it would suit him to have the air warm and moist and to have the place full: he was always at his best with a large audience.

That bloomin' G again! Funny how it was bothering him today. He didn't know what was the matter with him lately. Still, he had got it beautifully last night; he'd got it, smack in the middle, a full, round, absolutely *steady* note that had made old Edwards sit up with a vengeance. But he hadn't been absolutely confident about it lately, that was the trouble. Well, indeed, it was coming to something, worrying about a little G; him, of all people. But there, it would be all right; he was always at his best when he was a little nervous.

Here it was at last, thank goodness.

They were announcing the tenor solo competition. To be taken after the adjudication on the three lyrics. Would they answer? Ron? T.J.? Danny Boy? Iorwerth? Up to the stage in readiness, please.

He gingerly fingered his black bow tie; must get it straight and quite flat against the collar. Fancy T.J. saying that the bow was supposed to be *outside* the wings. Swank, pure swank, just because he knew Walter Glynne. Over the wings, indeed! Good, he looked and felt all right. Hair tidy, cuffs showing just a little bit, only the middle button, and a crease like a razor, fair play to Lizzie Hannah. Now, take it easy. Keep cool, that was the ticket. Dignified, like.

He slipped a Vocalzube into his mouth and walked slowly along the aisle towards the stage.

'All the best, Dan *bach*!' Evans the Ironmonger as usual. What an enthusiast he was. *He* knew what singing was, if anybody did. Damn, he must get that G! People expected it of him. He mustn't let them down, and that's what would happen if he made a mess of the thing. Damn it all, he was shivering again. There's draughty bloomin' places these wings in the Welfare Hall were!

He adjusted his white scarf carefully over his collar again, and buttoned up his overcoat.

'Hullo, Ron boy? How are things with you, T.J.?' Easy, quiet confidence, that was the ticket. He nodded affably to Iorwerth; didn't know him—from down the valley somewhere, Llangyfelach way. Soft collar, brown suit, these youngsters didn't care a button how they looked. Yes indeed, T.J. did have his bow over the wings. Well, if that was the right way, it looked rotten. All bunched up like a cabbage and the stud showing. And his parting wasn't straight either. Never any style about T.J., and a face like a clock: fancy asking him to his face why he'd changed his stage-name from 'Dan' to 'Danny Boy'. So insensitive, somehow. 'Calling for you, Ron. All the best, boy.'

Not a bad voice, Ron's. Nice quality, but his intonation had never been good; always sharpening—there, he was at it now: 'and thy gra-a-a-a-cious mien'—bad, bad, very bad. Just that little bit off the note, but fatal, fatal. Yes, Pughe-Thomas had noticed it too. Trust him. Writing like mad....

The G. Yes, he'd do it all right; he was feeling fine again now. In the bag, Dan *bach*. He was going to be on top of his form after all. In good voice as they say. What a fool he'd been! He'd pull the place down with it. There was Ron coming to it now ... now ...

there! Poor, very poor. He got there, true, but it was thin, reedy, closing in instead of opening out....

'Well done, Ron boy. Good going.'

Poor old T.J.—as always! Tummy bobbing up and down, and singing with a copy again. T.J. all over. Couldn't carry his corporation after all these years and a memory like a sieve. A fine voice, of course, even if it was a bit brassy in the middle register. But no brains, no musical brains. Plenty of the other kind, the sly devil, but no real musical intelligence, just lucky enough to have a good set of vocal chords, that's all. That and plenty of cheek. 'Thy gra-a-a-acious mien'—yes, not bad, not bad at all. A bit stiff, perhaps, but it would pass—no, no, T.J.! Too hard, mun, you're pressing on it... 'and thy tre-e-embling hands'. Fat lot of trembling there! Too straight, too direct. Now for the G ... *now* then ... yes, very good, fair play. Wobbling a bit towards the end, but not bad, no, not bad.

'Fine, *fachgen*, very fine. Thanks, I'll want it!'

Well, here goes. Press the curl in front down a bit. Keep your tummy in. Springy step. Good, he felt fine. A big audience—always pink faces, and smoky in the back. Fine. Bow straight, trousers hanging nicely, mouth moist, throat absolutely clear, clean as a whistle. A bit of style. It was important. Style and bearing. A good stager. A bit noisy in the back there, that's right, close the doors, please; somebody walking in the wings now and stumbling; dead silence, right.

Good steady opening—fine—fine—fine. He felt great, top of his form. 'Thy gra-a a-a-acious mien'—(there, beat that, anybody—look at old Evans the Ironmonger smiling), fine, very fine, going well—and fair play to Miss Hopkins, with him all the way, very sympathetic, just right. One peep—hadn't written a note yet; good.

Old Evans still smiling and nodding. Now then: 'and thy tre-e-e-embling hands'—perfect, absolutely perfect, there, there was feeling in that, *passion* as they say. Artistry, that was the word, artistry—look out, Dan *bach*, here it comes, the G at last, now, *fine*, very, very fine, like a silver trumpet, smack in the middle, without having to grope for it, and *steady*, absolutely like a line all the way.

There. He knew it, pulling the house down, old Evans smiling all over his face and smacking his knee! Adjudicator writing: *a polished singer with a beautiful style, with a voice that conveyed the passionate tenderness of this song most effectively—the G on the last page easily and triumphantly surmounted—an artist to his fingertips—an outstanding performance....*

Diawch, that Iorwerth could sing! Yes, indeed! ... Close that door there, you silly so-and-sos! This draught behind here! Yes, a fine voice, a bit raw here and there, yes, just a little: 'thy gra-a-a-acious mien'—very fine, boy, that bl—— why don't they keep that door—yes, yes, good, good, a little softer there, perhaps. It's *passionate* tenderness you want—not *quite* got the right feeling into it. Not mellow enough, can't get that *dark,* warm richness into it. Now for the G, now, splendid! A bit raw at the edges, perhaps, but plenty of body, yes, plenty of body, opening out on it too. Young blood, yes, he'd come, he'd come, he'd be knocking at the door very soon....

There. Now for Pughe-Thomas ... shut that door, you silly so-and-sos! This hall was a death-trap. Well, he knew his job, that was one thing. Used to, anyway. That adjudication of his in Morriston—when was it? 1931 or '32 it was, yes, '32, yes, that's right. *Dan: Here was a polished singer with a beautiful style, with a voice that conveyed the passionate tenderness of this song most effectively, full of the dark, warm richness of a summer's night. Moreover, the G on the last page was easily and triumphantly surmounted. Dan is an artist to his fingertips, and this was undoubtedly an outstanding performance.* Yes, a real masterpiece, the best adjudication he'd ever had.

Well, here goes. SHUT that bl—Witty chap, Pughe-Thomas. Very shrewd, but light touch, knew exactly when to be humorous....

Ron: A nice voice and singing very correctly; an unfortunate tendency to sharpen occasionally—his quavers were all right, but he didn't like the quavering, so to speak. Right every time, and the humorous touch. The G on the last page, he got there but I'm afraid it was a pretty narrow squeak in more senses than one—that was a good one! Typical of Pughe-Thomas, very smart.

A narrow squeak—double-meaning, like. A nice performance on the whole. Yes, a bit of consolation....

Funny how he knew all the answers beforehand, so to speak. T.J. next.

T.J.: Why on earth use a copy on this old song—an old war-horse like him! He ought to be ashamed of himself—there he goes again, blunt, straight talk, knows who he is talking to; a fine voice, good intonation, but would prefer less stridency in the softer passages—you don't go serenading with a trombone. Smart, smart. A fine G, but not sensitive enough....

Here it comes, look out. Danny Boy: A very experienced singer (of course!) with a good voice still ... *still*? What did he——? Here was a stylish singer with quite a lot to teach the younger generation. A voice of fine texture, but—yes, yes, yes, go on, man! —but he had a feeling that it was becoming—how shall I put it?—just a little threadbare here and there. Threadbare? What did he——? Still, it was a good voice, well controlled throughout. And yet, all through he felt that this singer was struggling, *wrestling* with something; not so much with this particular song, but with—with—should he say Anno Domini, that nasty old creature, you know, who will insist on forcing himself on our company when he isn't wanted? And unfortunately, he didn't come alone. There was his bosom pal, Signor Tremolo, that sly and insidious shadow who overtakes all singers in the end. Hell! But still, this was a good, finished performance. Mark that. The G at the end, for instance, was a good example of what an artistic performer could achieve—just a *little* out of the reach of his natural register these days, perhaps, and it was beginning to wobble a bit towards the end—that wobble, you know—but he'd got there, yes, he'd got there all right. Yes, on the whole this was a sensitive, intelligent, and *plucky* performance....

Iorwerth: a beautifully fresh voice—a song of youth, of love, of passion, the attributes of young love ... a young man's song ... Iorwerth ... Iorwerth....

He bent down for his hat, but he straightened up suddenly. He forced himself to smile. Damn it, his face was like a piece of cardboard! Smile and look unconcerned, you fool. Get that It's-all-in-the-game-better-luck-next-time expression. You must, you must. Don't look so dazed, you idiot. Why don't you listen to people, say? Lizzie Hannah hinted enough last week, but of course, *you* had to lose your temper. You're getting old, Danny Boy. Danny Boy, indeed! Lizzie Hannah told you enough about that too—go on, clap, you fool—harder, harder!

Mustn't go out too soon. Look too pointed. Pughe-Thomas, the witty adjudicator. And his bosom pal, Signor Tremolo. Witty, that was. Witty, they call that. Make the crowd laugh, like. You're getting old, Dan *bach*, you and your black coat and vest and striped trousers and pretending that you wanted them for Morgan's funeral. Morgan's funeral, my eye! You and your Come-to-Jesus collar. All tricks and style and no voice. That's what it amounts to. You're sunk, and you know it, so chuck it, for God's sake. Anno Domini is after you, Dan *bach*. Anno Domini and his insid—insiduous old pal, Signor Tremolo.

You're plucky, though. That's something, anyhow. Plucky, you, plucky, you, a National winner. A plucky performance. There's a thing to say. Plucky. Yes, plucky, *myn diawl*. . . .

HARRI PRITCHARD JONES

The Miracle

Translated from the Welsh by the author

Good God, how many more stairs can there be? What a place to have to come to on a day like this. Cow-muck even among the snow, all over my shoes too. I bet the lads back in the hospital are having a whale of a time. It's only about ten years since they put up this tenement, and look at the mess it's in already. It'll take a generation or two for these people to learn to live respectably after the troughs they were given when the English were here. God, I'll get dizzy if I look over these balconies again; one for each floor of a dozen flats, then stairs leading to more balconies, each with its own dozen, floor upon floor.

'Do you know where Mrs. Flynn lives?'

'Number 141, mister. What's your business there, mister?' answered a choir of unwashed cherubs. Another floor, so. Here we are: 131–142; to the right then—'38, '40, '41—here we are. Nobody at the door waiting. Hm.

'Oh, it's you,' said the sunken face wearing a three-day beard which answered the door. Then, looking at Alun's bag, he added: 'Come in, Doctor, you're very welcome.' Alun went inside to a room without a carpet, full but bare, with another door at the opposite end of the room promising a kitchen or a bedroom. There was a table, two high chairs, one easy one, a fireplace, a gas stove in one corner, and a double bed in the other. Against one wall lay a small mattress, and there was a piece of new linoleum on the hearth. On the window-sill, almost hiding behind the disintegrating curtains, there was a little crib lit by a candle. In came a stocky old woman, her face all wrinkled: the grandmother, obviously.

'She's in the jakes. She'll be in to you now,' said she, wiping her hand on her apron before offering it to him. The father strode over to the radio and put a stop to it.

'She hasn't gone very far, you know, Doctor,' said the old one, clearing the table, 'but the waters are gone these two hours, and I was thinking we'd better be phoning you in good time since it's sure to be a busy day for you today.'

'That's grand; labour's started then.'

'It has; the pains are coming every twenty minutes or so, Doctor. You'd better go out for a while, Bob, and bring a noggin of Jameson's back with you.' The father straightened up from his slouch, took hold of his cap, looked tenderly towards the far door, then out he went.

'He's out of work this two years, the creature. I've sent off the other children to the neighbours. There's plenty of water on the boil for you, Doctor,' said the old one, starting to fuss. 'I'm an old hand at it, as you can see,' she started up again, laughing gently down her nose. Alun took out the contents of his bag, a handful at a time, and laid them out neatly on the table. The rubber mat and apron and gloves, the coarse cotton-wool, Dettol, the net scales, sterile dusting powder, thread, a small forceps and a scissors. He left the obstetric forceps hopefully in his bag.

'This is the sixth, isn't it?'

'That's right, Doctor, she had twins on the third.'

'How old is she now?'

'Thirty-five. I had ten of them myself, but I buried two in America, and I've three sons working over in England. You're not Irish are you, Doctor?'

'No. Welsh.'

'There do be a lot of you from overseas at the Rotunda, doesn't there?'

'Yes, there are, from all over the place. Ah, here she comes.'

In came the pale mother, shoulder first, through the far door, putting her hand on the mantelpiece to steady herself.

'Come over to the bed, Mrs. Flynn.' The doctor took her by the hand and led her as if she were a child learning to walk. She straightened up suddenly in pain as she got to the bed, and then sank limp on to it.

'You can have an injection to lessen the pain the moment the nurse gets here.'

'Thanks, Doctor.'

The old one came back into the room bearing a large enamel bowl, steaming like a censer. She put it on the table, taking care not to touch or splash the instruments on it, and then went over to hold her daughter's hand.

'Lie on your back now, Mrs. Flynn, if you're able to, so I can listen to the baby's heart. There we are, easy does it, there's no hurry at all,' said Alun as he thought of that party getting into its stride.

'Now then, Mrs. Flynn.' He gently palpated the uneasy swelling in the mother's belly, searching for the baby's head and shoulder and back. 'Grand. Game ball! It's in the right position,' he added, feeling the baby's back lying towards the mother's left loin, the shoulder and the neck deep in just above her pubis, and the head already on its way along its intended path. He listened with his stethoscope over the baby's back and heard a rapid beat, then felt with his hand the pulse at the mother's wrist: the two were not synchronous; it was the baby's heart he could hear then. It's alive. My watch: one, two, three—twenty-six in fifteen seconds—one hundred and four. Fine, no hurry.

'There you are, Mrs. Flynn dear, everything's grand. I'll just examine you from below, just to make sure.'

Glove and Dettol. 'Turn over on to your left side, will you please? There you are.'

The neck of the womb open to two fingers-breadth. Only about three-quarters of an hour to an hour to go, with any luck.

'On to your back again now, that's fine. You won't be long now. Ah, here's the nurse I'd say.'

The door opened to reveal a gaberdine raincoat and cap, and the nurse turned her face towards them.

'There's a good few stairs up to this place!' Her face was flushed by the cold as well, a small, commonplace, kind face.

'You're welcome, Nurse,' said the old woman. 'I'll go and get you a cup of tea. You're sure to be frozen stiff after coming through that snow.'

'God bless you. How's she getting on, Doctor?'

'Two fingers-breadth and contractions every twenty minutes or so. The baby's fine: V2, foetal heart rate a hundred and four. The sixth. Would you take her blood pressure, and give her a sixth of Omnopon for me, please?'

'I will surely, Doctor. Hello, Mrs. Flynn,' she greeted the mother.

After taking off her coat and starched cuffs and rolling up her sleeves, she got out a syringe and a phial from her bag. She wrapped the cuff of the sphygmomanometer around the mother's arm:

'A hundred and twenty over eighty, Doctor. I'll give her the injection now.'

'Thanks a million, Nurse.' Alun, also, took off his coat and put on his rubber apron, rolled up his sleeves, put his rubber gloves conveniently near by on the table and sat down to wait.

The old woman went out on to the back balcony to throw away the dirty water out of the bowl. Nearly everybody was inside in their homes, as might be expected today, except the woman of 137, who was pretending to sweep her doorstep with one eye on 141.

'Jesus, Mary, and Joseph, what a day for it, isn't it?' started the old one. 'You've finished the dinner, I see. It won't be much of a dinner we'll be getting today, just like three years ago. I'd say they'd best be leaving off now, Mrs. Cullen, wouldn't you? They're old enough, God knows, and there isn't any more room here anyway. But there you are, you can't tell them anything. The poor creature's without work, and not much for him to do with his time, God love him. It's well for us that Nuala had her fourteenth birthday last month. She can leave school now and get work for herself. I was at it yesterday in that new supermarket they've got in Moore Street, asking after work for her. Four quid extra would go a long way towards feeding and clothing the new one—and we can only pray to God and His Holy Mother that it will only be one this time.'

'That woman from the Saint Vincent de Paul's after being here again, asking about our means and what we wanted special for the feast like. I gave her feast, I can tell you. I told her where she got off, that it was money for milk and nappies we were wanting, not some fancy paper to prettify the house and silly little things for the childer. God forgive me, but she's a right busybody is that one. It's like as if she pulls herself all in when she comes into the house, and she's afraid of sitting down with us. She's married to some auctioneer, I think, and I bet he doesn't leave her half enough to do with herself. She's only about two childer, and those away in some posh school. What the hell does her sort want coming here to interfere with the likes of us, while some stranger is being paid to run her home for her.

'There'll be room for the new one in the pram anyway, thanks be to God, with little Grania and the shopping. But God only knows where we'll find a place to sleep. The older ones see too much for them as it is, and I wouldn't like to think what goes on half the time on these dark stairs at night. Thanks, all the same, for taking the lads this morning for them to have a little bit of the feast-day, and for those little presents for them, Tomós was full of himself, the creature. I meant to thank you too for telling me about those cheap nappies, the seconds at McBirney's sale.

'Look at Bob there, coming out of the back of Swift's. He's lucky to get in at all today, but then he's a good customer in his way, I suppose. Where's he off to now I wonder? Straight across to Ryan's, by God. Do you think he's getting worse looking? There isn't much food in that drink for all they say, and he doesn't be getting much meat these days, just the odd bit of bacon and cabbage.'

Ryan's Select Bar, by Jesus! They're all the same, just all the same. I'll have a couple of pints to celebrate, and a few more tomorrow likely, to celebrate the new little one, God love him. Thanks to the Man of the House and those that's got work for themselves, God bless them. The dole will go up, and the Children's Allowance. God forgive me for letting Nuala leave school and go out to work, but it's so much easier to get work if you're a girl the way it is in these new little factories. And God knows how little comes into the house these days. Maureen gives me as much as she can, but it's begging the pints I'm at since the redundancy. Jesus, I'd like to be able to buy things for the kids for today, and give something to Maureen. I'm just a bit of driftwood really, aren't I. It would be far better if I'd gone off to England the time Dermot went, and be sending money home.

Though God knows, it's a queer life he has too, living and drinking in Camden Town and sending most of his wages back to Linda. There's one thing, they haven't had any more since he went off. Who knows but Maureen and the childer might have been able to follow me there. But then, it'd be very hard to leave the Coombe, all the lads, The Pipers' Club and all that. Having to come over by train and that old boat for funerals and such-like, with a little square bag and a piece of black on my sleeve.

Why don't they open these places today? It's just messing like this every year. I'd swear I could hear a melodeon and a fiddle going in that back room. Ah, here's Phil to open for me at last.

It was five tasteless cups of tea later in Alun's life when the mother's voice, quiet from her labours, said:

'I think something's happening, Doctor.'

Alun jumped up and over to the bed: the mother's face in a peaceful anguish, her body flowing out; a tremble like the Creation. Her fingers pinched his arm painfully. With the palm of his hand he steered the crown of the baby's head as it slowly appeared from the well of her body. The nape of the neck came into view, and then he allowed the neck to straighten gradually revealing a forehead and nose, a mouth and chin. Alun's hands remembered how to turn the baby from side to side as he brought out the shoulders in turn, the hips, legs, feet—and a cry. There, it's born! As the doctor tied the umbilical cord in two places and divided the life into two, the mother's anguish turned into tears of pride, the heart of those pale cheeks blushed, and in a while, after she had passed the after-birth, she was allowed to hold the baby to her bosom in a pledge of succour.

The doctor and the nurse washed their hands; a cigarette each.

'Well, there you are, Mrs. Flynn: another son for you, six pounds and ten ounces, and a lot more washing besides! We'll be back to see you tomorrow.'

'Thank you, Doctor, for everything—and you, Nurse. God bless you both. What would we do without the likes of you?'

The old one went to fetch the father off the balcony, and they all welcomed the new baby in whisky.

'Well, Nurse, we'd better be going.' The drink had reminded Alun of the party back in the hospital.

As they hurried down the stairs, they passed three little ones on their way to see what had happened.

'That last one's as dirty as an Arab,' said Alun. 'What a hell of a way to spend Christmas, isn't it, Nurse? We can only hope some merciful Samaritan will have kept a drop for us.'

MARGIAD EVANS

A Party for the Nightingale

Miss Trinkett, Miss Boyce, and Miss Bently were all living in Trinkett Cottage that May, where Miss Boyce had passed her childhood. One warm night Miss Boyce went along the Valley by herself and returned with the news that she had heard the nightingale while standing in a patch of nettles under a hawthorn tree. Miss Trinkett remarked she supposed the nettles were not necessary to the experience; and Miss Bently proposed a picnic. They could ask Ally, she said: Ally was a poet, and everyone knew that poets had never actually heard the song of the nightingale, had they?

And that was why Algernon Henry Orb was walking along the grass lane to Trinkett Cottage, in his summer suit, carrying the primus and mildly driving his nephew Newton before him. Mr. Orb was forty-nine and Newton was nine-and-a-nibble, a slender ugly child who wore the sunlight like a lizard.

Mr. Orb's summer suit was something he had cut, grown, and sewn himself. It was of linen, with some jagged lines in it, the colour of a grey wall: the seams were like cracks in the mortar and the pockets were lumpy from the churning of his nervous hands.

When they arrived at Trinkett Cottage they found four women all squeezed as tightly into the porch as if they were growing too thickly and needed to be thinned out. Their arms were enlaced and from their cotton sleeves there stuck out, here and there, an anonymous handshake for Newton.

'Now, Newton.' This was Mrs. Carr, the vicar's wife. Newton sighed. He touched the fingers. Miss Boyce, who had never seen

Mr. Orb's summer suit before, and who was in love, was startled aside from her vision. The rest were habituées.

'Hot, hot, hot,' said Miss Boyce, jumping out of the group and spreading her lovely empty arms. She was the only one who wasn't carrying a basket or something twisty.

'Now have we got everything? Yes, here's the tea-pot—and my knitting. That's the *ink,* Rhoda—be careful. That's the way. Across the field, Ally. Newton—now . . . Altogether—that's it.'

Capable Miss Bently led them out of the garden. Mr. Orb walked between Miss Trinkett and Mrs. Carr. Mr. Orb did not like Mrs. Carr: he did not like her dark green shiny dress with its turn-down white collar and rustling under-thought as of starched petticoat. He himself preferred something more floating—graceful, such as Miss Boyce's buoyant light blue, in which as she ran with Newton he fancied he could see bubbles breaking. Nevertheless he talked: he talked more than anybody, in a voice that was so like an essay, one could almost see the words in print.

'I remember in "A Nest of Nightingales" . . .' he was saying.

'A nest of nightingale's eggs, you mean,' Mrs. Carr said.

Mr. Orb opened his mouth: 'I was speaking of Russia. I mean, of a Russian short story—or was it French?—yes, of course. Théophile Gautier's. There were two beautiful girls—Isabeau and Fleurette. They sang against the nightingale—and they died. Yes, what beauty! But speaking of such things always makes me think of Russia. As it were. Russia must be a lovely country. Don't you think so? Now Chekhov——'

But Miss Boyce had returned to them: 'The oil's dripping out of the primus. Look it's all down your *plus-fours.* Here, give it to me,' and dropping aside she whispered to Miss Trinkett: 'Just look at him—did you ever see such an idiot? Why does he wear those *dreadful* sandals? They must be *full* of paraffin, and they make his feet look all big toes.'

'That's his toe-nails,' Miss Trinkett replied vaguely.

'Don't,' Miss Boyce besought.

'Really, Rhoda, do be nice,' Miss Trinkett whispered. 'I shall simply have to get you by yourself one day and tell you what a charming creature Ally really is.'

'He'd rather do it himself.'

'Oh, Rhoda. Oh dear!'

'Don't worry. I won't hurt him,' Miss Boyce said bitterly. Mr. Orb strode on to the stile:

'Every thing has flowered.
Now let wildness—'

sang he, as he scrambled over it after everybody else. He was now some way behind, but he continued to talk to Newton, who didn't listen.

'Here, Bently, don't scramble so,' puffed Miss Trinkett. 'You've simply *got* to wait for Ally. Hang it, woman, it's *your* picnic. Go back for him.'

They waited on the edge of the hillside where the Valley dropped. Mr. Orb arrived, saying: 'It really, really is somewhat beautiful, isn't it, don't you agree?'

'Affected fool,' hissed Mrs. Carr. 'I wonder if there are any adders here?'

'Yes there are—millions,' said Newton, and his eyes finished what he was wishing to add.

But Mr. Orb was quite sure it was beautiful now, and he was silent as he looked down into the still, shimmering vale. There were the greater hills all pushed back against the sky, as if for this greenness to grow and bloom, and for this scent of warm leaves to rise to the sun. Oh, what did he wish, seeing it there below, without houses, without people but only this luxuriant, ravishing glow of peace?

'Bluebells!' screamed Newton, tearing away, 'and the brook. I'm going to walk in the brook. Not paddle,' he explained.

Presently they were all at the bottom, filing sedately one behind the other, talking themselves along like the stream at their side. There was a rustling and a murmuring of clothes and brambles snapping and snarling at dresses. The sun was in their eyes and there were hard lines on their faces which were the colour of pinkish stone. The pure light and the living gloss of the leaves made them look false, overcoloured, over-bright, and yet threadbare. Only Newton matched it, when he darted oblique, in the bluebells: 'Uncle, may I pick all these?'

'You may, you may.'

'And are we going to have tea soon? I don't want to be found dead with nothing in my innards. Are there birds' nests in mountains?'

'Yes, yes. No, no, no.'

'Of course there are,' said Miss Bently: 'Eagles' nests.'

'Eyries,' said Mrs. Carr.

Miss Trinkett swung her basket. Music strutted through her head: 'We're nearly at the place.'

Soon Newton shouted: 'I've seen the nightingale! It's a yellow bird, isn't it a yellow bird? Are its eggs yellow, Uncle Al? If I find its nest can I have an egg?'

Mrs. Carr stopped: 'Now, Newton, you've picked enough flowers. The nightingale is *not* a yellow bird and so you haven't seen it. Its eggs are olive green. And if you find them you're not to touch them, is he, Mr. Orb?'

No, no, indeed, everybody said. Suddenly, stepping into armour of shadow under the trees Miss Bently held up her brown hand: 'Sh—isn't that it, Rhoda?'

'Yes,' said Miss Boyce—'Listen, do be quiet. We may not hear it again.'

Their faces became strained—they dare not move their hands and their twisted, silent bodies looked as if they were caught in mid air. There was another squirt of song and then silence. This silence came right up close to their ears and breathed down their open mouths.

'Oh,' whispered Miss Trinkett, 'oh wasn't that lovely?'

'Is that the nightingale?' Newton asked. 'I'm going to build a dam!'

He jumped down the bank, pulled off his shoes, and stepped carefully into the water. Softly he curled his toes on the swirling red sand: 'Oh, look at the dust!' he murmured.

Gradually the others began to bend towards the warm ground. They might have been falling slowly, magically asleep, only the nearer the grass they descended the more bustle they began cautiously to make. Mrs. Carr put down the kettle. 'Now, Mr. Orb—the primus——' 'The bird has flown,' they said.

'Yes, we'll stay here in the shade. It'll come back presently when it's used to us,' said Miss Bently. Their voices grew firmer.

But Mr. Orb was still standing. All at once he said poetry:

'The ear has visions! Of these tones
thy notes are given
and from onrushing heaven
which streams with rivery radiance through the soul,
like water's root which through the trickling woods
whispers its gods
and cadences both sweet and unrevealed declares
within the living grotto of the ears.'

(Mrs. Carr struck a match discreetly.)

'What is thy faith of bliss, what singing pain?'

asked Mr. Orb, and rapidly continued:

'What unhelped, utter victory in final phrase unbares
itself in sousing sound? Oh Nightingale, what gain?'

He sat down.

'Well, I've never heard that one,' Miss Trinkett remarked.

'Oh I have!' Mrs. Carr exclaimed.

'It's my own,' said Mr. Orb, lying down.

'Have you ever heard the nightingale before?' said Miss Boyce.

Mr. Orb shut his eyes: 'Not actually—no.'

'There,' cried Miss Bently: 'I told you so.'

There was a pause. The kettle whistled. The young leaves streamed over their heads. Many birds were singing.

'Well,' said Miss Trinkett, 'I don't think much of it. The nightingale I mean—not your poem, Ally.'

'Neither do I. Can't think, if that's it, why people think so much of it. It must have been Keats Keats heard, not the nightingale,' said Miss Bently. But Miss Boyce wriggled herself out into the sunshine: 'I think it's lovely,' she said rather wildly, and she let her long arms rest lightly on the hot grass. The others sat in the shade that was moist and warm as flesh, and where the sunlight, veering through the hazel trees, bored into their bodies, they felt patches of contentment.

'Lovely,' said Miss Boyce.

'Lovely—yes,' said Mr. Orb sadly, looking at the three grey women whose brittle hair was an ashy, dead-petal colour, in the depths of the light. Like everlasting flowers, he thought. Is there anything more dead than the everlasting? He threw out his arm and his hand touched Miss Boyce's foot:

'Every thing has flowered
but wildness . . .'

'Oh, let me be wild!' implored poor Mr. Orb. But Mrs. Carr tightened the pattern of the tea-things and twitched the cloth, and——

'Not now,' said she, 'even if they aren't the best tea-cups. Newton—tea. Wash your hands.'

Newton came rushing: 'Ho,' he said. His shirt was blotted with wet like shadow marks. 'Look at me,' he said to Miss Bently and Miss Trinkett: 'Feel how wet I am. I washed my hands with mud. I want a drink. Uncle Ally, will you come and see my dam? I'm going behind that tree to do something first.'

'Well, you needn't tell us. And you could go a bit farther off,' suggested Miss Bently, who adored Newton and never offended him.

After the sandwiches and the little plain cakes were eaten, everyone crawled out into the sun. Newton carried off the tea-pot to catch minnows in. Miss Bently knitted, Miss Trinkett went to sleep, and Mrs. Carr got out her pen and paper and began to sketch. Mr. Orb glanced at her, and then he rolled over and hid his face in the ground.

'Uncle, Uncle, come and look. I've caught some minnows, and I'm pouring them through the spout. They love it,' Newton shrieked.

'Presently, presently,' moaned Mr. Orb, not animatedly.

The remembrance of her unhappy love overcame Rhoda Boyce with relief, with radiance, even though he was in India and married as he had promised her he would be. She got up and walked away, and only looked back to think it was ugly seeing so many people together in a place that was meant for none.

Soon Mrs. Carr made a blot. She felt furious and looked sharply about her for something to blame. A chaffinch perched high above them kept shouting at half-minute intervals its loud, annoying, and insensate tune. 'Choo-wee choo-wee, chee-chee-chee, chutt, choot-choot choot,' sang the chaffinch, as though it were tumbling it all out of a bag. The nightingale, far away, answered softly.

'It's that chaffinch. I can't bear it. Don't you hear it, Miss Bently? Shocking. Sickening. So monotonous. *All* the birds are singing. We ought to have come at night. It's such a muddle. I can't hear anything but chaffinch, and I *do* so dislike them,' said Mrs. Carr.

'Oh dear,' said Miss Trinkett serenely. Miss Bently groaned over her knitting. Nobody suggested moving or searching for the nightingale. And Mr. Orb, gazing up at the chaffinch, laughed.

'Go it, go it! Well done. Go on,' he encouraged, aggravatingly.

'I do hate it! I could wring its neck,' said Mrs. Carr viciously. And once more, again and again, the chaffinch mocked. The magpies rattled, the butterflies eddied round islands of air, and far away the call of the cuckoo sounded like a tremor in the earth.

'Go it, go it,' roared Mr. Orb outrageously. 'Ha-ha. Cheer up.'

'It's like a lunatic,' said Mrs. Carr, but just then Newton shouted: 'Uncle Ally, Uncle Ally, do come. There's such a lot of birds. Heaps of birds flew in my face. What shall I do?'

'Nothing. Leave 'em alone, for God's sake,' said Mr. Orb. 'They're young blackbirds,' he said, scrambling down the bank. 'Uproar,' he heard Mrs. Carr saying, and Miss Trinkett woke up and said: 'More tea?'

'Why did we ask her?' she muttered to Miss Bently, leaning to her ear. 'How very disagreeable she's being!'

'Yes,' Miss Bently muttered back; 'and she's making Ally rebellious too.'

'That's Rhoda, I think,' Miss Trinkett said, and she looked towards Miss Boyce who was lying on the hillside higher up the stream, with her arms wreathed about her head.

'I hate Mrs. Carr,' Newton was whispering. 'Why is she here, Uncle?'

'Dreadful things happen,' said Mr. Orb, 'every day.'

He would go and sit by Miss Boyce, he thought. Rhoda.

'Well, I hate her, and I wish the nightingale would fly down and peck off her nose,' said Newton.

> *'Why be as other than these flowers be,*
> *Why crouch and cringe for punishment?*
> *Let the seed snap, the bent bud break*
> *Beneath the singing of the scent,'*

sang he, strolling away.

Miss Boyce had not been perfectly happy by herself, but she had been perfectly complete. She had peeped for nests in the bushes, but not with a child's dexterity. She was too tall, she told herself; the eye-level was gone and she had an odd feeling that in these fields where she had once been really young, she had become a clumsy stranger. She had risen physically, to senior rank, and in many moments she wished herself backwards—wished she hadn't visited. So she looked into a clump of grass for a lark's nest, but there wasn't one. There never was, nowadays. It was very lonely. Miss Trinkett's companion was music, and Miss Bently's her knitting, and Mrs. Carr's the sound of her own education. What was Mr. Orb's? Miss Boyce wondered, glancing back at the party. Apollo, she told herself, with his lyre. And then she shook her hand, for the sound of the word Apollo moved her like gentle fire, and linked her with the sun and the lovely rounded light upon the valley. She sat down weakly, and thought of hard square daylight, white rooms in India; India the hospital where they were incessantly and slowly operating on her heart...

And as she sat there she suddenly became aware of the nightingale's singing that was streaming out from an oak tree, and the tree was covered and all lit up with greeny-gold flowers like moss, which she was curious to touch. But she would not frighten the song, she said. They were right; the bird had flown from the party; it had flown to her because here in her native place she was invisible and quiet.

It was so whole, so perfectly beautiful, the song, that at first she was lost in it, her mind silenced. The first break of notes came fast and wildly, at unbelievably intricate speed, running downhill;

then that was followed by three or four clear staccato calls, when the song brought itself up by its own command. Then the bird really began. Long, smooth cadences were laid upon the air, were stroked out to their shining tips, were divided thought by thought until it became impossible for the listener to decide which was the harmony—the sounds themselves or the inset pauses let into the voice. Yet it was not 'music'. There could be no human term for it, no comprehending what made the arrangement of the tones. Then for a short while, as by decision, it ceased, and Miss Boyce breathed.

She knew it would begin again. She knew it would not be over, for the world was charged with it. And, on the brink of its return, there whirled in the silence of her ears, a tintillation as of light, as of shining discs still turning and hovering on the thread of that vibration. Her first thought was to call the others, but she glanced at them, and did not. Why should she, she said; who cared? And at that moment the bird picked up its song once more, and again differently.

This time, it spent its phrases slowly, with melancholy distinctness, with a sort of sad eagerness, like a gambler who sees his gold dwindling. The notes were intricate at times, and were met by a piercing echo, out of the ground or sky, which joined to them without seam, and lengthened them to a sensitiveness unbelievable. The 'music' was now far more evocative: she did not know it, but already her few moments of pure listening were over, and her mind was acting scenes again. Now the beautiful sounds had become only another illustration of her passion's series of possibilities, as everything else that was lovely in the land and trees and skies.

'Why didn't I know? Oh why? What a fool I've been,' she was saying, as she sank back against the pillow of the hill, Rhoda Boyce, again. And so she shut her eyes and opened them, seeing the blue sky in blinks like a great butterfly hovering over her face. And the hum of stillness that came (or seemed to come) out of the earth under her brain, seemed the *sound* made by the mesmeric blue over her eyes. With it she heard the song of the nightingale as the centre of all the detached bird voices, moving here and there as phrases move inside an orchestra, lighting first these instruments, then those. At last her eyes ceased to open and, falling asleep, she heard only a soothing monotony of earth and life.

She was woken by a touch on her hand. Mr. Orb was sitting by it. She started up with an angry cry: 'That was hateful.' Her voice was so loud that unnoticed the nightingale dived through the oak-tree and flew away.

'I'm sorry,' said Mr. Orb wretchedly.

Miss Boyce sneered: 'Haven't you a quotation ready?'

'"What love can do for lovelessness." Oh yes, if you're interested,' said Mr. Orb.

'That'll do. But I guess it's your own. Isn't it? Can you quote from yourself?'

Mr. Orb smiled: 'I always do,' he said expressionlessly.

'Love!' cried Miss Boyce. 'I suppose you always quote *that*. What an old-fashioned poet you are!'

'Yes, it's my age,' said Mr. Orb.

'How can you bear it?' said she.

'It's very painful,' said he, and he went on, in a running tone, rubbing a grass against his skin:

> '*Oh Love! No habitant of earth thou art—*
> *An unseen seraph we believe in thee,*
> *A faith whose martyrs are the broken heart . . .*'

'That's Byron, though.'

'Love!' cried she again. 'I didn't mean *that*. I meant those women. How can you endure—so—so many? Your friends—well. Wreathing you. With defence. All the time, whatever you do—"Oh Ally's always kind." *Kind*. "Ally's always gentle." Yah,' said Miss Boyce.

'Always gentle to the ignorant,' said Mr. Orb.

Miss Boyce turned to him and suddenly she laughed: 'Come off it. Well, we must go back to the party. You must cultivate some enemies, Mr. Orb.'

'I do,' said he, 'when they let me.'

'Shall we find Newton?' she said.

They did. He had taken off all his clothes and tied them round his neck. Miss Bently and Mrs. Carr were waking Miss Trinkett.

Newton, straddling his dam, and painted with mud, approached them confidentially: 'Uncle Ally, make Mrs. Carr let me have a tea-cup for these few extra minnows. They're my spare stock. I don't want to lose them. I don't want to leave them behind.'

'We'll try,' said Mr. Orb.

They scrambled up the bank. 'Altogether now,' Mrs. Carr was saying. They shook the rug: 'No, Newton. I've packed the cups. Aren't you going to dress?'

'Well...' yawned Miss Trinkett.

'Never mind.' Newton glared. 'I've had a very good time, and I've got ten and this little bird...'

'You naughty child! Let it go at once,' they screamed.

'Newton, that really makes me sick. How could you be so cruel?' said Miss Bently.

The boy smiled subtly: 'I am rather cruel.' And he tilted a look at them all. 'I don't mind,' he said inscrutably; 'nobody need worry.'

For a moment the party stood, facing the boy as if they saw in him a strange, cool danger. Behind the leaves, and passing them rapidly, sounded the quick, intelligent, foreign talk of the water. The valley was sloped with shadow.

'I'm going home,' said Miss Boyce.

They turned: 'But we none of us heard the nightingale! Oh dear, aren't we awful?'

Miss Boyce said nothing. 'Let us get away. Oh let us get away from here and leave it alone,' she thought in anguish, almost in prayer.

GLYN JONES

It's Not by His Beak You Can Judge a Woodcock

It was nearly midnight. There was a frosty stare to the big stars and the moon above the farmhouse gleamed like a splash of whitewash. Not a blade or a twig moved in the frozen Nantwig fields and the only sound was the grass crackling like cake under a pair of heavy boots. In the distance the Reverend Gwilym Nanney was coming down to the farmhouse for the second time.

Gwilym was a simple man. He spoke little. He was good at making fishing-flies from the neck-feathers of a cock. Sometimes he mixed up the points of his sermon, but he would carry a can of milk every day to a drunkard like Jim Saer and pray with him until the beer was overcome. He gave his money away. He gave away his jacket to Theo the tramp who came cuckooing through the parish in the spring. People marvelled at their vicar's big naily boots and at his grey flannel shirt, just like their own, when he took off his coat to help with the hay of a widow or a farmer gone into the decline. Gwilym was tall, but on his large bones no flesh had ever found a resting-place. He had the long chin, the bulging chest, and the lifted shoulders of the asthmatic. From the middle of his white face the cold gristle of his nose pointed sharply up, the tip of it nibbled at the air all the time he was speaking. To visit Nantwig in the freezing weather he was wearing his round hat and his black overcoat down to his boots.

He tramped over the crust of the field and there at last, in a bowl full of trees, the light of the farmhouse shone. The whole glitter of a lake came flooding into Gwilym's moon-wet eyes. His hump of a chest wheezed but his long and knock-kneed legs moved faster. During the last three weeks an idea had entered his mind like something brought by a far-off pigeon. When he reached the middle of the farmyard he stood a moment under the oak tree watching the smoke coiling out of the farmhouse chimney like a brandished rope and thinking of what had happened in that house on his last visit. But he was clear now as to what he should do, and he would do it.

It was three weeks since the last time Gwilym had been called to Nantwig. That night, when he went into the house, he saw that the big iron double bed had been moved down into the middle of the kitchen and a great furnace of a fire stoked up in the chimney. An oil-lamp, the flame turned low in the frosted globe, was placed on the window-sill and by its light he caught a glimpse of Phoebe Harris, the saffron-faced wife of Nantwig, peeping at the doorway that led into the parlour. But at the sound of his boots on the kitchen flags she disappeared and soon her stockinged feet could be heard on the boards low above his head. Gwilym took off his round hat and placed it on the brass bed-knob where a pair of cord breeches were hung up by the braces. Then he stood gripping the bars at the foot of the bed and slowly recovering his breath.

There facing him, propped up by the pillows, a sullen look on his big red face, was Ahab Harris, Nantwig, wearing a frayed nightshirt of red flannel. Ahab, a heavy man, had pitched into the yard off the roof of the stable and was dying in full flesh. But Gwilym could still feel blazing through the bedrails the bullying furnace of Ahab's strength, the power that comes from a gigantic frame, a bull's bellow, and a bulging nose-bone. Ahab's fleshy face, through which whisky had driven a mass of red pathways, was still fiery red, the skin looked hot enough to crack open and let the flames inside blaze out. The front of his head was bald but half-way up the scalp a torrent of thick black hair gushed out and fell behind him. He watched Gwilym with close-together eyes, too small for his huge head, while his black eyebrows, a pair of thick furry wings, shot up and down all the time like the brows of a monkey. As Gwilym watched him in silence a purring sound came out of him like the buzz of a huge cat snoring.

What was in the heart of this Ahab, Gwilym wondered, this

mocker, this flagrant adulterer, this drinker for whom there was often not room enough on the roads? Ahab was as worldly a man as any between heaven and floor, carnal and violent, never would he put his shoulder under the ark, never ponder the unsearchable riches, never once of a Sunday or week-night had he sought the lake-bank of the Means. What could he want? When Gwilym had got enough breath into his lungs the tip of his nose began its restless scribble against the air as he spoke.

'Good night, Ahab Harris,' he said. 'You wanted me.'

Ahab blinked out at him.

'Yes,' he talked in his arrogant voice. 'That's right. I want to talk to you.'

'What's the matter?' Gwilym asked.

'I was fastening some loose tiles on the stable roof and I fell into the stack-yard. Nothing serious.'

Gwilym nodded and the heavy, cunning brick-skinned face stared back at him. 'You look well,' Gwilym said.

'Why not?' Ahab answered. He grinned. 'In a week from now I'll be in town with the chestnut mare under my thighs again.'

There was a pause. Ahab spat at the fire, and it boiled on the bars. Suddenly he scowled at Gwilym.

'Don't you think now, Nanney,' he said, sullen and threatening, 'from what I am going to tell you that I am moving out of Nantwig stiff in a few days with my feet in front of me. No, no. I will stand on the graves of a good many yet, yours included. But I want you to do something for me.'

Gwilym said nothing. Then Ahab spoke about his will. He said what Phoebe and the children were to receive. They were a judgement on him and it was little. But there were some things he did not wish to put down in black and white. And he wanted Gwilym to promise that he would see these things were carried out. He paused and then dropped his voice. 'Come here,' he whispered, glancing up at the ceiling, 'I want to explain to you.'

Gwilym took his hands off the sweating bars and went round to the bedside.

'You have been with religion these forty years now, Nanney,' Ahab said, 'and I know you are like a gunbarrel. Now listen. Although I am not clothed I am in my right mind. Remember that. Across the *nant* I have five fields. You know them. Good fields. No rushes. No stones. No need to cut thistles. The best of Nantwig. They are on Twm Tircoch's side of the brook. And Twm wants to buy them. But I won't sell them to him. Do you understand, Nanney? I wouldn't give a hair of my nose to Twm Tircoch. And I refuse to sell him my fields. If I am under the big stones before Phoebe she is not to sell them to him. Now remember.'

'Thomas is a faithful churchman,' said Gwilym, 'and a good neighbour.'

'You are right,' Ahab answered. 'Twm is a faithful churchman and a good neighbour. There's nothing wrong with Twm. Only the air still goes in and out of him. Only he feels the stroke of the blood in his veins. And he sings hymns. *Yr argian fawr* that little voice! I would sooner listen to a bandsaw. That is all. He wants my fields. I don't know why. Perhaps he thinks the railway will wish to come through them some time. Perhaps he likes the look of them under heavy hay. I won't sell them to him. I won't. But I want them sold. *Yr Israel Fawr* yes, I want them sold. Do you understand? And do you know why? To provide for a widow. No, no, not Phoebe. Not her. My real widow. The one in Hills Street in town. Mrs. Watkins forty-two.'

Gwilym remembered her. He had seen her one mart day, a big purple pigeon of a woman with a mop of red hair, standing under the arch that leads to Hills Street. 'That's Ahab Nantwig's fancy,' someone said. She saw Gwilym looking at her standing with her big hip out and her hand on it like a trollop. 'What the hell are you staring at?' she shouted across at him.

'Stoke the fire if you are cold,' Ahab called out, 'stoke the fire, man.'

Gwilym was sweating with heat and anger. His bleak nose looked warm. He picked up the big iron poker and with one blow broke the back of the fire so that it roared up the chimney. Then he came back to the bed.

'Listen,' Ahab went on. 'I want those five fields sold, and the money paid over to Mrs. Watkins. They are good fields. They will fetch a good price.'

A long and thick silence followed. Gwilym was too angry to

speak. His big ears had become bright red and stiff, they shone like slices of lacquered wood. He looked up at the black ceiling near his head. It was so hot the hung bacon was sweating. What words was he to use in protest against giving to a red-haired harlot the best of Nantwig, the undercut and all the thigh slices? Five fields of ungathered hay velvet under the breeze, or ploughed red with the gulls like pebbles upon them. All for a hard whore who wouldn't shed a tear even of gratitude. In his distress the long grey hairs brushed over his bald head fell down in a bunch and hung at the side of his face like a mass of creeper the wind has clawed by the roots off a ruin.

The bed creaked. 'Answer me,' Ahab shouted, with temper red in the webwork of veins netting his face. 'Answer me, Nanney. It's like drawing teeth to get you to speak. Do you promise or not?'

Gwilym bent his head to one side as though before the blows of a big wind. He heard the glass globe of the oil-lamp ringing at the loudness of Ahab's Welsh. How could he lay the seal of his blessing on this? But would he do more than blue himself if he fought against a hard man like Ahab? And dimly he knew what might happen to Phoebe and the children if he refused. He saw himself putting his head in a beehive but for the sake of Phoebe he nodded. 'I promise,' he said.

Ahab grunted. 'Put the belly of your hand here on my heart and swear it,' he said.

Gwilym bent forward. He placed his hand on Ahab's breast and felt the heat blazing out through the red nightshirt as though his palm were laid against a furnace door. Ahab's huge hand then covered his own, hot and soft as a poultice, while he swore he would see the five fields were sold, but not to Twm Tircoch, and the money received for them paid over to Mrs. Watkins.

He finished and Ahab's great red, upholstered face was no longer sullen. He grinned. 'Good,' he said, 'and now that we've got the gambo over the hill, what about you, Nanney, what will you take as your share of the whitemeat?'

Gwilym shook his head. 'The church, Ahab Harris,' he said. 'Give something to the church.'

Ahab laughed. The bald front of his head shone like a coal-shute in the lamplight. 'The church?' he said. 'What does the church want with money? I always thought the gospel was free?'

With considering Gwilym considered this. With his huge bare hands he picked up some glowing coals fallen on to the hearth and put them back on the fire. 'The gospel,' he answered at last, 'is free. But we have to pay for the paraffin oil and the sweeping brushes.'

A sound boiled up into Ahab's throat like a huge bubbling of porridge. He opened his great mouth and laughed. It was a laugh that filled the house and had in it the note of a roof-cock triumphant over ten hens. Nanney the harmless, the dull as a bullock, had promised. All was well.

Nanney came out from under the oak tree which stood in its gaiter of white-washed wall and went towards the house. He had finished considering. A light shone from the kitchen window. He tapped at the back door, lifted the latch, and went in.

There was silence in the room, Phoebe was sitting one side of the fire and Twm Tircoch the other. The big bed had gone back upstairs and the table, with the lamp standing on it, had been returned to the middle of the room, for Ahab had been dead a fortnight. Gwilym took a stool and sat between Phoebe and Twm with his hat on his knee. Before him was a nice kitchen fire on which grew a good crop of flames like yellow bristles.

'It's a bitter night,' he said.

'You are right, Mr. Nanney,' said Twm in his thin voice, 'and me thinking it was going to rain because the cat was so playful.' When Twm realized what he had done he stopped short, blushed, and fell silent.

Phoebe nodded. She was a small and thin woman, her wrinkled skin bright yellow as though it were catching a powerful reflection from a sheet of brass. Because of Ahab's death she was wearing a black dress but her canvas apron was still on, steaming in the heat of the fire. On her head was a gold hair-net like a soft birdcage. Gwilym could see the snow was heavy on her heart. Her face was sad and her eyes were red with weeping.

For a time the three sat in silence. Phoebe wished to ask a question but she did not know how to begin. In her embarrassment she bent forward and brushed off Nanney's shoulder a patch of brown cow-hairs left there when he had milked Elin Tŷ-fri's cross-bred that afternoon. 'Mr. Nanney,' she said at last. 'What were his wishes?'

Gwilym paused before answering. Would he be able to explain? He turned to Twm Tircoch sitting at the other side of the fire. 'Thomas,' he said, 'you wanted to buy Ahab's fields on your side of the brook. Is that right?'

Taken unawares Twm looked startled and the colour went up his plump face to the roots of his hair. He was a big blusher of a man with a thin voice; he was shy and he used to tell the neighbours that although he was all right with the dog he didn't know what to say to the baby. He wore a suit of bulging corduroy and the laces of his boots and all his buttons were under heavy strain. He had no collar and tie on and his stud was a cuff-link. Gradually his blush passed but all over his head his untidy hair stood up as though his scalp had been glued and he had passed through a heavy shower of craneflies.

'Yes, yes,' he said. 'And I do now. That's why I came over tonight. I hope Phoebe will give me the first chance. I will pay her a good price.'

'Ahab's wishes, Thomas,' said Gwilym, 'were that his fields on the Tircoch side of the brook were to be sold.' He paused again and looked at Phoebe. 'Phoebe,' he said, 'the night I came here to see Ahab three weeks ago, do you know what I promised Ahab?'

Phoebe shook her head. 'He never told me his business,' she said.

'I promised,' Gwilym went on, 'that I would see the five fields were sold, as the will says, but I also promised to see you did not sell them to Thomas here.'

For a moment Twm looked up in a vague way, like one suddenly conscious of a draught. Then he went red from the tight of his neckband to the roots of his hair. 'What wrong did I ever do to Ahab?' he said.

Phoebe sighed. 'When they are sold,' she said, 'what is to become of the money? I suppose it is not to come to me and the children?'

Again Gwilym looked about, thinking of words to use so that

Nantwig should not fall to the dogs and the ravens. 'Phoebe,' he said, 'have you heard of Mrs. Watkins forty-two?'

Phoebe began to cry.

'She,' said Gwilym, 'is to have what is received for the five fields. I have promised it.'

There was silence in the room, except for the sobbing of Phoebe.

Twm got up to go.

'Sit down, Thomas,' said Gwilym. 'Phoebe, you must sell the fields. It is in the will.'

Phoebe nodded.

'Who will buy them?' Gwilym asked.

Phoebe raised her head. She shrugged her shoulders. 'Anyone,' she said. 'Plenty will be ready to buy them. They are good fields, as good as any in the parish.'

'Well then,' said Gwilym, wondering if this was where his plan would go under the water. 'Now listen, Phoebe. Will you sell those fields to me?'

Phoebe stared. 'To you, Mr. Nanney?' she said. 'But the fields are large. And very good. And what will you be wanting five fields like that for?'

'Phoebe,' Gwilym repeated, 'will you sell them to me? All right. That is settled. I will buy the fields from you and I will give you a shilling each for them.'

'A shilling——' said Phoebe, and Twm began: 'But Mr. Nanney——'

'Will you agree?' said Gwilym. 'I will give you a shilling each for them. Remember, what you receive for the fields goes to Mrs. Watkins forty-two. If I give you a shilling each for them that is what Mrs. Watkins will get—five shillings.'

Phoebe sat with her mouth open. Gwilym turned to Twm. Slowly he was unhooking the three-weeks-old load from his heart. 'Thomas,' he said, 'you were not allowed to buy the fields off Phoebe. Will you buy them off me? For a good price?'

Twm nodded. 'And what will you do with the money, Mr. Nanney?' he asked.

'All but five shillings I shall give to Phoebe,' he said. 'Do you agree?'

Twm nodded.

'And now,' said Gwilym suddenly, 'let us pray.'

The three stood up. Gwilym thanked God that He had made some as cunning as serpents and as harmless as doves, that out of the mouths of babes and sucklings should come forth wisdom. As he prayed he felt his legs so cold he could have sat down for an hour before the fire with his feet stuffed in between the bars. He brought his prayer to a close. 'The Lord giveth and the Lord taketh away,' said Gwilym. 'Blessed be the name of the Lord.'

'Amen,' said Phoebe.

'Amen,' said Twm.

ALUN LEWIS

Ward 'O' 3(b)

I

Ward 'O' 3 (b) was, and doubtless still is, a small room at the end of the Officers' Convalescent Ward which occupies one wing of the rectangle of one-storied sheds that enclose the 'lily-pond garden' of No. X British General Hospital, Southern Army, India. The other three wings contain the administrative offices, the Officers' Surgical Ward, and the Officers' Medical Ward. An outer ring of buildings consist of the various ancillary institutions, the kitchens, the laboratory of tropical diseases, the mortuary, the operating theatres, and the X-ray theatre. They are all connected by roofed passage-ways; the inner rectangle of wards has a roofed verandah opening on the garden whose flagstones have a claustral and enduring aura. The garden is kept in perpetual flower by six black, almost naked Mahratti gardeners who drench it with water during the dry season and prune and weed it incessantly during the rains. It has tall flowering jacarandas, beds of hollyhock and carnation and stock, rose trellises and sticks swarming with sweet peas; and in the arid months of burning heat the geraniums bud with fire in red earthenware pots. It is, by 1943 standards, a good place to be in.

At the time of which I am writing, autumn 1942, Ward 'O' 3 (b), which has four beds, was occupied by Captain A. G. Brownlow-Grace, Lieut.-Quartermaster Withers, Lieut. Giles Moncrieff, and Lieut. Anthony Weston. The last-named was an R.A.C. man who had arrived in India from home four months previously and had been seriously injured by an anti-tank mine during training. The other three were infantry-men. Brownlow-Grace had lost an arm in Burma six months earlier, Moncrieff had multiple leg injuries there and infantile paralysis as well. 'Dad' Withers was the only man over twenty-five. He was forty-four, a regular soldier with twenty-five years in the ranks and three in commission; during this period he had the distinction of never having been in action. He had spent all but two years abroad; he had been home five times and had five children. He was suffering from chronic malaria, sciatica, and rheumatism. They were all awaiting a medical board, at which it is decided whether a man should be regraded to a lower medical category, whether he is fit for active service or other service, whether he be sent home, or on leave, or discharged the service with a pension. They were the special charge of Sister Normanby, a regular Q.A.I.M.N.S. nurse with a professional impersonality that controlled completely the undoubted flair and 'it' which distinguished her during an evening off at the Turf Club dances. She was the operating theatre sister; the surgeons considered her a perfect assistant. On duty or off everybody was pleased about her and aware of her; even the old matron whose puritan and sexless maturity abhorred prettiness and romantics had actually asked Sister Normanby to go on leave with her, Sister deftly refusing.

II

The floor is red parquet, burnished as a windless lake, the coverlets of the four beds are plum red, the blankets cherry red. Moncrieff hates red, Brownlow-Grace has no emotions about colours, any more than about music or aesthetics; but he hates Moncrieff. This is not unnatural. Moncrieff is a University student, Oxford or some bloody place, as far as Brownlow-Grace knows. He whistles classical music, wears his hair long, which is impermissible in a civilian officer and tolerated only in a cavalry officer with at least five years' service in India behind him. Brownlow-Grace has done eight. Moncrieff says a thing is too wearing, dreadfully tedious, simply marvellous, wizard. He indulges in moods and casts himself on his bed in ecstasies of despair. He sleeps in a gauzy veil, parades the ward in the morning in chaplies and veil, swinging his wasted hips and boil-scarred shoulders from wash-place to bed; and he is vain. He has thirty photographs of himself, mounted enlargements, in S.D. and service cap, which he is sending off gradually to a network of young ladies in Greater London, Cape Town where he stayed on the way out, and the chain of hospitals he passed through on his return from Burma. His sickness has deformed him; that also Brownlow-Grace finds himself unable to stomach.

Moncrieff made several attempts to affiliate himself to Brownlow-Grace; came and looked over his shoulder at his album of photographs the second day they were together, asked him questions about hunting, fishing, and shooting on the third day, talked to him about Burma on the third day, and asked him if he'd been afraid to die. What a shocker, Brownlow-Grace thought. Now when he saw the man looking at his mounted self-portraits for the umpteenth time he closed his eyes and tried to sleep himself out of it. But his sleep was liverish and full of curses. He wanted to look at his watch but refused to open his eyes because the day was so long and it must be still short of nine. In his enormous tedium he prays Sister Normanby to come at eleven with a glass of iced nimbo pani for him. He doesn't know how he stands with her; he used to find women easy before Burma, he knew his slim and elegant figure could wear his numerous and expensive uniforms perfectly and he never had to exert himself in a dance or reception from the Savoy in the Strand through Shepheard's in Cairo to the Taj in Bombay or the Turf Club in Poona. But now he wasn't sure; he wasn't sure whether his face had sagged and aged, his hair thinned, his decapitated arm in bad taste. He had sent an airgraph to his parents and his fiancée in Shropshire telling them he'd had his arm off. Peggy sounded as if she were thrilled by it in her reply. Maybe she was being kind. He didn't care so much nowadays what she happened to be feeling. Sister Normanby, however, could excite him obviously. He wanted to ask her to go to a dinner dance with him at the Club as soon as he felt strong enough. But he was feeling lonely; nobody came to see him; how could they, anyway? He was the only officer to come out alive. He felt ashamed of that sometimes. He hadn't thought about getting away until the butchery was over and the Japs were mopping up with the bayonet. He'd tried like the devil then, though; didn't realize he had so much cunning and desperation in him. And that little shocker asking him if he'd been afraid to die. He hadn't given death two thoughts.

There was Mostyn Turner. He used to think about death a lot. Poor old Mostyn. Maybe it was just fancy, but looking at some of Mostyn's photographs in the album, when the pair of them were on shikari tiger-hunting in Belgaum or that fortnight they had together in Kashmir, you could see by his face that he would die. He always attracted the serious type of girl; and like as not he'd take it too far. On the troopship to Rangoon he'd wanted Mostyn to play poker after the bar closed; looked for him everywhere, couldn't find him below decks, nor in the men's mess deck where he sometimes spent an hour or two yarning; their cabin was empty. He found him on the boat deck eventually, hunched up by a lifeboat under the stars. Something stopped him calling him, or even approaching him; he'd turned away and waited by the rails at the companionway head till Mostyn had finished. Yes, finished crying. Incredible, really. He knew what was coming to him, God knows how; and it wasn't a dry hunch, it was something very moving, meant a lot to him somehow. And by God he'd gone looking for it, Mostyn had. He had his own ideas about fighting. Didn't believe in right and left boundaries, fronts, flanks, rears. He had the guerrilla platoon under his command and they went off into the blue the night before the pukka battle with a roving commission to make a diversion in the Jap rear. That was all. He'd gone off at dusk as casually as if they were on training. No funny business about death then. He knew it had come, so he wasn't worrying. Life must have been more interesting to Mostyn than it was to himself, being made that way, having those thoughts and things. What he'd seen of death that day, it was just a bloody beastly filthy horrible business, so forget it.

His hands were long and thin and elegant as his body and his elongated narrow head with the Roman nose and the eyes whose colour nobody could have stated because nobody could stare back at him. His hands crumpled the sheet he was clutching. He was in a way a very fastidious man. He would have had exquisite taste if he hadn't lacked the faculty of taste.

'Messing up your new sheets again,' Sister Normanby said

happily, coming into the room like a drop of Scotch. 'You ought to be playing the piano with those hands of yours, you know.'

He didn't remind her that he only had one left. He was pleased to think she didn't notice it.

'Hallo, Sister,' he said, bucking up at once. 'You're looking very young and fresh considering it was your night out last night.'

'I took it very quietly,' she said. 'Didn't dance much. Sat in the back of a car all the time.'

'For shame, my dear Celia,' Moncrieff butted in. 'Men are deceivers ever was said before the invention of the internal combustion engine and they're worse in every way since that happened.'

'What is my little monkey jabbering about now,' she replied, offended at his freedom with her Christian name.

'Have you heard of Gipsy Rose Lee?' Moncrieff replied inconsequentially. 'She has a song which says "I can't strip to Brahms! Can you?"'

'Course she can,' said Dad Withers, unobtrusive at the door, a wry old buck, 'so long as she's got a mosquito net, isn't it, Sister?'

'Why do you boys always make me feel I haven't got a skirt on when I come in here?' she said.

'Because you can't marry all of us,' said Dad.

'Deep, isn't he?' she said.

She had a bunch of newly cut antirrhinums and dahlias, the petals beaded with water, which she put into a bowl, arranging them quietly as she twitted the men. Moncrieff looked at her quizzically as though she had roused conjecture in the psychoanalytical department of his brain.

'Get on with your letter-writing, Moncrieff,' she said without having looked up. He flushed.

'There's such a thing as knowing too much,' Dad said to her paternally. 'I knew a girl in Singapore once, moved there from Shanghai wiv the regiment, she did. She liked us all, the same as nurses say they do, And when she found she liked one more than all the others put together, it come as a terrible shock to her and she had to start again. Took some doing, it did.'

'Dad, you're crazy,' she said, laughing hard. 'A man with all your complaints ought to be too busy counting them to tell all these stories.' And then, as she was about to go, she turned and dropped the momentous news she'd been holding out to them.

'You're all four having your medical board next Thursday,' she said. 'So you'd better make yourselves ill again if you want to go back home.'

'I don't want to go back "home",' Brownlow-Grace said, laying sardonic stress on the last word.

'I don't know,' Dad said. 'They tell me it's a good country to get into, this 'ere England. Why, I was only reading in the *Bombay Times* this morning there's a man Beaverage or something, made a report, they even give you money to bury yourself with there now. Suits me.'

'You won't die, Dad,' Brownlow-Grace said kindly. 'You'll simply fade away.'

'Well,' said Sister Normanby. 'There are your fresh flowers. I must go and help to remove a clot from a man's brain now. Good-bye.'

'Good-bye,' they all said, following her calves and swift heels as she went.

'I didn't know a dog had sweat glands in his paws before,' Brownlow-Grace said, looking at his copy of *The Field*.

The others didn't answer. They were thinking of their medical board. It was more interesting really than Sister Normanby.

III

Weston preferred to spend the earlier hours in a deck chair in the garden, by the upraised circular stone pool, among the ferns; here he would watch the lizards run like quicksilver and as quickly freeze into an immobility so lifeless as to be macabre, and the striped rats playing among the jacaranda branches; and he would look in vain for the mocking bird whose monotony gave a timeless quality to the place and the mood. He was slow in recovering his strength; his three operations and the sulphanilamide tablets he was taking had exhausted the blood in his veins; most of it was somebody else's blood, anyway, an insipid blood that for two days had dripped from a bottle suspended over his bed, while they waited for him to die. His jaw and shoulder-bone had been shattered, a great clod of flesh torn out of his neck and thigh, baring his windpipe and epiglottis and exposing his lung and femoral artery; and although he had recovered very rapidly, his living self seemed overshadowed by the death trauma through which he had passed. There had been an annihilation, a complete obscuring; into which light had gradually dawned. And this light grew unbearably white, the glare of the sun on a vast expanse of snow, and in its unbounded voids he had moved without identity, a pillar of salt in a white desert as pocked and cratered as the dead face of the moon. And then some mutation had taken place and he became aware of pain. A pain that was not pure like the primal purity, but polluted, infected, with racking thirsts and suffocations and writhings, and black eruptions disturbed the whiteness, and coloured dots sifted the intense sun glare, areas of intolerable activities appeared in those passive and limitless oceans. And gradually these manifestations became the simple suppurations of his destroyed inarticulate flesh, and the bandaging and swabbing and probing of his wounds and the grunts of his throat. From it he desired wildly to return to the timeless void where the act of being was no more than a fall of snow or the throw of a rainbow; and these regions became a nostalgia to his pain and soothed his hurt and parched spirit. The two succeeding operations had been conscious experiences, and he had been frightened of them. The preliminaries got on his nerves, the starving, the aperients, the trolley, the prick of morphia, and its false peace. The spotless theatre with its walls of glass and massive lamps of burnished chrome, the anaesthetist who stuttered like a worn gramophone record, Sister Normanby clattering the knives in trays of lysol, the soft irresistible waves of wool that surged up darkly through the interstices of life like water through a boat; and the choking final surrender to the void his heart feared.

And now, two and a half months later, with his wounds mere puckers dribbling the last dregs of pus, his jaw no longer wired up and splintered, his arm no longer inflamed with the jab of the needle, he sat in the garden with his hands idle in a pool of sunlight, fretting and fretting at himself. He was costive, his stockings had holes in the heel that got wider every day and he hadn't the initiative to ask Sister for a needle and wool; his pen had no ink, his razor blade was blunt, he had shaved badly, he hadn't replied to the airmail letter that lay crumpled in his hand. He had carried that letter about with him for four days, everywhere he went, ever since he'd received it.

'You look thrillingly pale and Byronic this morning, Weston,' Moncrieff said, sitting in the deck chair opposite him with his writing-pad and a sheaf of received letters tied in silk tape. 'D'you mind me sharing your gloom?'

Weston snorted.

'You can do what you bloody well like,' he said, with suppressed irritation.

'Oh dear, have I gone and hurt you again? I'm always hurting people I like,' Moncrieff said. 'But I can't help it. Honestly I can't. You believe me, Weston, don't you?'

Disturbed by the sudden nakedness of his voice Weston looked up at the waspish intense face, the dark eyebrows, and malignant eyes.

'Of course I believe you, monkey,' he said. 'If you say so.'

'It's important that you should believe me,' Moncrieff said moodily. 'I must find somebody who believes me wherever I happen to be. I'm afraid otherwise. It's too lonely. Of course I hurt some people purposely. That dolt Brownlow-Grace for example. I enjoy making him wince. He's been brought up to think life should be considerate to him. His mother, his bank manager, his batman, his bearer—always somebody to mollycoddle him and see to his wants. Christ, the fellow's incapable of wanting anything really. You know he even resents Sister Normanby having to look after other people beside himself. He only considered the war as an opportunity for promotion; I bet he was delighted when Hitler attacked Poland. And there are other people in this world going about with their brains hanging out, their minds half lynched—a fat lot he understands.' He paused, and seeming to catch himself in the middle of his tirade, he laughed softly. 'I was going to write a letter-card to my wife,' he said. 'Still, I haven't got any news. No new love. Next Thursday we'll have some news for them, won't we? I get terribly worked up about this medical board, I can't sleep. You don't think they'll keep me out in India, Weston, do you? It's so lonely out here. I couldn't stay here any longer. I just couldn't.'

'You are in a state, monkey,' Weston said, perturbed and yet laughing, as one cheers a child badly injured. 'Sit quiet a bit, you're speaking loudly. Brownlow'll hear you if you don't take care.'

'Did he?' Moncrieff said, suddenly apprehensive. 'He didn't hear me, did he? I don't want to sound as crude as that, even to him.'

'Oh, I don't know. He's not a bad stick,' Weston said. 'He's very sincere and he takes things in good part, even losing his arm, and his career.'

'Oh, I know you can preach a sermon on him easily. I don't think in terms of sermons, that's all,' Moncrieff said. 'But I've been through Burma the same as he has. Why does he sneer at me?' He was silent. Then he said again, 'It's lonely out here.' He sighed. 'I wish I hadn't come out of Burma. I needn't have, I could have let myself go. One night when my leg was gangrenous, the orderly gave me a shot of morphia and I felt myself nodding and smiling. And there was no more jungle, no Japs, no screams, no difficulties at home, no nothing. The orderly would have given me a second shot if I'd asked him. I don't know why I didn't. It would have finished me off nicely. Say, Weston, have you ever been afraid of death?'

'I don't think it's as simple as that,' Weston said. 'When I was as good as dead, the first three days here, and for a fortnight afterwards too, I was almost enamoured of death. I'd lost my fear of it. But then I'd lost my will, and my emotions were all dead. I hadn't got any relationships left. It isn't really fair then, is it?'

'I think it is better to fear death,' Moncrieff said slowly. 'Otherwise you grow spiritually proud. With most people it's not so much the fear of death as love of life that keeps them sensible. I don't love life, personally. Only I'm a bit of a coward and I don't want to die again. I loathe Burma, I can't tell you how terribly. I hope they send me home. If you go home, you ought to tell them you got wounded in Burma, you know.'

'Good God, no,' Weston said, outraged. 'Why should I lie?'

'That's all they deserve,' Moncrieff said. 'I wonder what they're doing there now? Talking about reconstruction, I suppose. Even the cinemas will have reconstruction films. Well, maybe I'll get a job in some racket or other. Cramming Sandhurst cadets or something. What will you do when you get home?'

'Moncrieff, my good friend,' Weston said, 'we're soldiers, you know. And it isn't etiquette to talk about going home like that. I'm going in where you left off. I want to have a look at Burma. *And I don't want to see England.*'

'Don't you?' Moncrieff said, ignoring the slow emphasis of Weston's last words and twirling the tassel of his writing-pad slowly. 'Neither do I, very much,' he said with an indifference that ended the conversation.

IV

The sick have their own slightly different world, their jokes are as necessary and peculiar to them as their medicines; they can't afford to be morbid like the healthy, nor to be indifferent to their environment like the Arab. The outside world has been washed out; between them and the encircling mysteries there is only the spotlight of their obsessions holding the small backcloth of ward and garden before them. Anyone appearing before this backcloth has the heightened emphasis and significance of a character upon the stage. The Sikh fortune-tellers who offered them promotion and a fortune and England as sibilantly as panders, the mongoose-fight-snake wallahs with their wailing sweet pipes and devitalized cobras, the little native cobblers and peddlers who had customary right to enter the precincts entered as travellers from an unknown land. So did the visitors from the Anglo-India community and brother officers on leave. And each visitor was greedily absorbed and examined by every patient, with the intenser acumen of disease.

Brownlow-Grace had a visitor. This increased his prestige like having a lot of mail. It appeared she had only just discovered he was here, for during the last four days before his medical board she came every day after lunch and stayed sitting on his bed until dusk and conferred upon them an intimacy that evoked in the others a green nostalgia.

She was by any standards a beautiful woman. One afternoon a young unsophisticated English Miss in a fresh little frock and long hair; the next day French and exotic with the pallor of an undertaker's lily and hair like statuary; the third day exquisitely Japanese, carmined and beringed with huge green amber stones, her hair in a high bun that only a great lover would dare unloose. When she left each evening Sister Normanby came in with a great bustle of fresh air and practicality to tidy his bed and put up his mosquito net. And he seemed equally capable of entertaining and being entertained by both ladies.

On the morning of the medical board Brownlow-Grace came and sat by Anthony among the ferns beside the lily pool; and this being a gesture of unusual amiability in one whom training had made rigid, Weston was unreasonably pleased.

'Well, Weston,' he said. 'Sweating on the top line over this medical board?'

'What d'you mean?' Weston asked.

'Well, do you think everything's a wangle to get you home or keep you here like that little squirt Moncrieff?'

'I don't think along those lines, personally,' Weston said. He looked at the long languid officer sprawled in the deck chair. 'The only thing I'm frightened of is that they'll keep me *here*, or give me some horrible office job where I'll never see a Valentine lift her belly over a bund and go grunting like a wild boar at—well, whoever happens to be there. I got used to the idea of the Germans. I suppose the Japs will do.'

'You're like me; no enemy,' Brownlow-Grace said. 'I didn't think twice about it—till it happened. You're lucky, though. You're the only one of us four who'll ever see action. I could kill some more. What do I want to go home for? They hacked my arm off, those bastards; I blew the fellow's guts out that did it, had the muzzle of my Colt rammed into his belly, I could feel his breath, he was like a frog, the swine. You, I suppose you want to go home, haven't been away long, have you?'

'Six months.'

'Six months without a woman, eh?' Brownlow-Grace laughed, yet kindly.

'Yes.'

'I'm the sort who'll take somebody else's,' Brownlow-Grace said. 'I don't harm them.'

Weston didn't reply.

'You've got a hell of a lot on your mind, haven't you, Weston? Any fool can see something's eating you up.' Still no reply. 'Look here, I may be a fool, but come out with me tonight, let's have a party together. Eh?' Surprisingly, Weston wasn't embarrassed at this extreme gesture of kindness. It was so ingenuously made. Instead he felt an enormous relief, and for the first time the capacity to speak. Not, he told himself, to ask for advice. Brownlow-Grace wasn't a clergyman with a healing gift; but it was possible to tell him the thing simply, to shift the weight of it a bit. 'I'm all tied up,' he said. 'A party wouldn't be any use, nor a woman.'

'Wouldn't it?' Brownlow-Grace said drily, standing up. Weston had a feeling he was about to go. It would have excruciated him. Instead he half turned, as if to disembarrass him, and said, 'The flowers want watering.'

'You know, if you're soldiering, there are some things you've got to put out of bounds to your thoughts,' Weston said. 'Some things you don't let yourself doubt.'

'Your wife, you mean?' Brownlow-Grace said, holding a breath of his cigarette in his lungs and studying the ants on the wall.

'Not only her,' Weston said. 'Look. I didn't start with the same things as you. You had a pram and a private school and you saw the sea, maybe. My father was a collier and he worked in a wet pit. He got rheumatism and nystagmus and then the dole and then parish relief. I'm not telling you a sob story. It's just I was used to different sounds. I used to watch the wheel of the pit spin round year after year, after school and Saturdays and Sundays; and then from 1926 on I watched it not turning round at all, and I can't ever get that wheel out of my mind. It still spins and idles, and there's money and nystagmus coming into the house or no work and worse than nystagmus. I just missed the wheel sucking me down the shaft. I got a scholarship to the county school. I don't know when I started rebelling. Against that wheel in my head. I didn't get along very well. Worked in a grocer's and a printer's, and no job was good enough for me; I had a bug. Plenty of friends too, plenty of chaps thinking the same as me. Used to read books in those days, get passionate about politics, Russia was like a woman to me. Then I did get a job I wanted, in a bookshop in Holborn. A French woman came in one day. I usually talked to customers, mostly politics; but not to her. She came in several times, once with a trade union man I knew. She was short, she had freckles, a straight nose, chestnut hair, she looked about eighteen; she bought books about Beethoven, Schopenhauer, the Renaissance, biology—I read every book she bought, after she'd gone back to France. I asked this chap about her. He said she was a big name, you know the revolutionary movements toss up a woman sometimes. She was a Communist, a big speaker in the industrial towns in North France, she'd been to Russia too. And, well, I just wanted her, more and more and more as the months passed. Not her politics, but her fire. If I could hear her addressing a crowd, never mind about wanting her in those dreams you get.

'And then the war came and most of my friends said it was a phoney war, but I was afraid from the beginning that something would happen to France and I wanted to hear her speaking first. I joined up in November and I made myself such a bloody pest that they posted me to France to reinforcements. I got my war all right. And I met her, too. The trade unionist I told you about gave me a letter to introduce myself. She lived in Lille. She knew me as soon as the door opened. And I was just frightened. But after two nights there was no need to be frightened. You get to think for years that life is just a fight, with a flirt thrown in sometimes, a flirt with death or sex or whatever happens to be passing, but mostly a fight all the way along. And then you soften up, you're no use, you haven't got any wheel whirring in your head any more. Only flowers on the table and a piano she plays sometimes, when she wants to, when she wants to love.'

'I've never been to France,' Brownlow-Grace said. 'Hated it at school, French I mean. Communists, of course—I thought they were all Bolshies, you know, won't obey an order. What happened after Dunkirk?'

'It was such burning sunny weather,' Weston said. 'It was funny, having fine weather. I couldn't get her out of my mind. The sun seemed to expand inside the lining of my brain and the whole fortnight after we made that last stand with Martel at

Cambrai I didn't know whether I was looking for her or Dunkirk. When I was most exhausted it was worse, she came to me once by the side of the road, there were several dead Belgian women lying there, and she said "Look, Anthony, I have been raped. They raped me, the Boches." And the world was crashing and whirring, or it was doped, wouldn't lift a finger to stop it, and the Germans crossing the Seine. A year before I'd have said to the world, "Serve you right." But not now, with Cecile somewhere inside the armies. She'd tried.'

'And that was the end?' Brownlow-Grace said.

'Yes,' said Weston. 'Just about. Only it wasn't a beautiful end, the way it turned out. I had eight months in England, and I never found out a thing. The Free French didn't know. One of them knew her well, knew her as a lover, he told me; boasted about it; I didn't tell him; I wanted to find her, I didn't care about anything else. And then something started in me. I used to mooch about London. A French girl touched me on the street one night, I went with her. I went with a lot of women. Then we embarked for overseas. I had a girl at Durban, and in Bombay: sometimes they were French, if possible they were French. God, it was foul.'

He got up and sat on the edge of the pool; under the green strata of mosses the scaled goldfish moved slowly in their palaces of burning gold. He wiped his face which was sweating.

'Five days ago I got this letter from America,' he said. 'From her.'

Brownlow-Grace said, 'That was a bit of luck.' Weston laughed.

'Yes,' he said. 'Yes. It was nice of her to write. She put it very nicely, too. Would you like to read it?'

'No,' said Brownlow-Grace. 'I don't want to read it.'

'She said it often entered her mind to write to me, because I had been so sweet to her, in Lille, that time. She hoped I was well. To enter America there had been certain formalities, she said; she'd married an American, a country which has all types, she said. There is a Life, she said, but not mine, and a war also, but not mine. Now it is the Japanese. That's all she said.'

'She remembered you,' Brownlow-Grace said.

'Some things stick in a woman's mind,' Weston said. 'She darned my socks for me in bed. Why didn't you say she remembered darning my socks?'

Brownlow-Grace pressed his hand, fingers extended, upon the surface of the water, not breaking its resistance, quite.

'I don't use the word,' he said. 'But I guess it's because she loved you.'

Weston looked up, searching and somehow naïve.

'I don't mind about the Japanese,' he said, 'if that were so.'

V

Dad Withers had his medical board first; he wasn't in the board room long; in fact he was back on the verandah outside 'O' 3(b) when Weston returned from sending a cable at the camp post office.

'Did it go all right, Dad?' Weston asked.

'Sure, sure,' Dad said, purring as if at his own cleverness. 'Three colonels and two majors there, and the full colonel he said to me, "Well, Withers, what's your trouble? Lieutenant-Quartermaster, weren't you?" And I said "Correct, sir, and now I'm putting my own body in for exchange, sir. It don't keep the rain out no more, sir." So he said, "You're not much use to us, Withers, by the look of you." And I said, "Not a bit of use, sir, sorry to report." And the end of it was they give me a free berth on the next ship home wiv full military honours and a disability pension and all. Good going, isn't it now?'

'Very good, Dad. I'm very pleased.'

'Thank you,' Dad said, his face wrinkled and benign as a tortoise. 'Now go and get your own ticket and don't keep the gentlemen waiting. . . .'

Dad lay half asleep in the deck chair, thinking that it was all buttoned up now, all laid on, all made good. It had been a long time, a lifetime, more than twenty hot seasons, more than twenty rains. Not many could say that. Not many had stuck it like him. Five years in Jhansi with his body red as lobster from head to toe with prickly heat, squirting a water pistol down his back for enjoyment and scratching his shoulders with a long fork from the bazaar. Two big wars there'd been, and most of the boys had been glad to go into them, excited to be posted to France, or embark for Egypt. But he'd stuck it out. Still here, still good for a game of nap, and them all dead, the boys that wanted to get away. And now it was finished with him, too.

He didn't know. Maybe he wasn't going home the way he'd figured it out after all. Maybe there was something else, something he hadn't counted in. This tiredness, this emptiness, this grey blank wall of mist, this not caring. What would it be like in the small Council house with five youngsters and his missus? She'd changed a lot, the last photo she sent she was like his mother, spectacles and fat legs, full of plainness. Maybe the kids would play with him, though, the two young ones?

He pulled himself slowly out of his seat, took out his wallet, counted his money; ninety chips he had. Enough to see India just once again. Poor old India. He dressed hurriedly, combed his thin hair, wiped his spectacles, dusted his shoes and left before the others came back. He picked up a tonga at the stand outside the main gates of the hospital cantonment, just past the M.D. lines, and named a certain hotel down town. And off he cantered, the skinny old horse clattering and letting off great puffs of bad air under the tonga wallah's whip, and Dad shouting 'Jillo, jillo,' impatient to be drunk.

Brownlow-Grace came in and went straight to the little bed table where he kept his papers in an untidy heap. He went there in a leisurely way, avoiding the inquiring silences of Weston and Moncrieff and Sister Normanby, who were all apparently doing something. He fished out an airgraph form and his fountain-pen and sat quietly on the edge of his bed.

'Oh damn and blast it,' he said angrily. 'My pen's dry.'

Weston gave him an inkbottle.

He sat down again.

'What's the date?' he said after a minute.

'12th,' Moncrieff said.

'What month?' he asked.

'December.'

'Thanks.'

He wrote slowly, laboriously, long pauses between sentences. When he finished he put his pen away and looked for a stamp.

'What stamp d'you put on an airgraph?' he asked.

'Three annas,' Moncrieff said patiently.

Sister Normanby decided to abolish the embarrassing reticence with which this odd man was concealing his board result. She had no room for broody hens.

'Well,' she said, gently enough, 'what happened at the board?'

He looked up at her and neither smiled nor showed any sign of recognition. Then he stood up, took his cane and peaked service cap, and brushed a speck of down off his long and well-fitting trousers.

'They discharged me,' he said. 'Will you post this airgraph for me, please?'

'Yes,' she said, and for some odd reason she found herself unable to deal with the situation and took it from him and went on with her work.

'I'm going out,' he said.

Weston followed him into the garden and caught him up by the lily pool.

'Is that invitation still open?' he asked.

'What invitation?' Brownlow-Grace said.

'To go on the spree with you tonight?' Weston said.

Brownlow-Grace looked at him thoughtfully.

'I've changed my mind, Anthony,' he said—Weston was pleasurably aware of this first use of his Christian name—'I don't think I'd be any use to you tonight. Matter of fact, I phoned Rita just now, you know the woman who comes to see me, and she's calling for me in five minutes.'

'I see,' Weston said. 'O.K. by me.'

'You don't mind, do you?' he said. 'I don't think you need Rita's company, do you? Besides, she usually prefers one man at a time. She's the widow of a friend of mine, Mostyn Turner; he was killed in Burma, too.'

Weston came back into the ward to meet Sister Normanby's white face. 'Where's he gone?' she said.

Weston looked at her, surprised at the emotion and stress this normally imperturbable woman was showing.

He didn't answer her.

'He's gone to that woman,' she said, white and virulent. 'Hasn't he?'

'Yes, he has,' he said quietly.

'She always has them when they're convalescent,' she said, flashing with venom. She picked up her medicine book and the jar with her thermometer in it. 'I have them when they're sick.'

She left the ward, biting her white lips.

'I didn't know she felt that way about him,' Weston said.

'Neither did she,' said Moncrieff. 'She never knows till it's too late. That's the beauty about her. She's virginal.'

'You're very cruel, Moncrieff.'

Moncrieff turned on him like an animal.

'Cruel?' he said. 'Cruel? Well, I don't lick Lazarus's sores, Weston. I take the world the way it is. Nobody cares about you out here. Nobody. What have I done to anybody? Why should they keep me here? What's the use of keeping a man with infantile paralysis and six inches of bone missing from his leg? Why didn't the board let me go home?'

'You'll go home, monkey, you'll go home,' Weston said gently. 'You know the Army. You can help them out here. You're bound to go home, when the war ends.'

'Do you think so?' Moncrieff said. 'Do you?' He thought of this for a minute at least. Then he said, 'No, I shall never go home. I know it.'

'Don't be silly, monkey. You're a bit run down, that's all.' Weston soothed him. 'Let's go and sit by the pool for a while.'

'I like the pool,' Moncrieff said. They strolled out together and sat on the circular ledge. The curving bright branches held their leaves peacefully above the water. Under the mosses they could see the old toad of the pond sleeping, his back rusty with jewels. Weston put his hand in the water; minnows rose in small flocks and nibbled at his fingers. Circles of water lapped softly outwards, outwards, till they touched the edge of the pool, and cast a gentle wetness on the stone, and lapped again inwards, inwards. And as they lapped inwards he felt the ripples surging against the most withdrawn and inmost ledges of his being, like a series of temptations in the wilderness. And he felt glad tonight, feeling some small salient gained when for many reasons the men whom he was with were losing ground along the whole front to the darkness that there is.

'No,' said Moncrieff at last. 'Talking is no good. But perhaps you will write to me sometimes, will you, just to let me know.'

'Yes, I'll write to you, monkey,' Weston said, looking up.

And then he looked away again, not willing to consider those empty inarticulate eyes.

'The mosquitoes are starting to bite,' he said. 'We'd better go now.'

BOBI JONES

The Last Ditch

Translated from the Welsh by Elizabeth Edwards

'It looks like any other rural village as far as I can see.'

'So it is, of course. But there's one thing I want to show you.'

Dr. Joël Lefèvre opened his door, and I alighted from my side.

'Were you up here in connection with your studies of the culinary customs?'

'Yes. And compiling an Ati-tofa craft vocabulary.'

'Was anyone left, this close to Montreal?'

'One. An old fellow. Matama. He's the one I want you to see.'

We went up the only street in the village. The houses were similar in style to those we had seen everywhere else, but somewhat shabbier. Near the centre of the village and close to a shop where wooden images of the Virgin Mary were sold, we halted and looked about us.

'It was somewhere near here. Follow me.'

He turned back to one of the houses near by, and in its rear was a solitary zinc-roofed shed, a very crude structure resembling a prehistoric tortoise, with the planks that formed its shell sagging inwards: the roof and walls were engaged in a menacing competition as to which should collapse first.

'This chap's a character. An uncompromising old warrior. He refuses every grant from the Government towards building his own civilized house; refuses all assistance—money as well as pension. Refusal is the crux of his nature. That's the truth of the matter, he refuses everything.'

'Is he the only one still speaking the language in this section of the tribe?'

'Yes. He speaks it to everyone, if he speaks at all. And his vocabulary is remarkably pure. He creates new compound-words and so forth, in order to express unfamiliar technical concepts.'

'But how is he able to carry on if there is no one who understands him?'

'Obstinacy. He couldn't care less that there's no response. He'll refuse to exchange one word of French with anyone. If we fail to understand what he says, that's our misfortune.'

'And his bad luck.'

'This fellow doesn't live in a world of good or bad luck. He chose a universe of misfortune from the outset as it were, and he exists and moves within the confines of those terms.'

By this time we were on the threshold, and as Joël raised his hand to knock, the door was opened by a dark-haired young man, a relative of the old Indian, I presumed. He raised his hand and whispered.

'He's very poorly.'

'Since when?'

'Three weeks ago. He's dying.'

'What's the matter with him?'

'The same old trouble. Obstinacy.'

'Has the doctor seen him?'

The young man's answer was a look of helplessness and a tightening of the lips. 'By now he's refusing even a bite of food. He's looking at the wall and dying. Come in and see him.'

We slipped into the dark shed. On some straw near the far wall I could see a bed-ridden form mouldering under blankets, and a mass of white hair cascading downwards to mingle with his beard around his face.

'O lach, olama di,' said Joël, greeting him.

The body moved, and the beard quivered slightly, and a quiet snort came from its centre, but quite unintelligible to Joël and myself.

Joël continued, as he later explained to me, to tell the old Indian that he had brought a friend from Wales to see him, and he then asked me to say something, translating on my behalf to the bundle on the floor.

'The Welsh are Indians of a kind,' I said. 'They too have been deprived of their laws and their rights as a nation. Their language is being eroded by foreign pressures. They too are trying to be obstinate, coining technical terms and so on. At the same time we hope to win back the right to rule ourselves. Indeed, the nation's psychology is starting to regain some strength these days, and a new hope, a new dignity is returning.'

Throughout my discourse not a sound issued from the hidden form. His silence was merciless.

'Has he heard me?'

'Yes, and understood.'

'Oh!' I exclaimed, rather disappointed.

'I'm expecting the doctor again,' said the young Indian.

'Is there any point?'

'No, but the doctor himself insists on coming.'

By now, the form was completely still and silent but for its breathing.

'Matama,' said Joël, 'I have published your latest list of fishing terms in the *University Bulletin*, the same journal in which your hunting terms appeared.'

There was no response.

We heard a movement by the door, and the ginger head of the young doctor came through, grinning like a Cheshire puss at everyone.

'And how's the entertaining old gossip this morning?' he asked, approaching the patient.

There was no answer.

The doctor addressed us: 'You're strangers in these parts?'

'I've been here several times,' said Joël, 'but my friend comes from Wales.'

At this, the heap near the wall bestirred himself and turned towards us, raising himself laboriously on to one elbow and directing his eagle glance at the four of us.

We stood amazed.

'*Ralach Galsdi Amarat,*' said he ferociously, and spat, then sank back again, his breathing now more irregularly wild.

He rolled his body from knees to head into a tight ball. He neither protested nor drew away when the doctor approached him with his stethoscope to sound his chest.

The doctor returned to us.

'Five minutes,' he said.

We stood in a row, waiting. But no further sound came from the ungainly bundle. At the end of five minutes the breathing stopped, stopped without any fuss, without a sigh. One moment he was with us, and the next he was no longer; not one sound, nothing but utter stillness.

I turned to Joël, 'What was all that towards the end?'

'A curse on your foul Wales,' he said.

During the journey back to the city of Quebec Joël Lefèvre was silent for quite a while. But when we arrived at Trois-Rivières, he started to speak again of Matama.

'I have known him for twenty years, you know. It was here in Trois-Rivières that I first saw him at a fair. He'd had a varied history for some years before I came across him.

'For the first years of his adult life he was a professional boxer, and the occupation suited him admirably, because he could give vent to that urge of his which you saw, to revenge himself on, to hate, or to show his disgust for the strangers who stole this continent from the Indians. But like many others of his race, the whisky tot caught up with him and he became its slave. He got fat and paunchy, and of course he started losing his fights. He was then about twenty-eight years old, unable any longer to get any arranged fights. Eventually he left his trainer and wandered off westward, and then north to Alaska, so they say. He was not taking care of himself—never washing or shaving, never cutting his hair; sleeping where he could and begging whisky money; wandering far and wide, from degradation to degradation. Yet still proud.

'By the time he reached his fortieth birthday he was an old man, with his unkempt hair and beard snow white, his forehead and cheeks wrinkled, and his shoulders sagging above his belly. Following fairs was what he liked to do. In them he used to meet up constantly with new drunkards from new areas, and he was able to persuade them to hand out some charity to him when they were under the influence of drink. The nomadic life of the fair also appealed to him.

'On that night in Trois-Rivières—that is, the night I saw

him—a boxing ring had been put up, and an American by the name of Buck Wallace challenged all and sundry to venture three rounds with him. Already five of the toughest lads of Trois-Rivières had been flattened by him. Although I understood enough about boxing to know that this Wallace would be no match for a reasonably good opponent, he was safe enough against the amateurs of this area—and any other area the fair was likely to visit.

'Matama must have measured him up similarly, and the prize of fifty dollars undoubtedly had him licking his lips, because after Wallace had floored his fifth opponent, the poor old Indian—amid derisive laughter—made his way through the crowd towards the ring. When Wallace saw this white-haired stupe climbing into the ring, he indicated with his fist that he would not accept such a contest.

' "Come on, you coward, you dirty Yankee," shouted the Indian from his cocoon of filth. And he insisted that the seconds made haste to tie the gloves over his fists. He had the appearance of a man well over sixty years old, not only because of the colour of his hair and the aged look of his face, but also his legs were skinny and his belly paunchily ugly. He was centuries old. But everyone soon noticed by his style, by the positioning of his arms and his movements around the ring, that he was motivated by whisky and that this was not his first venture into such surroundings.

'Wallace danced confidently out of his corner, and Matama gave him a clout which sobered him abruptly. He didn't wait for the American to regain his composure, but followed up with a neat blow to his midriff and then two clean punches to his chest—wham—wham—and the man who had been lord of Trois-Rivières only a moment before was writhing against the ropes. The crowd was flabbergasted and they shouted their heads off as the old man charged in on his prey, everyone completely enchanted by the old pensioner turned Knight of the Round Table. A left hook towards Wallace's temple followed, but he had managed to duck and to use his fleetness of foot to move back out of reach of this dangerous old'un who kept on adding insult to injury with each passing second. He also got an opportunity to hit back, but Matama moved his head slightly and the blow landed uselessly in the air. Another clout to Wallace's right ear, and a merciless punch to the same place again. The old boy, though his feet moved rather slowly, could weave his way subtly across the ring. By this time Wallace was more wary: he held back somewhat, and then pranced hesitantly forward, throwing out a straight left to Matama's eye. He, in turn, failed to evade it, and a swelling appeared on his eyebrow. One, two, three, more blows—bam—bam—bam—to his body, and the old man lost a bit of his steam under the attack. Both were by now more cautious, the young man quicker, the old more definite with his punches. Wallace prodded Matama's navel, and he retreated a yard or two. Much of the American's fist work was threshing the air by now as the old Indian ducked and evaded. The bell went to end the round, just as the old man returned to the attack and pounded his opponent's chest.

'The second round started quietly. During the first half-minute it seemed that each was waiting for the other to open up. Then suddenly, having lost his patience, Wallace charged into the old Indian, jabbing left, left and aiming for his chin with the right. But the other pulled away quickly, retaliating with a strong punch to his opponent's eye, which opened up like a poppy, and the blood flowed sweetly on to the canvas. Wallace tried to raise his fists in front of his face to defend himself, but the old fox had smelt victory. He followed up with a cross to the nose and the defender's fists dropped: then the hail of his gloves fell on the poor wretch's face, and he retreated to his corner unable to cover himself. He sank on to one knee, and the referee started to count: Wallace was not unconscious, nor had he lost any of his faculties, but he had suffered a truly grim beating, and his facial flesh was an ugly pulp. A few people around the ring booed, others mocked, while some were hopefully urging him on. But it was all over for him.

'Following the verdict, the Indian crouched in the centre of the ring and then leaped into the air, raising his right hand and shouting *"Ocwlw"*, according to tribal custom. The old shame had again hidden itself from view inside his fists.

'After this he was hired by the fair's manager to travel with the fair, and with his white hair and aged appearance, the old Indian was a special attraction, challenging each boxer to three rounds with him in the ring. He continued thus to travel the length and breadth of Canada and through the northern states for at least five years, until he arrived at Vancouver one summer. And there, he was shattered by a man eighteen years his junior, who had boxed professionally over a period of years. His right eye received such cruel treatment on this occasion as to cause him to lose his sight, and the eyeball was split in two.

'He crept from the fight at the end with his eye closed. And without complaint or explanation he sneaked away into the darkness, and made his way back towards the territory of his tribe.

'He had not given up his drinking habits, and he continued to deteriorate physically. He was innately strong, of course, and that was a blessing, for his body had to withstand cruel winters and deplorably insufficient nourishment for years.

'By the time of my second encounter with him, about four years ago, he was more or less as you saw him on his deathbed. I got no welcome from him for months, not until he realized that my only reason for bothering him was pure knowledge concerning the language and customs of the Indians, and that I was a great admirer of their fine civilization. But even then he was not very willing to answer except formally and briefly. He would never expand. He took refuge behind his fists. He had no real confidence in even his Indian neighbours, and he scorned their quasi-American way of life.

'But do you know, this old fighter knew by heart hundreds of nursery rhymes, thousands of proverbs, old harvest verses, funeral and wedding songs; and goodness knows how much about hunting and fishing, cooking and time-keeping customs, and the history of his tribe for many generations. On the face of it he was a worthless drunkard, jetsam thrown overboard by misfortune, a corrupt prodigal. But in the course of studying his culture, from afar, as it were, I came within hearing range of some unbelievable dignity and beauty, and I succeeded in penetrating his defence just a little.'

Joël was anxious to attend Matama's funeral, and I accompanied him, mainly out of curiosity, on the following Saturday. But I was disappointed, because not one of the tribe was familiar with the old Ati-tofa method of conducting a funeral. He was buried according to the cheapest method of the Americans.

After the service, we went to the house of one of his neighbours for a little chat before leaving.

'Mind you,' said the neighbour, 'he was not one of us. We don't live in that manner. He wasn't a true-blue Ati-tofa. He came here from the West somewhere. A strange fellow, and dirty you know. He consistently refused to speak to us.'

IDWAL JONES

China Boy

1

I first beheld Pon Look twelve years ago, and even then he was the oldest human creature in Fiddle Creek township. It was on top of Confidence Hill one August day, when the pines were withering in the terrific heat and the road was a foot deep in white dust. Pon Look came over the brow of the hill, from below.

He waddled like a crab, leaning on a staff, and extreme age had bent his body at a right angle to his stunted legs. His physiognomy was fearsome, like a Chinese actor's in a print. His head was sunk forward, so that his ears were in line with his shoulders, and the protuberant chin was adorned with sparse, silvery hairs. For all he had the aspect of a crippled galley-slave, he progressed smartly, slewing that head continually from side to side with a strange grace. He seemed to be propelling himself through the heat waves with that sculling movement. He had something alive, which he held in check with a rope. It was a large, feline animal, with a bobbed tail and a funny wicker hat fitting over its head, like a muzzle. At intervals this beast leaped into the air, and, uttering frantic cries, tore furiously at the muzzle with its forefeet. It had eyes as glittering as topazes. It was a superb catamount. Pon Look no more minded its antics than if they were the antics of a mosquito.

I offered Pon Look a cigar. His face wreathed instantly with smiles, and he took it shyly. Laughter wrinkles creased his smooth high forehead.

'You are taking your pet out for a breath of air?'

'Pet?' he queried. Meanwhile the catamount was whirring insanely in the dust, at taut rope, with the velocity of a squirrel in a cage. 'Pet?'—oh, no—I jus' catch heem now in the canyon.'

'What are you going to do with him?'

Pon Look gave a fierce yank at the rope. 'Oh—I tame him first. Then in two weeks, if not fliendly, I kill him.'

Heaven only knows how Pon Look, dried-up like a cricket, captured these monsters. Certain it was that he was wise in the arcana of nature, and cunning in the manipulation of willow forks, ropes, knots, and all the little tricks of leverage. Once a month, at least, he rattled down the steep road in his buckboard, with a wildcat, a cougar, or a brown bear in the crate behind. These beasts he sold to merchants in the Chinatown of San Francisco, who liked them because they drew crowds before the shops.

Though he sold his spoils for a bagful of money, he invariably came back to Fiddle Creek without a dime. He had his little failings. Fan-tan, bottles of *ng-ka-py,* dinners of pickled goose for his old cronies, bouts with the poppy, and nights of amorous dalliance—that was how the money went.

As a sort of watchman, he tyrannized over a domain of three square miles, covered with chaparral, snake-infested and repellent in summer, and no more desirable in the rainy season. It had once been called Summerfield's Place. Some bank held it in lien, or it was held in mortmain. It is of no consequence. On top of this hill Pon Look lived alone.

When he was born, I never learned, nor could he himself guess. Even his beginnings were as shrouded in mystery as his end. In Fiddle Creek and Tamales there were ancients who had come to this part of California in the fifties, but had to admit grudgingly that Pon Look was there before them. A Digger Indian squaw averred that he was there before she was born. At the time of this declaration she was sixty, so I am probably not wrong in setting Pon Look's age at this meeting as about eighty-five. The school-children in Sonora looked upon him with as much awe as Boston infants would a resurrected Pilgrim. Still, Pon Look was sometimes articulate.

He began his career at the age of ten, as stable boy to La Penelli. A few old prints, a casual note in a diary written by an Argonaut who had applauded her exploits—that is all one can find concerning La Penelli. This person was a gymnast who performed in John Rowe's Olympic Circus in Kearny street in 1850. That was the first outdoor entertainment in San Francisco. One Sampson was its star, clown, harlequin, and chariot driver. But what the pioneers most applauded was the lady act, wherein the ravishing Penelli turned somersaults on the back of a galloping white horse. This being the only female exhibition in the city, Rowe made considerable money, until the equestrienne got drunk, and the secret was out. It was Sampson, who had disguised himself with a white wig and an ingenious system of padding. The Olympic habitués were furious, and there was talk of lynching the proprietor. To make things worse for Rowe, one Foley set up a rival circus a block away, and exhibited freaks—the best being Iron Jaws, who could bite through six pieces of pioneer pie at one time. This feat he performed daily until some disgruntled patron inserted a tin pie plate in the strata and wrecked his maxillary leverage.

The circus business declining, Sampson withdrew with his horse and China boy, and took to loafing in the Boomerang Saloon, the rendezvous of British gentlemen. Here roast beef, Yorkshire pudding, and pale India ale were procurable. Once a week, a genuine Stilton cheese, venerable with age, double-creamed and mouldy, was roasted on the spit. *The Times* and *Galignani's Messenger* were on file.

The spoken drama was looking up; Sampson went in for Shakespearean roles, and set off with a barnstorming troupe into the foothills. Pon Look drove the coach, with scenery and costumes lashed behind, all over a dozen counties. Twenty months later, after an altercation with the rest of the company, Sampson absconded with the funds, and started back for England. Pon Look, who went back to the city, spent weeks in futile search for his master, but Sampson had gone to the bottom of the sea in the ill-fated *Brother Jonathan.*

II

The youth mooned in the alleys of Chinatown, half dead with grief, and smitten with a nostalgia for the hills. He apprenticed himself to a Cantonese cobbler who kept a booth near the plaza, and worked with such diligence that he mastered the craft in eight months, and made for himself covertly a pair of fine high boots. They were wrought of Chili oxhide, oak-tanned, and embroidered with dragons. He burnt a hundred candle-ends stitching on that pair of boots. They had to be good, for he had a hard road ahead of him.

Without saying good-bye to a soul, Pon Look tramped back into the hills, going by the devious Mariposa route into the region of the Southern Mines. He wore a coolie hat, flat-crowned, and a dolman, like an actor. At some of the camps the miners were kind and gave him bread; at other camps he was stoned, and bloody-eyed gaunt dogs were turned loose on him. He passed wanderers who limped by in tattered shoes, or else dragged along weary and swollen feet bound in rags. They cursed, never because they were hungry or hopeless, but because of their feet. The sharp quartz slashed their soles, and split open their toes like figs, so that they left blood in their tracks. Pon Look rejoiced that he himself was well shod.

One day he heard loud singing by the side of the road, and there on a rock sat a venerable old man with a snowy beard. He held an open book, and his aspect was so benign that Pon Look paused in reverence.

'Well, well, John—stop and rest a while,' said the old man, holding out both hands in greeting. His head was bare, he carried a heavy staff, and his feet were swathed in burlap. 'Come and have a cup of tea.'

Pon Look was touched. The aged one built a fire of pine cones, and brewed tea, which he shared with the boy from one pannikin. Between draughts he roared scraps of hymns. Pon Look was taking another swallow of tea, when his skull was struck with such violence that he fell senseless. It was night before he awoke. The beautiful old man was gone, and so were Pon Look's fine boots.

He shunned the road after that, and made his own path through the woods and over the hillsides. He would have thrown away his dolman to ensure himself against further attack, but the pockets were handy to carry bread and rice in. Towards nightfall, as he was about to cross a road, sounds of lamentation fell upon his ears. He concealed himself behind a clump of juniper. A man came riding on an agile grey pony. He wore a Mexican sombrero, with a horse-hair strap under his prow of a nose. His teeth were protruding, like a rat's; his wizened face was pockmarked; his eyes were a dead black, and humorous. To the pommel of his saddle was attached a long rope wound in bights about the necks of eight Chinese who tripped and stumbled behind. Pon Look trembled at the sight. What would be their fate? Later he could guess, for he learned that the rat-toothed man was the bandit Murietta, a merry and bloody personage.

Clearly, he had to be discreet above all else. For days and nights he kept off the trails, and never ventured across country until he had first surveyed the land from a height. The second week he fell in with a party of fifteen Cantonese, foot-sore and staggering under the weight of their loaded baying-poles. These, too, groaned and whined, being under the command of a harsh giant, a hairy Manchurian who set the pace, for he was unencumbered and had long legs. This captain had been a dealer in jargoon, moonstones and beryls in Foo-Chow, and was on his mad way to explore the upper reaches of the Tuolumne in search of like things. He permitted Pon Look to tote a heavy sack of millet in recompense for company and safe convoy.

This was the party that made the great strike of Summerfield Flat. That night they had encamped in a narrow valley littered with boulders and gravel, a strip of land so barren that it sustained merely chamiso bush and a few lodge-pole pines. In digging for a fire-pit, a shovel turned up a strip of blackened metal. It was gold. Forthwith, with yells and sweating, everybody plied tools, and the Flat was discovered to be paved with shards and shields of gold, an inch thick, flattened by glacier action, and under no more than two feet of ground. By dawn, when they had dug and piled up tons of gold, a great and appalling discouragement came over them. Even the jargoon merchant was filled with inquietude. What was so plentiful must necessarily be valueless. All hurried away from that spot of disillusionment.

The big Manchu and his party in time returned, loudly cursing the day they had set forth, for luck was against them. They found the Flat throbbing with tumult and life. It was plowed deep, swarming with men like maggots in a honeycomb. Over six million dollars' worth of gold was being taken out. The Cantonese, screaming like magpies, beat their captain with staves, and he crawled away, out of his wits with chagrin.

It was then that Pon Look got a glimpse of the truth that was to abide with him to the end of his days: adventure and travel are the futile expedients of the foolish to escape from themselves. His companions scattered, but he stayed on.

III

Across from the Flat was a narrow pass in a long mountain of black, igneous rock. The mountain was in a semi-circle, and encompassed many square miles of the only green land in the countryside. It was moist from hidden springs, and the virgin soil, overlaid with a humus of centuries, was phenomenal in its richness. Old Man Summerfield owned it. He was a hard-scrabble Vermont farmer who lived in a good house with his haggard wife. He waylaid cattle from the ox-trains, and decoyed them into the enclosure. They bred calves, and he grew passably rich. He dwelt in antipathy with his neighbours, who at night frequently took pot-shots at him. It was on the domains of this ogre that Pon Look trespassed. The owner came riding out with a rifle.

'What do you want here, you yellow limb? Get off my place!'

'A job,' responded Pon Look.

After some reflection the farmer manoeuvred Pon Look, as if he were a stray ox, and drove him to the cow-house.

'Live there,' he snarled. 'You'll find some sacks to sleep on.'

Pon Look entered upon his duties, and became known as Summerfield's China Boy. There were twenty-five head of cattle, and it was his function to ride about on horseback and keep a wary eye on them, and if they showed symptoms of bursting, to dismount and stab them in the belly with a trochar. Because of the succulence of the grass they would overeat and suffer from bloat.

He acquired a sympathy with these animals, and in his solicitude would keep them moving incessantly, and try to retain them where the grass was somewhat less luxuriant. One night a handsome black bull escaped through the pass and vanished. Probably it got carved into steaks by unscrupulous neighbours. Old Man Summerfield frothed through his beard. He raged at Pon Look.

'What am I paying you board for, hey? To lose cattle for me? If that happens again—you get kicked out!'

The boy was aghast. There was every likelihood that it would happen again. It was then that he conceived the idea of building a wall around the ranch. It was a felicitous idea. Along one side of the low cliff was a talus of lava boulders; material right to hand. The stuff was in every size, from pebbles the bigness of a fist to rocks the size of a huge hog, and all rounded by aeons of time. The most of them resembled footballs, and were known locally as nigger-heads.

He built a stone-boat, trained a cadgy old ox to haul it, and began to close the pass. He built a wall six feet high, and three and a half wide, with a wooden gate in the middle. The quarry was a quarter mile distant, and his tools were a crowbar and an end of plank. The job was finished after a year of back-breaking toil and the cost of Pon Look's right toe. Old Man Summerfield was so proud of this entrance that he spent hours sitting on the gate so people could see him as they drove by.

It was a notably fine gate, portentous and eyetaking. It was a gate that connoted landed respectability, and its psychological effect was curious. Old Man Summerfield swelled with self-esteem. He loafed at the saloons in the camp, and leading talk to the job, arrogated to himself all the credit for its design and building.

'It's all in handling the ma-terial,' he would say. 'You got to know how to lay them boulders and lock 'em so they won't roll off like balloons. They's nothing like a good gate to keep the cattle in.'

'A better gate 'ud be one that kept other folks' cattle out,' some neighbour would remark, after Old Man Summerfield had left.

The China Boy's task was only just started. He now began to haul boulders to close in the southern and open arc of the circle. He lived on a diet of boiled beef and rice, which he cooked at his end of the cow-house, where he also slept. He arose before dawn, ate breakfast, then hitched the ox and boated a load of nigger-heads to the scene of operations. These he laid down before he returned to do the chores and attend to the milch cows. Not even after the rainy season was past was danger to the cattle over, and he had to be vigilant against the bloat. His masonry plan was to lay down the bottom tier, for the space of four miles, large boulders that required a trip apiece; then to superimpose smaller boulders, then loads upon loads of nigger-heads, until the wall was complete.

Progress was slow. The stone-boat ox would cough, then die very soon, and Pon Look had to train another one; or the vehicle would wear out, and he had to build another. Old Man Summerfield's wife, who had kept within the house and was wont to shout loud at night, gave up the ghost, so the master went to San Francisco to do some wooing, and being, as he said, 'a particular man to please,' it was three months before he returned with her successor. The boy did the work of two men in the meanwhile, but had to suspend work on the wall.

The new mistress was a fat shrew of a body, with a clacking tongue, and much displeased Pon Look by her interference. She made him beat carpets, trudge about the country to buy laying hens, and dig a garden. He submitted to it all, and arose an hour earlier, making a return trip with the stone-boat before sun-up. On one occasion, as he was passing by the house, she called to him to come in and wash the dishes. He said no. Whereupon she rushed at him with a broom and smote him violently as he stood in the yard. Pon Look took the blows without a murmur, and remained like a statue, with hands folded, while his mistress, still plying the broom, waxed hysterical.

There was no budging Pon Look. She spun round to beat at his face. It was serene, but pallid. The lips bespoke an obstinate resolve, but the eyes gleamed mistily at her with pity and forgiveness. Mrs. Summerfield's arms dropped, then she clutched at her throat, and staring at him walked backward into the house.

IV

When Pon Look returned to the cow-house that night, he found on his table a hot raisin pie. On the window-sill the next morning, Mrs. Summerfield found the pie plate, scrubbed with the sand so bright that it reflected the sun like a mirror, and upon it a handful of the white daisies that grew nowhere except near the bog a mile distant. Pon Look had dined that night, as usual, on rice and beef. The mystified hens, before going to roost, had filled their craws with pastry and raisins.

Thenceforward, Mrs. Summerfield treated Pon Look with a respect that was a compound of both affection and fear. On no pretext could he be induced to enter her house. She did not know what to make of him, so she left him alone. She ran the domestic establishment, but Pon Look, since the old man spent all day and half the night in the camp saloon, saw to the running of the ranch, the sale of the cattle and, of course, the construction of the wall.

'You don't have ter build that wall entire of rocks, China Boy,' she said one evening, when the indomitable mason, scrubbed, and in his fresh alpaca coat, stood surveying in the dusk the lengthening boundary of the ranch. 'Wire's just as good, and fence-stakes is cheaper than they was.'

Pon Look gave a smile so expansive that his eyes disappeared in the creases. 'Make 'um all stone, Mis' Sommyfeel'—begin 'um stone, and finish 'um stone, allee same niggy haid.'

She plucked timorously at her alpaca apron. 'Oh, well, it's you're doing it, not us.'

Yet she took a pride in the fabulous immensity of the task. The editor of the county-town paper drove over one day and watched China Boy wrestling with the boulders. The next week he published a page story on the Summerfield's stone wall. It was a monument to Mr. Summerfield's enterprise and vision, he said; a testimony to the will, the perseverance and crag-like virtues that made New England great, etc. He dragged in quotations from the Latin poets. This story attracted a surprising lot of attention. Old Man Summerfield bought several copies, and wore them to rags in making a boozy tour of all the saloons in the country. People came to see, and among them were women who owned family coaches. Mrs. Summerfield made social contacts in this way, and finally joined the Ladies' Aid Society, and bought a bombazine dress and a landaulette so she could ride over to the meetings. Her period of ostracism was over.

The year 1879 was memorable in the annals of the family. Pon

Look had completed the southern wall after the unremitting labours of twenty-seven years. Death enfolded Mrs. Summerfield that autumn, while she was pruning a rose-bush in her garden. Pon Look worked by lantern-light in the barn and built an enormous hexagonal coffin to house her frail body. It was so heavy that eight men buckled under the weight as they carried it to the hearse. Old Man Summerfield bought a new silk hat for the occasion, and was very proud of it. The minister held a service in the parlour, with no less than six families in attendance; and all throughout the widower nursed the hat on his knees, in full view of the admiring assemblage. Pon Look participated by looking in through the open window. He did not attend the funeral at the Odd Fellows' Cemetery, for there was much to do.

He trudged all over the ground with a tape-measure, and made mental calculations. He returned very late, and sat on the veranda to smoke a pipe in the moonlight. The old lady had latterly been quiet, and his thoughts were tinged with regret that she had gone. He was gratified that the master had taken things sensibly. A wind arose, and because it was cool, and he was afraid of the moon shining on his temples and making him mad, he got up to retire to the cow-shed. Between the lower bars of the gate something white caught his eye. He thought it one of the fluffy pom-poms that had been blown thither from the garden where the old lady had planted a clump of Holy Thistles. He drew nearer, picked up wonderingly a new silk hat, and found that the object was Old Man Summerfield's snowy head. Whisky and grief had done for him.

There was some wearisome business with the coroner. Pon Look wanted to attend the funeral, but could not, for some excitable men detained him for a week in a stone room with bars at the window. He was released with palliative back-slappings and a handful of cigars after the inquest. He had been put to a great inconvenience, for the rains were now on, coming down like firm and slanting spears without let-up for days and days. He had to slosh around in the bog to lay a timber road across which to sled his rock. The Summerfield heir, an elderly nephew, took over the place a month afterwards. He was a city man, with a waxed moustache and a square-cut derby. He drank somewhat, and was inclined to be companionable. China Boy avoided him, looking rigidly ahead every time they passed.

'How much longer that job, John?' he asked one day.

'No can say.'

'Well, then, how long did it take to build all that wall?'

'Oh—thirty—thirty-five year.'

'Good God!' murmured the heir.

He sat under the trees dismally, like a strange bird. Then he panned for gold in various corners of the ranch, and did other foolish things. He would sit hunched on the sacred gate, mope about whistling with a dirge-like note, or keep to the house and drink. He was a lonely and wistful interloper. All his actions lowered himself in China Boy's esteem, and he knew it. China Boy strutted about with aloof and cold arrogance, and the heir's morale ebbed. Finally he accosted the mason and came to an understanding. China Boy was to keep an eye on the place, market the stock and keep a percentage for himself. Then he packed up his things in a wicker suitcase, and went away forever.

The Chinaman had the place to himself now, and sold off most of the heifers so they wouldn't breed and rob him of time he could apply to building. The wall progressed handsomely. He had stretched barbed wire across the northerly side of the farm until the work should be finished. When that was done the place would be a paradise for cattle. They could cram themselves with lush grass in one part of the ranch, then chew the cud in the cropped field adjoining. That would be the end of bloat. China Boy worked incessantly, visited by no one except the banker who came along every quarter to represent the routed heir. In time the wall got itself done. It undulated for miles over uneven ground, but plumb, as straight as a furrow, without a single bend. The job had taken China Boy forty years to complete. By this time he was doubled with age, his pigtail white, and his hands rock-hard and stumpy.

V

It was in August, when China Boy went up to ring the nose of the little black bull, that he saw the ground was parched. Down he went on his knees in the middle of the field and pulled up a handful of soil. It was as dry as ashes. The cattle came around with their tongues, leathery and swollen, hanging out. Palsied with terror, China Boy arose, and shading his myopic eyes, turned round and round like a weather cock, and stared for a glimpse of green. The entire ranch was as brown as a brick. Drouth had laid waste the ground as if with torches.

He saddled a pony and galloped, pigtail a-flying, to the bank. The banker, when he heard the plaint, grumbled:

'I knew there was a hoodoo on the damned place. It's cooking hot, but I'll come down and see.'

Together they rode back. The banker drew up in the buggy before a new mine in the field adjoining the Summerfield ranch. Here were a tall gallows-hoist, with sheaves whirring, a mill from which poundings emanated, and an engine house with a high stick. The ditch alongside the road was filled with a roaring flood of water.

'Ye-ah,' he grunted, pointing at the ditch with his whip. 'That's what I expected. The shaft has tapped the springs underlying the Summerfield flat. Might as well sell off the cattle, the place will be as dry as a volcano from now on.' Then he scratched his head. 'I'll have to send down some goats, Angora goats. Mebbe they'll pay off the taxes. Guess we can cut down some timber, too. I'll have a look at it.'

China Boy got out and walked in a daze to the grove. The banker followed afoot, then paused when his guide appeared at the door of his cabin with a musket in his hands.

'Cattle can go,' China Boy informed him, 'but these trees they stay up, I watch 'um.'

And up they stayed. The story got about, for the banker, who had been taken by the handsomeness of the grove, told it on himself. 'An arbor-maniac, that's what he is. He made that wall business a life-long job, so he could live right there among those trees. Poor old chap, I'll have him pensioned off.'

The banker kept his word, but China Boy drove a hard bargain. His terms for being superannuated were the weekly dole of five pounds of corn flour, a piece of bacon, six cartridges and a quart of whisky, all to be delivered at the cabin.

Thereafter China Boy lived in the grove. Two hundred trees! Lordly sugar-pines, gold traced with black, like Porto-Venere marble. Five sequoias, so colossal that only after staring at them for twenty minutes did their size dawn upon you, and then with a finality that took you in the pit of the stomach like a blow. Wine-stemmed manzanitas, gnarled chaparral. The rest were all redwoods, with high fluted columns; and through their branches interlaced overhead the sunlight streamed in lines and cast disks of silver upon the dark trunks and the ochre ground twinkling with ants. It was something like the inside of a church.

There was a wood for you! Visitors came rarely. Bearded blanket-stiffs, homeless men, tarried for a night on their way to the Middle Fork of the Stanislaus. An occasional prospector, reverent among trees, stayed sometimes two days. China Boy was their invisible host. He peered at them through the foliage, as if he were a bird, but he never spoke to them, unless he perceived their shoes needed cobbling and he felt sure they could pay for the job, nothing less than a dollar, for even a philosopher must live. Aloof, and wrapped in an old army overcoat, he sometimes watched them all night, being afraid they would be careless with their pipes or forget to stamp out the embers of their camp fires.

His house, hidden away in the trees, was rather a nice one, of a single large room, very high, and built of brick. Decades before, he had come across an abandoned express office, and had carried it thither, piecemeal, a bushel of brick at a time, and set it up exactly as it was before, even to the legend board above the doorway: 'Wells-Fargo Express.'

It was a forest lover's house, with blackberry bushes climbing into the window, hedgehogs and grey squirrels sunning themselves on the step, and pine cones dropping like cannon-balls on the roof. It held a cot, a stove, a shoe-last, and a library that consisted in a wisdom-banner that hung on the wall. If he found you, after years of acquaintance, worthy enough, he would translate the wiggly ideographs thus:

'It is shame to be ignorant at sixty, for time flies like a mountain stream.'

Here in this tree sanctuary that was of hoary age long before the Sung dynasty had started, China Boy had gone to school. He listened to the wind wrestling with the tree tops, to the language of the birds, the cries of the coyotes and owls, and other sounds that made the air articulate and vibrant. He loved to sit in the middle of his grove at night, still and pensive amid the falling leaves, like a rheumy-eyed hamadryad.

At intervals he straggled afoot to Sonora, with shirt-tail out and the sun warded off by an umbrella: quite the gentleman of leisure. But these excursions bored him finally, and he desisted, except when he had to call at the bank to complain about the quality of the whisky. It was surprising what an educated palate he had. He wouldn't let the grocer's boy depart until he had first sampled the liquor ration.

Two years ago he trapped a pair of fine wildcats, and carted them off to town, and tarried overlong. Some campers came to the grove and were careless with their fire. China Boy's woods made a gorgeous blaze, singing and burning for ten hours, with the grey squirrels plumping down roasted, and the philosopher's house turning to a black lump like fused glass.

The story made five lines in the county paper. The forest ranger said afterwards that he had seen the Old-Man-Mad-About-Trees pull up to the ruins in his buckboard, look on a few minutes, then drive away.

The banker was dubious. 'Must have checked out through old age in the city,' he said, 'else he would have come up to the bank. He drove an awful hard bargain over that whisky. He had me paying eleven dollars a bottle for the stuff I used to get for him at two before Prohibition. If anybody's ahead of the game, it's me.'

GWYN JONES

The Pit

Akerman came by the pits just after eight o'clock. There were four of them, and near each a high bank of rock discarded from the ore. These were now thinly grown with silver birches, feathered with young ferns, starred with saxifrage and wild strawberry flowers. The stones were about a foot to eighteen inches wide and thick, many of them embedded in livid moss, and those lying loose nearer the pit edge handsomely weathered. The first pit and the fourth coming from Coed-y-Mister had, said the countryside, been sunk in Roman times to meet the level running in under the hill at the Ystrad, and had been worked off and on through fifteen hundred years. The two middle ones had been cut through the rock by Lewis Tywern the ironmaster in Chartist times, and made him a wealthy miser, and had been abandoned as it grew difficult and expensive to fetch the ore out by basket from the pits or by tram through the level. Around two pits, one Roman, one Lewis Tywern's, there still hung from rotten posts the last rust-riddled strands of wires; the other two were open to the hillside, twenty yards from the disused path. In this path, which led from the Roman Steps to the ruined farmhouse of Coed-y-Mister, there were still visible beautifully smoothed stones grooved by the wire that had pulled the full trams to the shoots above the Ystrad. Because there was no fencing, occasionally a sheep went over and, once only, a dog. The largest pit of all, the one Akerman had visited three or four times, had claimed a child, but that was in the days when it was still being worked.

He went to the edge. From the curtain of trees opposite he heard the complaining of birds at his presence, and smiled. The pit was roughly circular, some eighty feet across. For three parts of its round it went steeply over smooth bluffs of ruddy stone mottled with moss, very warm looking in the apricot coloured light. In four places a tree went out from where its roots knitted frantically into a crevice, and there were tufts of greenery twenty or thirty feet down. On the fourth side there was a convex slope covered with last year's leaves, and then a drop to a ledge that he could just distinguish in the brown darkness which always filled the shaft. Carefully he stretched himself on the grass and worked forward till his face was clear of obstruction. Nothing to see. For as the setting sun slipped from the brow of the hill, it cast solid-seeming shadows into its heart.

Then he shouted. He had barely time to hear his voice die in the pit when with a frantic squawking a flock of jackdaws broke raggedly from the trees where they had been watching him and made uneven flight over the chasm. They wheeled and came back to the trees, but half of them, uneasy still, went off a second time with a loud clapping of wings and much jabber. Getting to his feet, Akerman shouted again just as they settled, whereon out they poured in full flock like a devil's chorus screaming across the pit, so that a ewe with two lambs to Akerman's right ran off all huddled. They swarmed up over his head, cursing and jeering, with a hundred insults telling him to take himself off. 'All right,' he called to them; 'but I'll be back tomorrow. I'm going down that pit.' He grinned, reading meanings into their cries. A reprobate with a hanging feather banked within a yard of his face. 'Don't worry,' he said, 'I'm going.' The last he heard of them as he set off towards the steps was a tetchy interchange of suspicion and one commanding squall. Hang-Feather was making a speech.

The Roman Steps led from the mouth of the level at the Ystrad to the ancient earthwork at Castell Coch. Much of it above the point where he joined the way was grass-grown, but in places he could see the series of wide flat steps at the sharper ascents, and there were ten-yard stretches of curbing on the model of the Roman roads he had seen in southern Italy. No wagons could have come this way, though; the iron ore must have been slave-carried in baskets. 'Seen a bit of misery in its time,' he reckoned, wagging his head.

He reached Castell Coch in twenty minutes. The stone house in which he was staying had been built within the earthwork itself. Castell Coch: Red Castle—in the evening one saw why it bore its name. The sun was just sinking, and here on the hill top the light was a lovely soft gold, and the stone outcrop seemed flushed with blood under a tough skin. And what a view! To the west he could see the debouchment of three valleys into the open Vale, and far away the oak trees of Coed Duon went in slow successive folds into fairyland. Behind him, when he turned towards the Ystrad, he found the brown dusk stretched up the hillside to the home meadow, but Cader Emrys wore a purple robe and a crown of light. Then, even as he looked, in a minute, the giant drew a dark hood over his head, and the sun left him.

As he stood there, Mrs. Bendle came from the house and crossed to the well. She looked towards the red and yellow streamers, shading her eyes, and saw him on the mound. He went down to her, telling himself not to hurry.

He hesitated. 'Bendle in?'

She had been treating him this way for a fortnight. 'By the fire. He's a terror for being kept warm, is Tom. Winter and summer, day and night.'

'Bed and board?' he asked, watching her. She was a fine, sly-faced woman, smooth and supple. Her throat was like milk, her hair raven-black. Akerman's age. As high as his mouth.

'If you say so, sir.' Her eyes flashed at him, her mouth drooped humorously, then she had turned to the well again.

'In his place I should want as much,' he challenged.

'As much, sir?'

'Cherishing at bed—and board.' He leaned over the well beside her. 'And don't keep calling me "sir".'

'But I ought to. It is proper.'

'I call you Jane, don't I?'

'Sometimes'—she smothered a laugh—'when my husband can't hear you.'

He knew he was colouring, but as the bucket came up he

reached for the handle, his grip locked upon hers. 'What I ought to do with you——'

'You'll tip the bucket!'

'Never mind about the bucket. There's plenty of water where that came from.' Setting his left hand to the bucket he caressed her soft round forearm with his right. 'Why didn't you come this afternoon?'

'Why should I—sir?'

'Because you promised you would.'

She pushed his hand away. 'Oh, no, I didn't!'

'Oh, yes, you did! But never mind now. Will you come tomorrow?' He had forgotten about the pit.

They were walking towards the house. She looked down at her feet. 'It's my day for mam and dad tomorrow.' She smiled sideways. 'And what would Tom say?'

He scowled, knowing himself a fool. 'Tom will say nothing—if he knows nothing.'

'It's bad you want me to be, I know. And tell my husband lies!'

He could have struck the slut. But she had pushed at the door, calling out: 'Tom, here's Mr. Akerman,' and he could do nothing but follow her inside with the bucket of water. 'Put it in the bosh. There's good of you, sir.'

Bendle said nothing. He was of middle height, very broad, indeed fattish, none too well shaven. Forty years old. He wore a shepherd's jacket, earthy looking trousers stuffed into short leggings, and heavy boots. His red hair was frizzed out at the sides, but the top of his head was quite bald. He was reading a three days' old newspaper, though whether he got anything from it in so bad a light Akerman couldn't know.

'Turns chilly on top here when the sun goes,' Akerman suggested, putting his hands towards the small fire.

'It's too late in the year for fires. They make more work,' said Mrs. Bendle, as she went into the scullery.

Akerman had picked up the poker. 'Someone has to make them, I suppose.'

Bendle put down his paper. 'It's women makes the fire and fools play with it.' He got up boorishly and clumped into the scullery after his wife.

Later, they had supper. Akerman's meal would have satisfied the former holders of the earthwork: brown bread, cheese, lettuce and an onion, a pint of milk. The other two drank tea. Only one part of the conversation mattered to Akerman. Mrs. Bendle was leaving at half-past seven in the morning to catch the train at Maes-yr-haf, four miles away. She did not know whether she would be back at eight or ten o'clock. Bendle could expect her when she came. First, and foolishly, Akerman thought of slipping out at dawn and waiting for her on the Steps; then he looked at Bendle. What he had said about fools playing with fire. Cutting the rind from his cheese, he thought of Bendle in a rage. Heavy shoulders, thick neck like this rind, bull head, shag eyebrows, he could see his powerful jaws going like machines. Awkward to handle if he came at you. He looked full at Mrs. Bendle. No cause for rage—yet.

The two men smoked while Mrs. Bendle washed up outside. Akerman offered his pouch: 'Good stuff,' he said. 'Try some.'

'Try some more, you mean.'

'You said that, not me.' He watched him press the tobacco down with a stumpy finger. 'I may go down one of Lewis Tywern's pits tomorrow. The big one.'

Bendle looked up. 'Why?'

'Curiosity. And habit. I've done a lot of cave work. I like it.'

'You won't find much to interest you.'

'What if I don't? Could you come with me?'

He shook his head. 'Got something better to do with my time.' He fell to puffing steadily.

'You've got a rope in the'—he pointed—'the shed there?'

'Ay. I got a rope.'

'Long enough, is it?'

'Ay. Plenty of rope.' He looked into the bowl. 'I'll give it you.'

In the scullery outside his wife had begun to sing. Akerman leaned back in his chair, listening and thinking. There was no savour to his pipe. He felt the strong beat of his heart; heard it too. Even her voice had a sly laugh in it; the lullaby was tender and caressing. He knew nothing of the Welsh words but found himself nodding as Bendle with half-shut eyes beat time to her singing with his pipe. 'Sing it again,' he called to her when she finished; 'Sing it slow.' She did so and Bendle hunched to the fire. 'When I was a crwt of a boy, no heavier than a bag of nails,' he said at the end, 'I remember my grannie singing that to my sister who died.' He began knocking out his pipe against the square palm of his hand, and blew as he stood up. 'I must see to that cow before I go to bed. There was a mistake for you.' He lit a lantern. 'Ten minutes I'll be.' He had hardly gone from the room with a pan of hot water when his wife came inside.

'It's in her belly, poor creature.'

'What is?'

She laughed. 'Her calf, what d'you think?' She began to rake out the fire, rounding out her hips as she bent in front of him. 'It make's you wonder, don't it?'

'What does?'

'Oh, nothing. Hasn't it been a nice day?'

'It might have been.'

She stepped away from him. 'It is so nice in the woods at night, lying among the flowers, looking up at the moon.'

So fierce a vision possessed him at her words that he had to stand up. 'I'm willing to try it,' he said, dry-mouthed.

'Only there's no moon!'

'There will be, in an hour. Will you come?'

'What a question—sir! Whatever would my husband say? Oh no, I couldn't do a thing like that, could I?'

'Listen!' He came quickly around the table and moved between her and the scullery door. 'Before he comes back——'

'We mustn't forget that he will come back, must we, sir?'

'And if you call me *sir* once again, I'll do something I'm wanting to do, at once, husband or no husband. Understand?' He thought she would have dared him, but warily she nodded, half-smiling, and rubbed the flats of her fingers across the table top. 'Come here,' he ordered.

'Why then?'

'Because I don't like you always dodging away from me. Come here!'

Slowly she came a little nearer. 'Yes?'

'What time are you coming back tomorrow night?'

She glanced, he thought uneasily, at the door. 'Why?'

'Because I'm going to meet you. And bring you home.'

'You can't do that,' she said. 'If I come by the eight train at Maes-yr-Haf I shall walk with the Trefach folk as far as the Ystrad.' She looked towards the door.

'Then I'll wait at the mouth of the level. And help you up the Roman Steps.'

'You mustn't talk such things. If my husband came in and heard you——'

'Who cares?' Her mouth, her throat affected him almost to drunkenness. 'To hell with him anyway!'

'No, no!'

Before she could draw back he had her by the shoulders. Their lips met, hers full and wet and soft, his dry and harsh and bruising. For one moment she clung to him hotly, kissing and taking kisses, and then she broke roughly away. 'No, no!' It was then they heard the scrape of a bucket on the scullery floor. Without a word, hands to hair, she was through the door that led to the stairs. Akerman, a wave of cold dousing the flame in his veins, turned to the table and was fiddling with the lamp when Bendle came in. 'Giving a bit of trouble,' he said steadily.

'Your fault, was it?'

Akerman stared at him. 'Possibly it was.'

'It's best to leave well alone. Where's the wife?'

'Gone to bed, I think.' He patted at a yawn. 'Not a bad idea, either.'

'No.'

'How's the patient?'

'She'll manage.'

'Then I think I'll have a glass of water and away to go.'

In the scullery, pouring water from the jug kept on the drainer, Akerman noticed a strange thing. Part of the plaster had broken away over the bosh that morning and the bit of shaving glass that hung there had been set at an angle against the rack. He saw that it reflected the living-room mirror, and what could be seen in the living-room mirror was the table edge where he and Mrs. Bendle had kissed. He managed one gulp of water and poured the rest down the sink, but when he came back into the living-room, Bendle had gone upstairs.

After a minute he followed him, holding his candle well aloft to illuminate every corner of the stairs and landing.

When he came downstairs in the morning, it was to find Bendle about to leave the house and his wife long on the way to Maes-yr-Haf. His breakfast was set ready on the table, the kettle steamed on the oil stove in the scullery. 'Good,' he said, and smacked his hands together.

Bendle dawdled. 'You serious about the pit?'

'I am.'

'I'd advise you not.' He used last night's phrase. 'Leave well alone, that's best.'

He seemed troubled. Akerman's anxiety about the scullery mirror grew less. 'Don't worry. But I'll borrow your lantern, shall I? I know all there's to know about caves and pits. No nerves to bother me. Start to worry when I don't get back.'

'Ah,' said Bendle. He pulled at his legging, frowned, then straightened up. 'And what time?'

Akerman poured out his tea. 'I may go off for the whole day. Expect me when you see me.'

'Like the wife, then?' Before Akerman could reply he had gone out, but at once reappeared. 'Don't say I haven't warned you.' With that he went for good and Akerman finished his breakfast and had a smoke before going to the shed for the rope. It was very strong, and there was plenty of it. Plenty of rope! He screwed up his eyes, remembering Bendle's phrase, remembering other phrases of his. He sat on the back door bench for some time, wondering. Mrs. Bendle was a slut and a cheat; so far he had made a fool of himself to no purpose. What was wrong with himself tramping four miles to Maes-yr-Haf and catching a train for a long way off from Wales? But his vanity was against it, and his desire. If he met her tonight at the mouth of the level, he'd fetch her to account before they reached Castell Coch. Then, tomorrow he would be off—not another day here—and so let her know what he thought the worth of her. Nice in the woods, looking up at the moon. He felt again her lips against his, the soft weight of her breasts, her loins under his hands. He would not go away before tomorrow.

He found and opened the lantern. The stub of candle was tilted right over, so he set it straight and went into the house for a better supply. He knew where everything was kept and slipped two candles into his jacket pocket. Then, thinking facetiously and yet with a hint of panic: 'I can always eat candles!' he stuffed several more alongside them. He made sure that he had matches, his own beam torch, his penknife, and odds and ends. He put half a loaf and a piece of cheese in his knapsack, and a flask two parts full of whisky. By this time he was growing out of taste with his venture and again sat on the bench out of the sun, wondering.

He'd feel a damned fool if he didn't go. 'Worse be one than feel one,' he said aloud. Alone as he was, he said other things aloud too, about Mrs. Bendle, perversely pleased with himself for doing this. He stood up. He would go just a little way down. No one could say he was afraid.

In twenty minutes he was at the iron pits. It was little more than ten o'clock. 'Hullo there!' he called, and the jackdaws dashed from the trees to revile him. While they swooped and swore, he worked out where the level would meet the pit shaft—somewhat to the left of the slope over the first ledge. Best have a look from there, but first he pitched a stone half-way across the crater. Pang! it came off a distant ledge; then pang! again but fainter, and at last a noise like breath sucked in between the teeth as it met water. Five hundred feet? Six? More? And how far down to the level?

With all the care in the world he passed his rope twice around a tree trunk as thick as his own body, growing near the brink, and then knotted it securely to a second tree six feet away. Slowly he paid it out into the pit. 'Here goes,' he said finally, and began his descent. With only his face above ground level, he hung awhile, staring around. He felt a hundred eyes on him. Climb back up, climb back up!

His feet made untidy tub-like holes in the leaf-laden slope, and then he went down the short drop to the first ledge. It was cooler here, but there was light enough for him to do without his torch. He stood for half a minute, his hand gripping a stout iron bar sunk into the rock, and looked up at the smooth penny of blue sky above him. Nothing would be more natural than that a face should peer over at him. But there was nothing—not even a jackdaw flying across the chasm. He now looked down, but had to wait till the glare left his eyes before he could see much. He fancied the opposite wall slanted towards him as it went farther down. 'Hm,' he began, and ended—'Jane Bendle!' though she had not been present to his mind when he began to speak. 'Well——' He gave his rope a turn around the iron bar, after dragging at it with all his might, and went over on the next stage. He had his torch tied to his button-hole with cord. At once he saw that his own wall was falling away from him and that the shaft was growing narrower. He was glad he had given the rope a turn around the bar; it made him swing that much less. Even so, he would be glad to reach the second ledge. Down another ten, twenty, forty feet—when would it—ah!

The wall of the pit, which had fallen right away from him, suddenly became a wide, flat terrace, on which he landed clumsily, striking his left hip and skinning the knuckles of his right hand. A flash of light rather than an oath went through his head, and then he was moving cautiously towards the back of the shelf. He was not surprised to find right in behind a small level stoutly timbered off. This must be a heading driven from the main road to the Ystrad. The rope secured, he lit his lantern.

There was little to see. The rock was bare as a shin-bone, and as dry. There were many boulders, though none of them, so far as he could judge, had fallen from the roof. From the level he could not even see daylight, and from the front edge of the platform the opening was a thin gash of white. Cloud going over, he judged it, and sat down, frowning into the darkness. He had done enough. He had had enough. He felt very cold, and cursed lumpishly.

Then something happened. He heard a rushing from above, stones and earth began to whang down the pit, the lantern went out as he snatched it up, there was a vicious rustle within a yard of him, and he was knocked a dozen feet as the rope went cracking under his knees. There was a loud groaning of timber from behind him, then silence, except for the clear, plangent notes of the last small stones falling.

For a minute he lay in the darkness, afraid to move lest he go over the edge. He endured a full paralysis of horror before he began to tremble and found his voice. 'What is it?' he asked huskily. 'What happened? Who is there?' With shaking fingers he struck a match, but it went out with the flare, and he failed three times before remembering his torch. It was still on the cord. 'Pray God——' he stammered, and clicked the button. The first thing he saw was his rope running *flat* and two-fold along the floor, and at sight of it he trembled so violently he could not direct the beam. He began to whimper, then to cry, and then he was shouting and choking and beating his fists on the rock under him. He did this for some time before the sounds brought him to his senses and he lay quiet, he did not know how long, in darkness.

Gradually he found courage. 'No good crying,' he said calmly. 'Light the lantern and see. That's the thing.'

He did this. His rope was still fast to the balk, but it had fallen from above and both ends were downwards from the platform. His lantern and knapsack were safe. A bubble of hysteria rose from his stomach to his throat, but he fought it and won. 'What——?' he asked. 'What——?'

He went to the entrance to the level. Could he get out that way? He flashed his torch along the timbers, sickened by their size and preservation. He looked inside. The walls so far as he could see were dry, the roof solid, the floor unlittered. The slow travelling light picked out some figures inside the gate, and he steadied it to read: 60 ft. He looked at this till it shone white on his
↓
eyeballs. What could be sixty feet down? 'The main level,' he said excitedly. He walked to the edge of the platform. Where his rope went over he saw two artificially-made grooves about eighteen inches apart, and a foot back two holes drilled in the rock. Lying flat, he thrust his head as far out as he dared, his torch flashed downwards. In half a minute he rose to his feet, grunting. He had picked out the top of an iron ladder about twenty feet down. Once only he looked up to the top of the shaft, put his broken knuckles to his mouth, and sucked them, and then, having satisfied himself that the rope would hold, lowered himself down-

wards. He went very slowly, and soon found the ladder. From here progress was easy, and even before he expected it he was on the next ledge. Landing, he gave his rope a tug. No Bendle this time to—but he felt that same bubbling of hysteria at the thought, and to drive it away began to talk about the pit in a loud, determined voice. There were lengths of rail here, very rusted like the ladders, pieces of timber, and the clean and frightening skeleton of a sheep. And at the back he found the mouth of the level.

It had been gated off like the smaller one above. As above, his torch went flashing inside. It was seven or eight feet high at the entrance. 'I've got to try it,' he said. He had grown very confident and so practical-minded that he pulled a contemptuous face at the notion that he throw a stone into the water at the bottom. 'Something else in hand,' he said severely. 'Get on with it, not mess about.' He carried a short length of rail back to the timbered level, tested and pushed and probed. It would be easy. He inserted the rail between the timbers and, using it as a lever, managed to force one of the horizontal pieces off the nails. He could now enter the level—if he wished to. Facing a grim moment, he began to sing: 'When the fields are white with daisies I'll be there.' I'll be there, Mrs. Bendle! But behind all this went images he dared not outface: of himself lost in the level, cut off by a fall of rock, coming out to another pit, plunged into bottomless water, poisoned by bad air, falling and breaking a leg, hunted by Something the black level might contain. So he sang to cheer himself, as he had whistled when a boy on a lonely country road, to keep away this Something.

What was the time? He looked at his watch. It was a quarter-past eleven. He had been down the pit more than an hour.

And now came a second noise from above. First a hissing, then a smash, then a heavier one, and as he crouched to the ground he saw a large, shapeless, whirling body go from the darkness of air to the darkness of water. He had just time to hear the chink and patter of tinier missiles before it struck bottom. The noise of the splash came up in rapidly overtaken waves, as though the water itself was washing upwards from shelf to shelf, tearing the air into gouts, sucking and buffeting like rollers trapped in a gulf. It subsided abruptly, leaving him battered with noise in a painful silence. Raising the lantern he saw a small piece of dark material on the edge of the platform and went towards it. It was his face flannel.

Bendle! The thought he had forced from his mind came back so strongly that he gasped like a swimmer taken with cramp. Bendle had followed him, Bendle had untied the rope, Bendle had gone back home and removed every trace of him, Bendle would tell his wife he had gone away that day. Bendle, Bendle, Bendle! He could see him standing above the leaf-deep slope, his bull neck thrust forward, heavy jaws clenched, listening so intently. He leapt up. 'Bendle!' he shouted. 'Bendle, Bendle—for God's sake, Bendle!' His voice clattered about the shaft, boomed back into his lungs, suffocating him. 'I never touched her, Bendle! I never! I never!' To be up there in the sunshine, under God's blue sky! To be free, free! 'I'll go away! I'll do anything! Kill me after, only help me out! Bendle, for Christ's sake, help me out!' He was dancing with terror and hope. 'Bendle! Oh, Bendle!' He choked with sobs, his chest split in two. 'Oh, oh, oh!'

Through the echoes of his shouting came a roaring from the shaft. A boulder tore down a yard from where he stood, a second smashed itself on the ledge above, the iron ladder clanged under a mighty impact. A multiplied crashing and rumbling filled his ears with the noise of an avalanche. Snatching at the lantern, he ran back to the level and climbed through the timbers, the bombardment growing madder each moment. From inside, the lantern threw gigantic bars of yellow light through the gating, and through these bars boulders and splinters hurtled incessantly. Rocks a foot or more square rebounded from the walls of the shaft, shot from its irregular declivities, playing hell's own tattoo before they thrashed into the water below. Some of them burst like bombs on his own ledge, spraying the sides with shrapnel, lumps of stone singing through the air and thudding against the heavy timber framework which protected him. Something went past him with a sigh, to rattle down the stone tunnel; from below an ocean of watery echoes lashed up at him; and through it all he could hear the tremendous sonorous song of metal struck like a harp. He dared not look out, and what he saw as he pressed himself to the floor and joist was Bendle, in bright day, throwing down the cube-shaped blocks of waste till the shaft reverberated as under a hammer.

The uproar continued for ten minutes, great stones cascading all the while to destruction. On the ledge outside nothing would have saved him. Whether Bendle had calculated as much he did not know, but he himself judged that most of the stones, rolled rather than thrown down the leafy slope, would leap away to strike the far wall level with the first ledge and thence smash off, whole or in jagged pieces, to fall sheer to the ledge he had descended from, or just missing that, to the one behind which he now cowered. At least twenty such crashed within as many feet of him, the last of them bounding, hardly splintered, against the rock face left of his head.

The silence when it came was shocking. His ears went on humming and roaring, and there was a muffled bludgeon beating bad time inside his head. At last he left his shelter. The ledge was screed with rubbish, the timbers sconched, the skeleton hit to pieces. 'All right, Bendle,' he whispered, actually fearful lest Bendle should hear him. 'All right.'

He went back into the level and trimmed a new piece of candle. Thank God he had plenty of candle! His hearing became normal again, his head cleared. He had, he reckoned, the third of a mile to go, and with a convulsive effort of mind brought himself to start. He must forget everything else except the will to save himself. 'When the fields are white with daisies——' he began, but bit the words off as the roar of falling boulders was renewed behind him. This time he smiled grimly. 'Fool,' he said, 'wasting his time.' If he got out soon, to go quickly back through the woods, surprise Bendle as he levered up his ammunition, push the fool over the edge to go bump, bump, bump to the bottom! And Mrs Bendle—— He laughed out loud. Trust him!

He was a fool to laugh in a level. A noise might set up tremors, those tremors strong enough to fetch the roof in. He looked up, very grave now. The height had decreased to little more than five feet already. As he lifted the lantern against the face of the stone, his foot kicked against something, so that he stumbled heavily. He panted, had to set his hand against the cold wall, for there were tramlines running ahead of him. 'Oh!' he cried. 'Oh!'

Then the roof came down to four feet six, so that he went clumsily doubled. The sides were cut clean and plumb, the floor was flat and worn. The air was fresh and there was a slight draught on his face. Here and there, just as in a coal mine or a railway tunnel, were manholes let into the sides, big enough for a man to shelter in. 'In less than an hour,' he said exultantly, 'in less than an hour I'll be out.' That cold air was coming straight from the Ystrad, and he had covered a hundred yards already! Almost as he spoke the tunnel went half right, and on the left he saw the opening of a subsidiary shaft running up and away in the direction he had come from. The level of the second ledge he judged it, and was puzzled by a buzzing in his ears. This grew louder with each step he took, and after twenty yards and a sharp turn became a dull rushing noise shaken intermittently like a pulse. Twenty more and the rock throbbed with it, the gush of a pent-up river seeking low levels seeming to push the air faster along the tunnel. It was on his right, no great distance away, the heavy baritone of fast-moving water. It grew colder, the sound a thunderous bass, and then he saw it. Through a fault in the rock a band of black water stretched foamless and unspilling. He had the fancy that if he advanced his fingers it would break them off like pencils. It had the might of a hundred times the flow in sunlight, this unflurried electric stream sucked into blackness. Alarmed, he hurried away.

After another hundred yards, the roof for a long stretch not more than three feet six, he came into a lofty hall. It went so high that his lantern did nothing to illuminate it, and even his torch could not find the centre of the dome. It was some fifty yards across, and circular, save for a huge bulge on his right. From a floor that grew increasingly irregular towards the rim there reared tremendous rounded bastions, so symmetrical that they gave the impression of being tooled by men. The light of the lantern fell softly from their brown masses as Akerman moved slowly around. A pantheon given to silence and emptiness, his footfalls the first in fifty years. He tried to imagine it aglow with lamps in its working days, when men no bigger than he trundled the heavy trams of ore and sent the only noises of an aeon around the vast hollows of its ceiling. 'We don't know we are alive,' he said wonderingly.

It was now, as he came back to the rails and found the other end of the tunnel, that he grew afraid. Bending to enter it he gasped, for he had imagined some huge, shapeless Being of the Hall behind him. He turned, shuddering, and snarled when he found nothing. 'Fool!' he grated, and bent again, and once more had to turn, the hair all alive on his neck. In these black antres who knew what might dwell? Shoulder demons, hunters from behind. 'Nonsense,' he said. 'Nonsense!' Men had worked here, crawling about like bees in a hive. Why, look! there was the haft of a mandril. He caught it up, a weapon, rubbed it against his face, careless of the dirt. 'Come on!' he said hoarsely, staring about him. 'You or Bendle—come on!'

But nothing came. The fist-blows of his heart slackened. 'All right,' he said, 'all right.'

Then, in the mouth of the level, a new panic brought him up stock-still. How did he know he was right? Were there other exits from the hall, with rails? Had he taken the right one for the Ystrad? Had he even gone the whole way round and was now retracing his steps towards the pit? This was a hundred times worse than terrors of the dark. Was the air still blowing against his face? With frightful vividness he thought of the piled-up hillside above him. Four hundred feet of unbroken rock under which to creep and creep till your lantern gave out and you were part of the dark for ever. The whole weight of it rested on his shoulders, compressed his chest so that he could not breathe. He drew his hand across his forehead, caved forward, caught at the wall for support. Breathe slowly, he told himself, breathe slowly! He must go back to the hall, work around it to the other mouth of the level and go on until he heard the waterfall. That would settle one doubt. Then he must return to the hall and come around it in the other direction, and if he found no other exit there was nothing to worry about. If there were other exits——. He threw the weight from his back and set off.

He had no fear of a Being of the Hall as he went back, after leaving the mandril haft at the mouth of the level. He came to an opening which he recognized as that he had left and, sure enough, after going some way along it, he heard the roar of the river. Back he came to the hall and around it, to his left this time. 'There you are,' he said, when he found the mandril haft; 'what did I tell you?' He was a fool to have doubted that the air still blew on his face. He went on.

There was an odd feeling in the middle of his body, as though a tennis ball had been stuffed under the V of the breastbone. 'Because I'm doubled up,' he thought and said, but it was growing bigger and harder. It took him half an hour again to recognize that he was hungry—this where a runnel of clear water was squeezed from under the rock and went gently along with him. He took out the bread and cheese and the flask of whisky, all of which he had forgotten. After eating, he took a couple of mouthfuls of the spirit and felt warm and confident. He was glad the little stream was going his way. It showed he was going downhill, towards the Ystrad. For several minutes after drinking he sat there in a golden tent of light, resting. His watch said half-past two, and at first he could not believe it. He had been down the pit four and a quarter hours.

After attending to his lantern he started off once more. He must be more than half-way. At the slowest reckoning he would be at the Ystrad by four o'clock. And then? It would be barred, he knew that, perhaps locked and double bolted, but once he saw the light of day he'd have no fears. At the worst, he had only to wait until eight o'clock, when Mrs. Bendle would come that way from Maes-yr-Haf.

Mrs. Bendle! Head bent, going sideways under the low roof, he thought of her till her naked body glowed before him in the darkness, white as bone. So nice in the woods at night, lying among the flowers, looking up at the moon. 'All right,' he said, 'all right.' He would be quits with Bendle then. He hissed, changing hands on the lantern, surprised to find himself alone as the vision of her milk-and-raven nakedness faded from in front of him.

Without warning the runnel squeezed back under the right-hand wall. Was he going up a slight incline? Still, there could be only the one way, so he kept on unworried. Easy going, plain sailing, nothing to it. So he thought elatedly, and only superstition prevented him saying so aloud. To match his mood, the floor dipped again on the sharpest gradient he had so far found. His breathing grew deeper and more laboured. Surely this was the last stretch towards the Ystrad. Any moment now he'd see daylight. All right, Bendle. All right, Mrs. Bendle. He heard himself panting and forced himself to walk slower.

In less than a minute the tramlines divided at a full set of points and led off at an angle of thirty degrees into two levels of equal size. For a moment he stood gaping, and then examined them carefully. There was nothing to tell him which was the right one. He had his first sensation of panic since leaving the great hall. Left or right? He made a futile attempt to assess the compass, and then felt the need of sitting down. In a very deep voice, which he did not recognize as his own, he began to assure himself that it did not matter which road he took, as both must lead to the same opening. It was now half-past three.

Finally he decided to go right, ridiculously equating left with wrong. After twenty yards there was a new forking off—in impossible directions, so it seemed to Akerman. He retraced his steps and made a sally down the left-hand tunnel. This ran true for forty yards and then, as he was congratulating himself, branched into two. He was very worried now, and had to get a grip on himself before deciding to take the right-hand turn. But in less than five minutes he came to a fall of rock and knew a year would be no better to him there than a day. Without delay he went back into the road to the left. Soon he was climbing again, steeply, and the rails had come to an end. He went on for a couple of hundred yards, twice bearing right, before deciding this would not bring him to the Ystrad. Once more he must go back and take great care with his turnings. But ten minutes later he came unexpectedly into a bigger level with tramlines. This both frightened and comforted him, frightened him because clearly he had failed to keep his bearings, comforted him because the main level to the Ystrad must be tram-bearing. Nor had he any idea whether to go left or right along this roadway. Fatalistically he went right, but before long discovered that he was going back along the level that had brought him so straightforwardly from the pit, so in a cold sweat he turned yet again and after half an hour found himself at the same main fork. He looked at his watch. It was a quarter to five. He had been down the pit six and a half hours.

He was very tired. He sat down and took a drink from his flask.

It did him good, for the flutters of panic seemed always to come from his stomach. 'Work it out,' he said: 'Let's work it out.' Evidently he must go to the right, unless the roadway blocked by the fall was the proper way to the Ystrad. In that case—he resisted the temptation to drink again, saw to the lantern, and, with his teeth chattering slightly, began to walk. At the parting from which he had already returned once, he decided to go left. He knew that freedom must lie within a hundred yards, perhaps a hundred feet, if only he could get to it. But he covered at least the greater distance before coming into a round rock chamber with a fourfold set of points and three other galleries leading from it. He felt certain as death that one of these was the way he wanted, and that this was a clearing house near the Ystrad end of the level. 'Which one then?' he asked, and noticed how shrill his voice was. 'Why don't they put directions?' One gallery looked exactly like the others, and all were menacing. Then, leaving this small chamber, he had exactly the feeling that had terrified him in the great hall: that some blacker shape in the darkness stretched out hands after him. 'Don't!' he cried. 'Don't!' and stood stiff and trembling and telling himself not to be a fool. But he had given the darkness life and a power of listening—listening to his footsteps, listening to his words, listening to the horrors that tightened around his heart. 'Don't!' he said a third time, his head on one side, and went blundering down a gallery. In ten minutes he was facing a dead end.

He had just resolution enough to follow the rails back to the rock chamber. From time to time he said in a broken voice: 'Must get out. Appointment with Mrs. Bendle. Must get out.' He went blundering down the next gallery, began to make little runs, bumped against the sides. His forehead was bleeding. 'Must get out!' he said, giddy and staggering.

He stood staring stupidly. There was a great yellow lake in front of him, and by holding up the lantern he could not see to the end of it. At his feet the rails dipped gently into it, and so shallow was the water that they travelled several yards before disappearing. 'Got to go on,' he muttered; and then: 'No, got to go back. Yellow water'; and went stumbling away. He was talking all the time now: about getting out, Mrs. Bendle, the tramlines, the Being who was Darkness. Several times he nearly fell, and his clothes were badly torn. 'Like a rat,' he sobbed, 'like a rat!' At the rock chamber he ran to the third gallery and went into it headlong. At once he fell sprawling, knocking the wind from his body, and the lantern was jolted from his hand and went out. Strangely, this restored some measure of self-control, and after scrambling for the lantern and lighting it, he sat still for several minutes. It was twenty past six. He was quite certain that if he were not out before darkness fell on the hill, he would not get out at all. This was not because by that time his candles would be at an end, but from the operation of a time limit he had subconsciously come to accept. 'Must move,' he told himself, and at once was in the rock chamber. 'Ah!' He went back into the gallery, walking quickly and at length dazedly. Surely he had been walking like this since he was born! The world above, the sunshine, the rain, the white clouds, these were all dreams of his. All creation centred in his head. But the birds, the little birds that flew and sang——. He began to sob, terrible dry-throated sobs, and then to howl like a dog.

He was at the yellow lake again. He looked at it and ran away. When he came to the rock chamber he entered another gallery at random and ran forward crying till once more he reached the yellow lake. Back he went the third time, and back he came to it. He ran crouching and fell often, and always found and lit the lantern. Several of its panels were now smashed, and its light was much dimmer. Sometimes he was mounting endless stairs, sometimes running from shadows that gambolled noiselessly behind him; sometimes he was tiny as a pinhead, sometimes swollen to the tight verges of the tunnel. Sometimes he saw Mrs. Bendle—not the delicious vision of her nakedness, but an elongated, swirling, slimy body, with green cheese-mould for hair, her breast wet and rotten, the eyes like cockles. Even when he could not see the face, he knew it was Mrs. Bendle, no other, who waited for him now at this corner, now around that. And wherever he ran, whatever he did, always he came back to the yellow lake.

The sounds he made were now part of the mine. They clashed about him, endlessly repeated, challenging him to cry and howl and whimper. No recognizable word came from him, yet he was never silent. And so long as one throb of strength was in him he would go on running, running, running.

Then the yellow of the lake, the yellow of the lantern swung up in a blinding, golden flame as he struck his forehead full on the rock, and for a long time he knew nothing.

At last he stirred, and in time sat up. There was a clashing of knives in his head; he felt cold as a toad. Through the dullness of his brain regret that he still lived cut like a razor. All his pains seized him together, and he could not light the lantern without crying out. His torch and knapsack were gone; he was down to his last piece of candle. The gentle light fell on the yellow lake, and, sickened, he turned away, resting the lantern on his naked legs, hoping to warm them. Soon he leaned back against the rock, his head nodding, and saw to his left two tiny green points of light. They moved, and he came to know it was a rat watching him. This was the first living thing he had seen since he descended the pit, and he felt a great love for it, and wanted to stroke it and nurse it. But as he moved the lantern it dodged past him into the water, and he saw it swimming ahead in line with the tramrails. His mouth fell open, his eyes glared under the bloody eyebrows, he shook like a mammet. He got up and walked into the yellow lake he had fled from so often. He went very slowly, drawing his foot along the inside of the rail not to miss the way. Now the water was to his knees, now to his thighs, now it set clamps on his belly; but he went on, lifting the lantern higher. Slowly the water rose to his chest. He could not have been colder in a coffin of lead. The roof was slanting steadily towards the water, the floor fell as steadily beneath his feet. The water now came above his armpits. Soon the roof was six inches from his head, the water to his neck; then it was three inches and he had to tilt the lantern. He made six strides in an eternity, and the roof rubbed his hair and the water touched his chin. For one unforgettable fraction of time he saw around him the yellow ochre and a slight swirl as of something swimming ahead, then the lantern went out and he let it fall from his fingers. The water now lapped his mouth, and he tilted his head back so that his nose and forehead scraped along the top. One stride—two—three—the water jolting into his eyes before the roof lifted miraculously from his face. Three strides each a century long, and his mouth was clear. His foot struck the tramline. To his shoulders, his chest, his waist, his knees, his ankles the bitter line sank, and he was slishing forward, his hands before his face lest he dash it against rock again. He fell on his hands and knees to follow the rails and crept on to dry ground, shivering so hard that from time to time he could not proceed. He moved forward with appalling slowness, and it was fifteen minutes later he came to a turn and saw a weak diffusion of light ahead. His tongue came out to lick his lips, but he was now past emotion and continued to crawl. It was not for twenty minutes that he looked up again and saw ahead of him a dull beam of light reddening the rock. He blinked and went on crawling and did not lift his head until he himself was part of that beam. He looked with curiosity at what he did not know were his hands, felt pleased and amused at them. The Ystrad entrance to the level was not ten yards away, and he went crawling towards it. Quite properly there was room for him to squeeze himself past a block of stone, fallen from where it pinned a stout paling, so through he squeezed, leaving half his jacket behind him. For a minute or two he sat playing with the dust, and then with animal patience dragged himself on all fours into the road. He looked up, and then down, and was not surprised to see Mrs. Bendle coming up the road from Maes-yr-Haf.

Bendle was with her. For their part they saw something half human flopping along the ground towards them. It was three-parts naked and unutterably filthy. The hair was grey, the face indistinguishable for blood, the hands raw. It had a voice, too, and squeaked as they came up with it: 'I came. I said I'd come.' Then it looked up at the man, 'He did it,' it cried. 'He made me like this!' It collapsed, sobbing, its face in the dust.

There was a long silence left to two thrushes over the level. Mrs. Bendle looked at the thing at her feet, then at her husband. 'We never——. We never——.' Her voice guttered out, and she panted for breath. In Bendle's forehead a thick red cord pulsed, and he clenched his right fist. He dropped on his knees. 'No,' said the broken mouth, 'oh, no!' But Bendle's fist unclenched, his thick hand stroked the bloody hair. 'Don't be afraid,' he whispered. 'I won't hurt you, machgen i.' Very gently he caught Akerman up in his arms. Then he rose, his burden to his chest, and after one strange glance at his wife set off for the Roman Steps and the house at Castell Coch. She, her face grey and rat-like, her fingers pinching at the buttons of her bodice, followed slowly behind, and it was so they disappeared, all three, into the quiet woods.

SIAN EVANS

Davis

Fred Davis opened the back door and spat on the manure heap thrown up against the kitchen wall.

'It's no use following me about,' he called into the hollow of the passage. 'Nagging night and day; it ain't my fault, damn you.'

He sighed heavily; his fat, sullen face sagged over a dirty white rag tied round his throat in lieu of a collar, his hands picked at the edges of his pockets; his hair, yellow and plentiful, hung in tags over a flat red brow.

A shrill voice answered like an echo. 'That's what you always say; you're lazy, *and* you know it. Just look at the garden.'

Voice and wife approached through the shadows; a woman thrust her face over the man's shoulder, at the same time pointing with a bony arm so that the fingers only appeared round the lintel of the door.

'Call that a garden; look at that hedge. I'd be ashamed to see my wife doing all the work.'

Davis shook himself and, turning round, muttered an oath.

'You clear off; leave me alone, can't you?'

His wife now stood on the weedy path, from which vantage-point she poured forth a string of invective and abuse.

'What's happening to us? Bills, no money, no beasts, the place rotting over our heads. Oh, you lazy pig, I wish to God I'd never married you. Too idle to mend the hedge or move the horse manure from off the path. God, the place is worse than a slum, and *yet* you won't do anything. I can't even find any vegetables to cook, but have to buy what I want. Look at all this garden, wasted, while you lean about all day. It makes me sick. I'm through.'

Her voice rose to a shriek, cracked, and was silent.

Davis started to shamble off towards the pigsties, standing at the far end of the path.

'You drive me crazy,' he mumbled. 'My life's hell.'

His wife tore at her hair as though with one frantic gesture to release all her bitterness.

'Hell, that's your destination all right; this ain't a patch on what God'll make you suffer in the world to come.'

She turned and disappeared into the house, slamming the door behind her. Davis leaned on the pigsty wall.

He noticed the cracks in the bricks and how the rotten gate swung from one hinge only.

Moss grew like slime on the walls, the roof leaked, stale pig manure and straw-sprouting grass littered the floor.

Again he sighed and the sound seemed ominous, as though by his own breath he stood accused.

God, he was tired. Couldn't she see what an added burden it was to think?

Of course she could, the bitch, that's why she kept goading him. Facing him with his demon till his hands were at his own throat.

He groaned; only with an effort could he bring himself to look at the house.

What had happened? The place was going to ruin.

He remembered how it had looked before his father, old Davis, died. White walls, clean paint, plants in the windows, thick doors fitting without the tremor of a draught, flower-beds under the windows, vegetables in neatly dug patches, pigsties with proper roofs.

The yard, too, looked different; in those days a gate divided the cowsheds, stable, and ricks from the open patch in front of the house; now yard and garden mingled in a puddly mess of straw, rotten stumps of cabbage, and manure.

It had been a prosperous enough place.

Well, something had happened, that was all. A gradual decay.

The garden full of weeds, that large hole in the hedge that made his wife so angry, the patch of horse manure in the middle of the path left when the horse broke in and finished the last of the vegetables, the cracking doors tied together with string.

The yard, unkempt as the garden, standing deserted save for a scraggy horse pulling out tufts of hay from the two remaining ricks, hens scratching in the flower-beds, turning over old tins, cans, and putrid scraps.

Yes, something had happened.

Davis made up his mind to remove the horse manure so that his wife shouldn't see it and scream at him every time she came to the door. He pulled out a cigarette, and while he stood smoking watched the sun disappear beneath the rim of the fields.

Another day gone, too late to do anything now. Tomorrow he'd tidy up the place and mend the hedge.

For a moment his heart seemed to lift in his side, his mind sprang lightly towards the future.

He'd get everything straight, he'd start work seriously.

Again his wife appeared at the door; a lighted candle burned in the passage, throwing a beam that revealed her shape and her thin attenuated arms waving like feelers towards the yard.

'Really!' she screamed, emphasizing each word with a fresh gesture. 'Can't you see that horse eating its head off in the yard? Anyone would think we'd got a dozen ricks to waste. Why don't you put it in the stable or shut it in the field? You've been standing out there for nearly an hour. I warn you, I've had about enough.'

Davis looked at her, at her small body that, even when still, appeared possessed by a demon of energy, at her hands rapidly unwrapping a scrap of bandage from round her wrist, and her face moving round words that poured from her lips in an endless stream.

'Why can't you do your share? Are you ill, or what? You don't care about anything, no pride ... no nothing.'

He bellowed suddenly in a voice choking with anger. 'It's your bloody tongue; you take the relish out of anything, work or pleasure. I'm going out, you've driven me out. You do everything yourself, then you can't complain; you always know best, nothing I do's right, you make a man mad.' He turned his back on her, setting off towards the road in a great hurry. His blood beat in his temples like pistons, he clutched at his chest uneasily. All this noise and excitement day in, day out; supposing he had a heart attack?

The thought made him feel sickish. When he had turned a corner in the lane he sat down on the roadside and held his head in his hands. No man could stand it.

A great depression fell on him. He kept asking himself questions, although the answers tormented him.

'What shall I do?'

'Work,' came the reply like a stone hurled at his head.

'What's the use?'

'Do you want to die, then?'

'No, by God!'

'If everything rots over your head, how will you live?'

'I don't know, something will happen.'

'No, it won't.'

He began to groan and mumble out loud.

'Things aren't so bad, I'll soon pull them round. I've seen many worse places about.'

Then he heard his wife's voice: 'You're lazy . . . bone lazy.'

He jumped to his feet. 'That's a lie, a damned lie. Nobody but a bitch would say a thing like that.'

He stopped shouting as suddenly as he had commenced.

It was nearly dark, a light mist covered the surrounding fields; standing back, the hills were black against a thickening sky. It looked like rain.

Davis turned and stared at the bank where he had been sitting. A distinct patch where the grass lay flattened revealed the spot.

He looked at it with surprise. 'I'm going dotty; anyone would think I'd been drinking. . . .'

He walked about for some time unable to make up his mind to go down to 'The Angel' for a pint. At last he made for home.

He remembered angrily that he had forgotten to milk the cows.

Never mind, it wouldn't be the first time; they'd have to wait a bit.

When he reached home his wife was washing the milking pails in the back kitchen.

He poked his head round the door, but she kept her head obstinately turned from him. Her tightly compressed lips showed that her silence was the silence of anger and contempt.

He returned to the kitchen and sat warming his feet by the fire. Presently he slept.

His wife woke him. 'Your supper's ready.'

It was late, nearly nine o'clock; he sat up with a start.

'All right; you needn't pretend to be surprised it's so late. You needn't say: "Why didn't you remind me about the cows?" because you knew all along I'd do it, like I always do.'

The woman set his plate down as she spoke. There were two red spots burning in her cheeks.

She polished the forks on a cloth and then they started to eat. Neither spoke. While she was making the tea Davis watched his wife sulkily, pulling at his hair with his hands and watching her every movement through half-closed eyes.

As soon as the meal was over she hurried out to the sink and started to wash up.

That night Davis couldn't sleep, but lay on his back staring at the chink of light showing through the bedroom window.

Outside he could hear the rustle of rain mixed with the lifting and falling of branches blowing in the wind.

If only with one sweep of his hand he could put everything right, if only from nothing wealth rose up like a thing solid to the touch, a thing one could snatch without effort and keep locked behind doors while one slept, ate, idled....

His thoughts drifted; he stirred and looked at his wife lying straight and stark beside him; the pallor of her face divided her from the surrounding gloom; her dark hair, braided in two plaits, hung outside the bedclothes.

He felt a dim desire, which, as his thoughts lingered, grew in urgency; he leaned over and touched her with his hands. 'Mary, let's be friends, for God's sake.'

As though through her sleep she had realized his passion, she at once drew away and answered harshly: 'It's useless, quite useless; we can't go on like this.'

He seized her arm and ran his fingers up to her bare shoulders; he could feel the blood beating slowly under his touch. There was a clanging in his veins, all his senses seemed gathering for a final revelation; everything was hastening, hastening. . . .

He muttered thickly. 'I'm sorry, Mary, don't be hard; I've thought it all out how I'll start tomorrow; I'll mend the hedge, tidy the garden; in a week I'll get the place straight, honest to God I will.'

His hands enclosed her breast, dimly he heard her cry. 'It's no good, no good.'

The lace curtains rustled, swept the fringe of the bed, then lay with a shudder, flat against the window.

Davis swore slowly, half asleep. 'I swear it; just you see in the morning.'

His wife answered with a kind of wild intensity. 'I don't mean to be hard. I try to believe in you, but you make me so bitter.'

Her voice broke; Davis fell asleep to the sound of her crying.

He awoke, and at once he was depressed.

Daylight filtered through the window; it fell on the bed, wide, flat, and tousled, on the white counterpane dipping to the floor, on peeling wallpaper and the wash-basin half full of dirty water, standing in the far corner of the room.

He yawned and closed his eyes. Why did the days come on him like a burden?

Downstairs he could hear his wife lighting the fire.

What had he said last night? Something about lighting the fire himself. Well, anyway it was too late now.

With a groan he remembered other promises. He closed his eyes; the warmth in the bed was like the heat from burning logs.

He heard his wife calling out that breakfast was ready. He must have slept again. He turned the clock with its face to the wall and again shut his eyes. His limbs felt like logs.

Drowsily he heard the cows passing under the window on their way to the cowsheds; their feet splashed in the mud, splash, splash, splash.

'Another minute,' he started to count slowly. Nearly sixty. What a fool he was to set a limit on time.

Rain ran down the windows and danced in bubbles on the aerial. One, two, three, no man could work in such weather.

Words ran in fragments to the tune of falling rain; they passed through his head, and the pulsing of his blood set a rhythm to utterance. 'Lazy, bone lazy, one, two, three. What were words?'

He buried his face deeper into the pillows. Once more he slept.

E. TEGLA DAVIES

Samuel Jones's Harvest Thanksgiving

Translated from the Welsh by Dafydd Jenkins

Samuel Jones of Hendre was a man who had seen in life many changes, and with every change its weariness, and with every weariness its tax on his faith. Often when he raised his eyes to seek the light he was blinded by the rush of the storm. And Hendre was like his life; for every blade of wheat that grew on his land there was a weed, and it was easier to grow gorse and thistles there than corn. Hendre was a farm in the shadow of the sun; so there was not for him much comfort in the luxurious prayers of Mr. Herbert of the Fron and his sort, men for whom the sun had never done anything but smile on them and on their land and its fruits, men who daily gave thanks for the smiles of Providence and because it was not with them as it was with many of their fellow-pilgrims, and who asked the Lord to be merciful to those fellow-pilgrims, with a hint that the fellow-pilgrims on whom Providence did not smile as it did on them were not wholly free from blame for that themselves. Mr. Herbert always called his God 'the Great King', and his highest conception of religion was to be loyal: he knew himself for one of the courtiers of the Great King.

And when the time came to arrange for the harvest thanksgiving, Mr. Herbert was the man who suggested dressing up the lonely old country chapel for the first time with the finest flowers and plants and fruits, as a sign of the Great King's generosity to them all. For it was seemly to be loyal. And having seen them acknowledging His gifts, the Great King would condescend to notice them in His grace, at the harvests which awaited them in the future. And Mr. Herbert was the owner of the most beautiful flowers, and the rarest plants, and the finest fruits, for he could afford to grow them. But he was loyal and respectful enough to admit that the Great King too had a hand in the work.

When the new plan was brought forward, Robert Owen of Tros yr Afon opposed it, because he did not believe in these new-fangled ideas, and because they were only Popery coming in through the back-door. He was the only man who spoke against the suggestion. Whether or not they agreed with Mr. Herbert, fear of him silenced all the others, except Samuel Jones of Hendre. He said not a word, not because he feared Mr. Herbert, but because he despised his blindness too much to venture to answer him; under feeling, Samuel Jones was stumbling in his speech. For he had not seen the Lord's face in these rich flowers and plants and fruits. If he had depended on them, his God's face would have been pale and weak. Mr. Herbert's gardens brought forth pomegranates, but Samuel Jones knew what it was to want for bread.

In the end Mr. Herbert won, and it was decided to decorate the chapel. For days before the festival the women were very busy carrying the fruits of the earth to the little old chapel, and arranging them as best they could in a chapel whose walls had not been designed for sheaves of wheat to hang upon, nor its windows to hold apples and oranges and turnips on their sills, nor its pulpit to hold loaves and bunches of grapes. And though the richest of the produce came from the Fron, the rest of the church was not going to come there empty-handed—except Robert Owen of Tros yr Afon and Samuel Jones of Hendre. And there was great variety —from the little red potatoes of Ty'n Clwt, and the 'old man's beard' of Moel y Wrach, to the pumpkins of the Fron greenhouses and flowers that had no Welsh names, and that had never breathed the air of Wales unaided. And the walls of the little old chapel were more ashen-coloured than ever beside the blush of these privileged flowers and fruits. Robert Owen of Tros yr Afon looked scornfully on all these things, condemning the whole thing loudly, and muttering between his teeth about country popes, but Samuel Jones looked at them with his head under his wing, and kept his own counsel.

When the decoration was complete, the old chapel looked like a heavy-footed, wrinkled-faced, countrified old maid who in the twinkling of an eye had thrown off her clothes in favour of the most fashionable London and Paris wear, and had filled her wrinkles with paint and powder, while the shape and movements of her body cried out against them.

Before the day of the festival, everybody looked in to see the sight, and it was extraordinarily fine in everyone's eyes. No one doubted that there would be great enthusiasm in the singing and the praying and the whole festival from beginning to end. Many a man went home from the sight fully believing that Mr. Herbert of the Fron was the most godly and the most inspired man in the whole countryside, for thinking of this idea: to bring the Great King's gifts to His own House, and in His sight to receive them back gratefully from His hand, instead of sweeping them thoughtlessly in from the gardens and fields. Samuel Jones too went to see the sight, and as he looked upon it, he cast his eyes back on his own past. Little ever had his body or his soul had of splendid fruits from the orchards and vineyards and gardens of life. He had been without them so long that he doubted whether they would agree with him if he had them now. The battle of his body and soul for their sustenance had been the battle of bleak land, and he would never have known the Lord if he had waited for the great harvests to lead him to Him. The God of these fruitful mercies was Mr. Herbert's God, not his; and he went home heavy-footed and weary-eyed. And a wave of bitterness came over his spirit, and swept away every tittle of thanks from his breast, leaving only the filthiness of the wave.

The night before the festival came at last, and the night before was a preparation for the great day. It was the night for the prentice hands to pray. The old hands were kept for the next day, and they were arranged according to their gifts, and carefully winnowed, so that only the great gifts remained for the last night. The sight before them was a great help in loosening the tongues of the prentice hands, and they gave thanks more freely than usual, if their language was halting and narrow, for these visible signs of the thoughtfulness of the Lord and His mercies towards them, though there was no hope that they, poor fellows, would ever sink their teeth in the fruits which smiled mockingly on them from the walls and windows. And they suggested that they didn't know what would have become of them if the Lord had frowned on them and withheld His hand, and they feared that their faith would have been shipwrecked had it not been for these signs.

Samuel Jones himself was one of the men of the night before, in the world of prayer, for he was clumsy-tongued and uncouth of speech. But though he was called upon, and though he wanted to go forward, he could not for the life of him do so tonight. He felt that the Lord's mercies round about him were mocking him and scorning him, siding with their Creator as respecters of persons. At the end of the service he got up before anyone else and went home alone, with his head bowed more heavily than ever. Though he went to bed, he did not sleep a wink, but tossed and turned all night, seeing the Lord's mercies staring at him from the darkness, laughing at him, with their eyes aflame like stars in every corner of the room. He saw what he had thought to be a rock, on which he thought he had climbed, and which he thought he had made the foundation of his life, shaking like a quicksand under his feet. He knew that if everyone else was right he was mistaken, but if he was right, all this sort of thanks was the vanity of people who had not faced life. It became a fight for him, and he fought the whole night, with the Great King half the time mocking him and the other half hiding His face from him. And when He did happen to show His face, it was the face of Mr. Herbert of the Fron. But after the long battle, he thought the face of the Lord had changed, and that he himself had at last found the true vision; and he determined to put it to the test. He rose when the dawn was beginning to mottle the sky, and went out to his fields. He cut all the thistles that were at hand and made a bunch of them. He went to the field whose gorse he could not master, and cut an armful of the gorse. Then he went to the field where he fought incessantly with thorns, and cut an armful of those too. Then he went to the hedge and lopped off the longest branches of the brambles and took them with him. After that he went to gather an armful of the weeds with which the farmers of the district fought a lifelong battle. He made a load of them all, and trailed straight off to the little old lonely chapel, whose frosted roof he saw shining in the distance in the pale light, when hardly anyone else in the district had begun to move. He hesitated a little on the threshold, and went in, for the door was not locked: no one would think of locking it between two services during the harvest thanksgiving festival.

He went in and put his load down. Then he collected all the flowers and plants and fruits and carried them to the cellar where the firewood was kept. He came back and began on the work he had come there to do. He dressed the pulpit with thorns and brambles, he put the gorse along the window-sills, and the thistles and weeds in bunches to hang on the nails here and there on the walls. Then he went to the other end of the chapel and looked at the sight. After that he turned on his heel and went home to his breakfast like a man coming home from the battlefield after a great victory.

Samuel Jones arrived early at the chapel for the ten o'clock prayer-meeting. The congregation was very large. It was always large at the harvest thanksgiving services, but the novelty of this meeting brought everyone with an inquisitive spirit there, however irreligious and unthankful he might be. When he got to the porch, each one put his head in through the chapel door first, before going in himself, to have a look at the sight. And the next thing was a sudden little sort of 'Oh!' as though someone had put a pin into him. And everyone who came in after this went through this rite, and turned back to the porch to whisper furiously to everybody who was there.

And Samuel Jones enjoyed the scene with a great enjoyment.

If the other decorations had been an attraction, these were much more so, for when the news of the transformation had gained wings, it went from one to another like wildfire, and people poured in, treading on each other's heels.

The hour for beginning came, but everybody stared one at the other—the elders in the big pew at the congregation, and the congregation at the elders and the new decorations alternately. Instead of signs of the Great King's blessings, there were signs of His curses on every side—for was not the great curse, 'Thorns also and thistles shall it bring forth to thee'? And in every breast were awakened bitter memories of the lifelong battles against opposing powers that were a burden on their lives in this bleak mountainous district. Every prayer that had been prepared for the meetings of the day was destroyed. And it was worse for the men who were to pray in the morning than for anyone, for the others would have a chance to revise their thoughts. And Samuel Jones, spying eagerly at the men who were to pray, muttered continually to himself, 'Now pray, you knaves.'

Mr. Herbert of the Fron looked bitter. He had never before had occasion to seek the Great King's face in thorns and brambles and gorse and thistles and weeds. But time was going, and he stood up to lead the meeting as usual. He could not think of a hymn that would suit an occasion like this; so instead of giving out a hymn himself, and calling someone forward afterwards, he called on William Jones of Gwern y Ffynnon to lead a hymn and to begin. But neither the chapter that William Jones had meant to read, nor the prayer he had composed, acknowledged thorns and brambles and gorse and thistles and weeds as God's mercies. And though he had a long list of those mercies to recite and work up enthusiasm with, since he had carefully learnt the names of as many of the exotic mercies as could be put into Welsh, he could not think of a tone of voice that would fit words like thorns and brambles and gorse and thistles and weeds. So William Jones shook his head. And Samuel Jones of Hendre rubbed his hands together between his knees and muttered to himself, 'Now pray, you knaves.'

Then Mr. Herbert called on Hugh Edwards, the stone-mason, who too had been shaping fine sentences during the last few days, including the words cucumbers and pumpkins and pomegranates, and had convinced himself that Mesopotamia was their natural home, so that he could bring that word in too. Hugh Edwards too shook his head. And Samuel Jones went on rubbing his hands and muttering, 'Pray now, enthuse now, Hugh.'

That was a head-shaking service, and Mr. Herbert came to the end of the men who ought to pray at the ten o'clock meeting without so much as one of them obeying his call; he was terrified of calling on any of those who ought to pray in the evening, lest he should offend them. And everybody again began to look one at the other. No one expected that Samuel Jones would be called on to take part, for he was one of the night-before men, and he had already refused. But after a long uneasy silence, during which everyone waited for everyone else, and stared at the strange decorations and made guesses at their secret; after Mr. Herbert had coughed suggestively from time to time, and puffs of laughter had begun to come from the children and the thoughtless; after Jane Daniel of Ddôl Ddu had tried to strike a tune and start a hymn, and had failed; Samuel Jones himself began to feel uneasy, and to see that all this was a challenge to what he thought of as his vision. After turning about in his seat and fidgeting and looking several times towards the door, and rubbing his hands together between his knees for a long time, and scratching his neck uncomfortably, he suddenly rose and went up at a half-trot to the big pew. He stood there and looked at the congregation, and the congregation looked at him, with something of stupidity in the look on both sides. For who ever heard of one of the night-before men taking part of his own accord the next morning, after refusing on his own proper night? Samuel Jones turned to look at the thorns and the brambles and the gorse and the thistles and the weeds, and shook himself. Then without giving out a hymn he turned to the Bible, opened it, and searched through it, and began to read, pouring his soul into every word and sentence. And the sentences took light under his touch. He did not read much, but these were the words:

'Although the fig tree shall not blossom, neither shall fruit be in the vines; the labour of the olive shall fail, and the fields shall yield no meat; the flock shall be cut off from the fold, and there shall be no herd in the stalls: yet will I rejoice in the Lord, I will joy in the God of my salvation.

'The Lord God is my strength, and he will make my feet like hinds' feet, and he will make me to walk upon mine high places.'

Samuel Jones shut the Bible with a snap, and went down on his knees, with cold sweat pouring down his face. After some stumbling the bonds of his tongue were unloosed, and his speech became like a flood. His vision flamed before his eyes, and he was as one who saw the thorns and the brambles on the pulpit, and the gorse on the windows, and the thistles and the weeds on the walls, as a splendid garment about the Lord, and the face of the Lord shining through them; and the Lord and he walked together in the garden of the Lord: but the flowers there were not ashamed of His garments.

The prayer meeting was held for the rest of the day, and the thorns and brambles and the gorse and the thistles and the weeds were not taken away. Many men prayed in their turn, but that festival is known to this day, in the tradition of the countryside, as Samuel Jones's Harvest Thanksgiving.

CARADOC EVANS

Joseph's House

A woman named Madlen, who lived in Penlan—the crumbling red walls of which are in a nook of the narrow lane that rises from the valley of Bern—was concerned about the future state of her son Joseph. Men who judged themselves worthy to counsel her gave her such counsels as these: 'Blower bellows for the smith,' 'Cobblar clox,' 'Booboo for crows.'

Madlen flattered her counsellors, albeit none spoke that which was pleasing unto her.

'Cobblar clox, ach y fi,' she cried to herself. 'Wan is the lad bach with decline. And unbecoming to his Nuncle Essec that he follows low tasks.'

Moreover, people, look you at John Lewis. Study his marble gravestone in the burial ground of Capel Sion: 'His name is John Newton-Lewis; Paris House, London, his address. From his big shop in Putney, Home they brought him by railway.' Genteel are shops for boys who are consumptive. Always dry are their coats and feet, and they have white cuffs on their wrists and chains on their waistcoats. Not blight nor disease nor frost can ruin their sellings. And every minute their fingers grabble in the purses of nobles.

So Madlen thought, and having acted in accordance with her design, she took her son to the other side of Avon Bern, that is to Capel Mount Moriah, over which Essec her husband's brother lorded; and him she addressed decorously, as one does address a ruler of the capel.

'Your help I seek,' she said.

'Poor is the reward of the Big Preacher's son in this part,' Essec announced. 'A lot of atheists they are.'

'Not pleading I have not the rent am I,' said Madlen. 'How if I prentice Joseph to a shop draper. Has he any odds?'

'Proper that you seek,' replied Essec. 'Seekers we all are. Sit you. No room there is for Joseph now I am selling Penlan.'

'Like that is the plan of your head?' Madlen murmured, concealing her dread.

'Seven of pounds of rent is small. Sell at eighty I must.'

'Wait for Joseph to prosper. Buy then he will. Buy for your mam you will, Joseph?'

'Sorry I cannot change my think,' Essec declared.

'Hard is my lot; no male have I to ease my burden.'

'A weighty responsibility my brother put on me,' said Essec. ' "Dying with old decline I am," ' the brother mouthed. ' "Fruitful is the soil. Watch Madlen keeps her fruitful." But I am generous. Eight shall be the rent. Are you not the wife of my flesh?'

After she had wiped away her tears, 'Be kind,' said Madlen, 'and wisdom it to Joseph.'

'The last evening in the seiet I commanded the congregation to give the Big Man's photograph a larger hire,' said Essec. 'A few of my proverbs I will now spout.' He spat his spittle and bundling his beard blew the residue of his nose therein; and he chanted: 'Remember Essec Pugh, whose right foot is tied into a club knot. Here's the club to kick sinners as my perished brother tried to kick the Bad Satan from the inside of his female Madlen with the club of his baston. Some preachers search over the Word. Some preachers search in the Word. But search under the Word does preacher Capel Moriah. What's the light I find? A stutterer was Moses. As the middle of a butter cask were the knees of Paul. A splotch like a red cabbage leaf was on the cheek of Solomon. By the signs shall the saints be known. "Preacher Club Foot, come forward to tell about Moriah," the Big Man will say. Mean scamps, remember Essec Pugh, for I shall remember you the Day of Rising.'

It came to be that on a morning in the last month of his thirteenth year Joseph was bidden to stand at the side of the cow which Madlen was milking and to give an ear to these commandments: 'The serpent is in the bottom of the glass. The hand on the tavern window is the hand of Satan. On the Sabbath eve get one penny for two ha'pennies for the plate collection. Put money in the handkerchief corner. Say to persons you are a nephew of Respected Essec Pugh and you will have credit. Pick the white sixpence from the floor and give her to the mishtir; she will have fallen from his pocket trowzis.'

Then Joseph turned, and carrying his yellow tin box, he climbed into the craggy moorland path which takes you to the tramping road. By the pump of Tavarn Ffos he rested until Shim Carrier came thereby; and while Shim's horse drank of barley water, Joseph stepped into the waggon; and at the end of the passage Shim showed him the business of getting a ticket and that of going into and coming down from a railway carriage.

In that manner did Joseph go to the drapery shop of Rees Jones in Carmarthen; and at the beginning he was instructed in the keeping and the selling of such wares as reels of cotton, needles, pins, bootlaces, mending wool, buttons, and such like—all those things which together are known as haberdashery. He marked how this and that were done, and in what sort to fashion his visage and frame his phrases to this or that woman. His oncoming was rapid. He could measure, cut, and wrap in a parcel twelve yards of brown or white calico quicker than any one in the shop, and he understood by rote the folds of linen tablecloths and bedsheets; and in the town this was said of him: 'Shopmen quite ordinary can sell what a customer wants; Pugh Rees Jones can sell what nobody wants.'

The first year passed happily, and the second year; and in the third Joseph was stirred to go forward.

'What use to stop here all the life?' he asked himself. 'Better to go off.'

He put his belongings in his box and went to Swansea.

'Very busy emporium I am in,' were the words he sent to Madlen. 'And the wage is twenty pounds.'

Madlen rejoiced at her labour and sang: 'Ten acres of land, and a cowhouse with three stalls and a stall for the new calf, and a pigstye, and a house for my bones and a barn for my hay and straw, and a loft for my hens: why should men pray for more?'

She ambled to Moriah, diverting passers-by with boastful tales of Joseph, and loosened her imaginings to the Respected.

'Pounds without number he is earning,' she cried. 'Rich he'll be. Swells are youths shop.'

'Gifts from the tip of my tongue fell on him,' said Essec. 'Religious were my gifts.'

'Iss, indeed, the brother of the male husband.'

'Now you can afford nine of pounds for the place. Rich he is and richer he will be. Pounds without number he has.'

Madlen made a record of Essec's scheme for Joseph; and she said also: 'Proud I'll be to shout that my son bach bought Penlan.'

'Setting aside money am I,' Joseph speedily answered.

Again ambition aroused him. 'Footling is he that is content with Zwanssee. Next half-holiday skurshon I'll crib in Cardiff.'

Joseph gained his desire, and the chronicle of his doings he sent to his mother. 'Twenty-five, living in, and spiffs on remnants are the wages,' he said. 'In the flannelette department I am and I have not been fined once. Lot of English I hear, and we call ladies madam that the wedded nor the unwedded are insulted. Boys harmless are the eight that sleep by me. Examine Nuncle of the price of Penlan.'

'I will wag my tongue craftily and slowly,' Madlen vowed as she crossed her brother-in-law's threshold.

'Shire Pembroke land is cheap,' she said darkly.

'Look you for a farm there,' said Essec. 'Pelted with offers am I for Penlan. Ninety I shall have. Poverty makes me sell very soon.'

'As he says.'

'Pretty tight is Joseph not to buy her. No care has he for his mam.'

'Stiffish are affairs with him, poor dab.'

Madlen reported to Joseph that which Essec had said, and she added: 'Awful to leave the land of your father. And auction the cows. Even the red cow that is a champion of milk. Where shall I go? The House of the Poor. Horrid that your mam must go to the House of the Poor.'

Joseph sat on his bed, writing: 'Taken ten pounds from the

post I have which leaves three shillings. Give Nuncle the ten as earnest of my intention.'

Nine years after that day on which he had gone to Carmarthen Joseph said in his heart: 'London shops for experience'; and he caused a frock coat to be sewn together, and he bought a silk hat and an umbrella, and at the spring cribbing he walked into a shop in the West End of London, asking: 'Can I see the engager, pleaze?' The engager came to him and Joseph spoke out: 'I have all-round experience. Flannelettes three years in Niclass, Cardiff, and left on my own accord. Kept the coloured dresses in Tomos, Zwanssee. And served through. Apprentized in Reez Jones Carmarthen for three years. Refs egzellent. Good ztok-keeper and appearance.'

'Start at nine o'clock Monday morning,' the engager replied. 'Thirty pounds a year and spiffs; to live in. You'll be in the laces.'

'Fashionable this shop is,' Joseph wrote to Madlen, 'and I have to be smart and wear a coat like the preachers, and mustn't take more than three zwap lines per day or you have the sack. Two white shirts per week; and the dresses of the showroom young ladies are a treat. Five pounds enclosed for Nuncle.'

'Believe your mam,' Madlen answered: 'don't throw gravel at the windows of the old English unless they have the fortunes.'

In his zeal for his mother's welfare Joseph was heedless of himself, eating little of the poor food that was served him, clothing his body niggardly, and seldom frequenting public bath-houses; his mind spanned his purpose, choosing the fields he would join to Penlan, counting the number of cattle that would graze on the land, planning the slate-tiled house which he would set up.

'Twenty more pounds I must have,' he moaned, 'for the blaguard Nuncle.'

Every day thereafter he stole a little money from his employers and every night he made peace with God: 'Only twenty-five is the wage, and spiffs don't count because of the fines. Don't you let me be found out, Big Man bach. Will you strike mam into her grave? And disgrace Respected Essec Pugh Capel Moriah?'

He did not abate his energies howsoever hard his disease was wasting and destroying him. The men who lodged in his bedroom grew angry with him. 'How can we sleep with your damn coughing?' they cried. 'Why don't you invest in a second-hand coffin?'

Feared that the women whom he served would complain that the poison of his sickness was tainting them and that he would be sent away, Joseph increased his pilferings; where he had stolen a shilling he now stole two shillings; and when he got five pounds above the sum he needed, he heaved a deep sigh and said: 'Thank you for your favour, God bach. I will now go home to heal myself.'

Madlen took the money to Essec, coming back heavy with grief.

'Hoo-hoo,' she whined, 'the ninety has bought only the land. Selling the houses is Essec.'

'Wrong there is,' said Joseph. 'Probe deeply we must.'

From their puzzlings Madlen said: 'What will you do?'

'Go and charge swindler Moriah.'

'Meddle not with him. Strong he is with the Lord.'

'Teach him will I to pocket my honest wealth.'

Because of his weakness Joseph did not go to Moriah; today he said: 'I will go tomorrow,' and tomorrow he said: 'Certain enough I'll go tomorrow.'

In the middle of an afternoon he and Madlen sat down, gazing about, and speaking scantily; and the same thought was with each of them, and this was the thought: 'A tearful prayer will remove the Big Man from His judgement, but nothing will remove Essec from his purpose.'

'Mam fach,' said Joseph, 'how will things be with you?'

'Sorrow not, soul nice,' Madlen entreated her son. 'Couple of weeks very short have I to live.'

'As an hour is my space. Who will stand up for you?'

'Hish, now. Hish-hish, my little heart.'

Madlen sighed; and at the door she made a great clatter, and the sound of the clatter was less than the sound of her wailing.

'Mam! Mam!' Joseph shouted. 'Don't you scream. Hap you will soften Nuncle's heart if you say to him that my funeral is close.'

Madlen put a mourning gown over her petticoats and a mourning bodice over her shawls, and she tarried in a field as long as it would take her to have travelled to Moriah; and in the heat of the sun, she returned laughing.

'Mistake, mistake,' she cried. 'The houses are ours. No understanding was in me. Cross was your Nuncle. "Terrible if Joseph is bad with me," he said. Man religious and tidy is Essec.' Then she prayed that Joseph would die before her fault was found out.

Joseph did not know what to do for his joy. 'Well-well, there's better I am already,' he said. He walked over the land and coveted the land of his neighbours. 'Dwell here for ever I shall,' he cried to Madlen. 'A grand house I'll build—almost as grand as the houses of the preachers.'

On the fifth night he died, and before she began to weep, Madlen lifted her voice: 'There's silly, dear people, to covet houses! Only a smallish bit of house we want.'

EIGRA LEWIS ROBERTS

Deprivation

Translated from the Welsh by Enid R. Morgan

As Lisi Blodwen arranged the tinned salmon for her tea, she reflected that every old maid and widow should have a cat. Not that there was any great pleasure to be had from a relationship with an animal, but at least one could pet a cat or sulk at it without hurting its feelings or raising its hopes. And a cat, thank heaven, could not afford to sulk. On reflection there was more and more to be said for having one. What would be the best kind? A pedigree cat, perhaps, of princely blood; a cat to adorn a hearth. But no; a true blue-blooded cat would need such fussing. What a strain to have to treat a cat as an equal. No, a cat without a family tree would be best, one that could be kicked out of the way, and kept at a distance.

The salmon was good, so good indeed that she felt she could eat it all at once. And why not? She could afford to be greedy now, or lazy, or sluttish. She could afford to take the brake off all her weaknesses. She decided to clear the plate. She was about to settle down to it seriously when she heard the hard heels of her sister Jane on the back cobbles. This was Jane's third call today. Indeed, she'd been hovering around the house like the plague for days now. Trying to reason with Jane two or three times a day took all the strength she had. Every time she heard the sound of feet in the yard her inside would turn to water and she would have to hurry to the lavatory. Jane's refrain today was that Lisi Blodwen should take down the photograph of Huw Llewelyn from the mantelpiece. It was useless trying to explain to Jane that seeing Huw's face on the shelf was the next best thing to having him here with her.

She pushed the plate an arm's length away. She was just wiping her mouth with her handkerchief when Jane stepped into the kitchen, rigid with authority. Lisi half expected to see her waving a search warrant.

'Having your tea?'

'Just finished.'

'Don't take any notice of me.'

'No, I've done very well. What about you?'

'I could do with a bite.'

'There's a plate of salmon.'

'It looks good.'

'I've just opened it.'

'I don't want to take your meal.'

'I don't want it. It's too much for one.'

'I should think so indeed. There's enough here for three.'

Blodwen watched her sister digging into the salmon. Little pink streams ran down her chin and she pushed a large tongue out every now and then to catch them. So that was the end of her salmon. She didn't have much heart for it now in any case.

'Clear the plate.'

'Yes, I might as well. It won't keep in this close weather.'

'Excuse me. I've got to go to the back for a moment.'

'Again?'

'People do go.'

'Yes—within reason. Really I don't know what I wouldn't like to do to that old man, hurting you like this.'

'You talk about him as if he were an old pig or something.'

'A pig has more respect for its sty than he ever had for you. I never liked the man.'

'I never heard you criticize him before this happened.'

'I didn't want to hurt your feelings.'

'I've still got those. Anyway, there's no point in scratching old sores.'

'Not on a corpse there isn't. That gets cleaned up quickly enough. But this old skeleton is still breathing. And he'll be back from his honeymoon soon, and that wife of his hanging on to him. The baggage that she is!'

'So she's catching it now?'

'She knew very well that he belonged to you.'

'I had no more right to him than she had.'

'After twenty years of courting? You'd better go to the back. I'll expect a bit more sense from you when you get back.'

Lisi Blodwen sat on the lavatory seat. Thank goodness for a place to sit down out of sight and sound of Jane for a moment. Really there wasn't anywhere better than the lavatory for relaxing and contemplating life's problems. She'd settled dozens of problems sitting here. Nothing to distract one, nothing but the sound of water snoring in the pipes. Two more days and Huw Llewelyn and his new wife would be back in town. The pair of them would be shopping in Tesco's on Saturday afternoon (Huw Llewelyn had had plenty of practice carrying those silly little wire baskets). They would be there in the cross-seats in Salem on Sunday night (one seat away from the deacons' row); they would be welcoming people to their house and be welcomed to others' homes. Would there perhaps be an invitation to Llys Arthur? It would be an awful job to stay in the front parlour without slipping out to the kitchen every now and again to keep an eye on the food. Perhaps that woman would need help in carrying the dishes through. She would hardly know how to put her hand on every dish. Let's hope she'll take care of the hot water jug, at least. Sixty years old and still without a crack. Huw Llewelyn's mother had bought it in the church bazaar for sixpence ha'penny. And the jug had outlived her. What a pity that people had to go, while things so easy to replace stayed on.

But it would be easier to endure being with the two china dogs and the big Bible in the front parlour than to bear the good-byes. Huw Llewelyn standing on the step of Llys Arthur with his arm round his new wife's shoulder, instead of helping his sweetheart to avoid the holes in the road between Llys Arthur and here, as he had done for more than twenty years. But there wasn't much danger of that happening. Thank goodness there was another way between her house and the town, and that she had refused to turn Methodist with Huw Llewelyn.

'Blodwen, are you ill?'

There was no peace to be had, even in the lavatory.

'Hurry up, will you?'

Where did they go on their honeymoon? But nobody would believe they were on their honeymoon when they saw Huw Llewelyn with his hair thinning on the crown. He never had had a crop of hair like some boys. But what he had he kept neat, and he combed it as often as a girl.

'Lisi Blodwen, I shall have to get a move on.'

'I'm just coming.'

She could see Jane in the window watching her cross the yard. Her face looked comic through the lace curtains, the blue of one eye through one hole, the red of a lip in another and a lock of untidy hair like a coconut shy crowning the lot.

'You didn't have to wait.'

'Thanks for the welcome.'

'I was only thinking of you.'

'It would be better if you thought about yourself. I've got a husband to bear my burdens. What will you do now?'

'You didn't have to bother about the dishes.'

'I only cleared away a little. You'll have all evening to wash them, won't you? Well, what are you going to do?'

'I've got enough to live on.'

'I'm not talking about money. You yourself, inside, is what's important. A thing like this could shatter you at your age.'

'I'll get through it.'

'Do you remember how losing her sweetheart wrecked Emma Hughes?'

'She was only a girl.'

'She had more cause to pull herself together. A pretty girl like her can bring the boys running. You've still not got rid of that old picture.'

'And I don't intend to.'

'People who come to the house will have a shock seeing him baring his teeth at them.'

'Nobody comes here except you and your family.'

'Ugh! Look at those eyes of his, tiny and slit like a china cat. What did you ever see in him, tell me?'

'Where did they go on their honeymoon?'

'Someone in the shop said they'd gone to the tip of Lleyn.'

'Aberdaron perhaps.'

'Yes, perhaps that was what they said. But the whole country's full of some Aber this or that. Didn't the two of you go there once when you started courting?'

'We didn't go farther than Pwllheli.' Quietly.

'Really? Well, you have made a mess of things. Quarter of a lifetime down the drain to a dreg of a man like that. You're on the shelf now, anyway, do you realize that? And poor mother died worrying she wouldn't live to see your wedding. How long ago is that?'

'Twelve years.'

'And you're still without a man.'

'That's a gruesome thing to say.'

'I don't know that it wouldn't have been better to have lived in sin than hold hands like school kids. At least you'd have something to look back on.'

'Yes, I would.'

'Twenty years of courting. Walking down Betws road, and enough room to drive a cart between you.'

'End of term meetings and the Sunday School trip.'

'And an occasional night at the pictures—home at eight.'

'A quarter past. Then we'd sit here for hours talking.'

'What about?'

'What does one talk about?'

'About rents and shop bills and the future for the kids.'

'We always found something to talk about. That was his chair.'

'As if I didn't know. Did you change chairs sometimes?'

'Never. We'd take our coats off in the lobby and then straight to our chairs. Huw Llewelyn that side and me the other.'

'Good God, and the bedroom above you. Tell me, have you got any glands?'

Lisi Blodwen felt a cramp in her stomach.

'I've got to go to the back again, Jane.'

'God save us. There won't be any of you left. Is it all right for me to go home?'

'Yes, of course.'

'I don't really like leaving you.'

Jane went with her to the back and stood at the lavatory door. Lisi Blodwen stood there too. There was something unseemly in opening the door in Jane's presence.

'Do you know where I could get hold of a cat?' she asked hesitantly.

'So it's come to that, has it?'

'Come to what?'

'That you've got to have a cat instead of a man in your life.'

'A cat can be a lot more agreeable than a man, so they say.'

'Well, it's not likely to take off and leave you on the rubbish dump anyway. And you can talk to it if you don't have anyone else to talk to. Do you remember how Auntie Dora used to be?'

'Who wouldn't?'

'She used to carry on talking to herself night and day; question and answer, just like the catechism. Yes indeed, a cat, at once. It's lucky that cats aren't so hard to come by as lovers. I'll call later if I hear of one.'

Lisi already regretted mentioning the cat. It wouldn't dawn on Jane that there were cats and cats, just like men and men. Jane wouldn't mind bringing along any old skeleton in tow. One of those creatures that skulk from wall to hedge at night, perhaps, with its fur full of fleas. It would be a disgrace to her hearth to let in a creature like that. Ugh, she had never had much to say for cats. But she could manage. Great God, she would have to manage.

She didn't have to go to the lavatory after all. Her inside steadied as soon as she said good-bye to Jane. She went back to the house and the kitchen. She looked Huw Llewelyn straight in the eye. It wasn't fair to judge people from the colour and shape of their eyes. Huw had old Ifan Llewelyn's eyes, and everyone testified to the fact that Ifan was as safe as the bank. And she'd never had any cause to doubt Huw Llewelyn. In fact his word was as good as a vow on the Bible. But it was a pity that he'd taken that woman to Lleyn, of all places. He must have remembered that little hotel he had fancied so long ago. 'I'll come here on my honeymoon,' he had said. There must have been a lot of changes in that hotel by now, but perhaps the inside would be like it was, old and solid, and its coolness like a balm on the flesh. She had lain the other side of the wall from her sweetheart, and the groan of his bed as he turned had sent the strangest shivers through her. She would have run to him had there been a welcome for her. She'd suggested it tentatively, but not tentatively enough to prevent shame from spreading in a blush on Huw Llewelyn's pale cheeks. 'We'll do everything properly,' he said. 'A ring first, and then bed; that's the way I was taught.' Of course Huw Llewelyn was right—cautious, wise Huw Llewelyn, the truest of men. She had done her best to be worthy of him.

Had he cooled towards her perhaps, after that night? But he'd courted her faithfully, without ever mentioning it. 'It would have been better if you'd lived in sin,' Jane had said. That's what she would have done. Jane was one to step first and look later. And Lisi couldn't remember her ever tripping up. And she herself, like a fool, watching every step. But she would have slept with him. One night in a little old-fashioned hotel, and the moon dangling outside the window, teasing them. One night she could have turned to now as to a book and read over and over again. On winter evenings with an empty chair opposite her, passing the summer night at the tip of Lleyn, lying safe and warm, shoulder to shoulder, thigh to thigh with her only lover ever.

Sometime in the evening Jane called again.

'Still sitting here,' she said sympathetically.

'There's no hurry.'

'Well I'm blowed. That picture's gone.'

'I put it on the fire just now.'

'You did a sensible thing, Lisi. The place is healthier already. I've got a cat for you.'

'What kind is it?'

'Just like any other cat for all I know. It hasn't opened its eyes yet. It will grow up with you.'

Splendid. She could put her foot down with it before it got cheeky.

'Don't give it too much room. I was thinking that perhaps that was what you did with that man.'

'Perhaps indeed.'

'Didn't he use to stretch out on the hearth as if he was the man of the house? But more fool you for offering him everything and getting nothing.'

'Nothing. When shall I have the cat?'

'The day after tomorrow if you like. They'll be glad to get rid of it. It would end up in the river otherwise. Not many people need a cat nowadays.'

Apart from old maids and widows, thought Lisi Blodwen. Especially old maids, for whom there was no point in looking forward or back.

'Damn that Huw Llewelyn,' she said aloud.

'Thank heaven,' said her sister Jane.

DAVID MONGER

The Man Who Lost His Boswell

A Short Story
(*Perhaps an allegory*)

There is only one thing in the world more difficult than acquiring a boswell, and that is losing one: they are all so well known and conspicuous that they cannot, in ordinary circumstances, be lost. And that is not the only reason: it is a well accepted fact among all true boswell owners that however deep the regard which a man may develop for his boswell it is but a pale shadow of the attachment which is given in return. These facts were perfectly well known to James Stewart when he embarked on the grave responsibility of becoming a boswell owner with such a comparatively light heart. Consequently, when he lost his boswell, his surprise was even greater than his annoyance and despair.

There are not only few boswells in this country, but very few in any other country, and in the case of China, Japan, Tibet, and the Argentine they are believed to be virtually non-existent, the reasons given being Confucianism, Buddhism, and the language difficulty, though the matter has never been satisfactorily explained to zealous inquirers. The few boswells which do exist are, as I say, so well known that anyone finding one would automatically hand it over to the police without a second thought. Complex and difficult rules exist protecting the rights of boswell ownership, and while these account for the collection of boswells in the Police Museum, due to people being unable to substantiate their claims, it also explains why Stewart knew that his loss could not be due to theft, not even by another boswell owner. This knowledge was no compensation for the loss, but it enabled him to proceed boldly in his effort to retrieve his loss, and he advertised in *The Times* and other papers, describing in minute detail what his boswell looked like.

So far as he was aware there were only three other boswell owners in this country—this was in 1936, when conditions were very much better. One dwelt in Scotland, one in Cornwall, while the third sojourned in London in between visits to the south coast. He had letters of sympathy from each of these, and all endeavoured to help his search in ways peculiar to their talents. The man in Scotland, who had been photographed on more than one occasion with his boswell, had an even larger and clearer photograph taken and published in certain weekly papers along with an article dealing sympathetically with Stewart's loss. The man in Cornwall, whose wireless talks on country cookery customs were the prototype of all that came later during the recent war, managed to speak of boswells from the London studio and described in detail Stewart's boswell and the importance of its loss. The sojourner in London, a most—if not the most—eminent dramatic critic, who was known never to go about without his boswell, devoted his columns in the Sunday papers to a description of boswells in general, and to Stewart's in particular. He went on to deal with those reasons—the very heart of the problem—why no one had ever been able to dramatize a story set round a boswell. Here, for the first time in the long history of boswells, was an extraordinary situation calling for the craft of the dramatist. It was true, he continued, that in the eighteenth century a novel had been written dealing with the search for a boswell; it was true that in the nineteenth century a man had actually devoted his life to such a search, and had lost it—his life—just at that moment when the boswell was in his grasp, but even this, thrilling and tragic as it was, was matter for the great novelist and not for the dramatist. But here, continued the dramatic critic, at long last, was material for a great play. Why had no one ever written on that great theme—the loss of a boswell? It was not difficult to understand. Millionaires might lose their fortunes, virtuous women their honour, kings might lose their thrones and Governments their majorities, Republics might perish and extinct volcanos erupt, but all these things, even if improbable, were nevertheless possible, and so they could be depicted on the stage, the resulting play causing no undue strain on the audience's credulity. But this matter of the loss of a boswell—imagine for one moment a play in which the Archbishop of Canterbury was shown running a private opium den for profit! The English playgoing public, church-going or not church-going, would not only blast it from the stage as infamous, but blight it for ever as being ridiculous. Thus, the loss-of-a-boswell theme had never been entertained by any reputable author, which fact gave the critic the opportunity to hold forth on the profound truth that life is, after all, stranger than the strangest fiction.

You will readily imagine that the publicity accruing from the newspaper articles and the wireless talks resulted in a deluge of letters descending on Stewart. Most of them expressed sympathy, many asked for his autograph, some asked for even more details on boswells, a few asked for subscriptions for charitable causes, two offered him funeral expenses at reduced prices, while only one was to the point. It said: *Meet me Charing Cross Tuesday at ten.*

It is possible that some of you of a timid or hesitating disposition might hesitate before undertaking a journey of several hundred miles to meet a complete stranger; it is possible that you might reason that such a vague message gave no undertaking that the purpose of the meeting was for discussion of the missing boswell; it is even possible that you might dismiss the whole message as romantic but absurd, but then, you haven't lost a boswell and you don't know Stewart!

Of course the message was vague. Did it mean ten in the morning or ten at night? Did it mean Charing Cross Station, Hotel, or Hospital? For no reason whatsoever Stewart did not pause in contemplation of these possibilities and at ten o'clock on the following Tuesday morning was standing under the clock in the casualty department of Charing Cross Hospital. It was not long before the conviction dawned on him that there are more pleasant places for waiting for someone than the casualty department of a great hospital and, seeing that it was now 10.25, he hurried out and dashed down the Strand, fully convinced that if someone had been waiting at the station then he would in all probability be rushing among the crowd on the other side of the street in the hope of catching Stewart at the hospital.

So, with hope fast fading, Stewart duly stood under the clock on the station and proceeded to light his pipe. It was while his right hand, grasping a lighted match, was around the bowl of the pipe, while the left cupped it to deflect the breeze, that a most extraordinary thing happened. A piece of paper was thrust into his hands: this had the effect of putting out his match and making him most annoyed, so that when, after but a brief moment, he looked around him he was unable to discover who, among the thronging crowd, had done this. He then had time to examine the folded paper, on the outer side of which were the pencilled words: 'Are you the man I've been waiting for? Have you lost your boswell? If so, go away, taking this paper with you. If not, drop the paper and I'll retrieve it when you've gone.'

Strange as it may seem, Stewart's reaction to this curt, though not impolite, note was one of surprise and, even more, curiosity. Disappointed though he was at not being able to discuss his loss, he, nevertheless, hurried away to the nearest coffee stall in the Strand and, ordering a cup of tea, and seating himself on the tallest stool, found time to read the epistle. This again was brief; it said: 'My friend. You were late. Others have been late. You must have been to the hospital. I assure you you'll never find your boswell there, though I understand why you thought so. Have you examined your own home?' Of course Stewart hadn't examined his own home, no one loses his boswell there—as you can well imagine. But, disappointed as he was at this unsatisfactory message, he determined to do all he could and returned home and examined it. Naturally, he found nothing and so, thinking the word 'home' might have been used rather loosely, he turned to the laborious task of inquiring in his own neighbourhood. First, he went to the police.

'Lost your boswell, eh?' said the inspector cheerfully. 'Interesting things,' he added, 'not that I've ever had much time for them. Seen the collection in the museum at Scotland Yard?' he asked, taking out a sheet of paper to make his notes. Stewart had to admit he hadn't seen it. The inspector, after inquiring whether it was one 's' or two, turned to Stewart and confided with a smile, 'I don't suppose you knew that it's illegal to own a boswell?' Stewart was startled, and said he didn't. 'Since the time of Henery the Eighth,' added the inspector, in the same manner. 'But we don't want it generally known, they're a trouble to have around, and we've had enough forced on us as it is!' He had a sudden inspiration, 'You know, Mr. Stewart, if you really want another one I'm sure they'd let you have one at the Yard. I mean, you are a real boswell owner.' Stewart assured him that only the return of his own would do and he departed firmly convinced by the inspector that only time was needed before the boswell would turn up.

His next visit was to the local J.P. This gentleman was, astonishingly, the owner of the local drapery stores, and when he wasn't selling what he mistakenly took to be silk, he was dispensing what he frequently mistook to be justice. Although he assured Stewart that he had his fingers on the pulse of local affairs, he had to confess that he had neither seen, nor heard of the loss of, the boswell. He was unshaven when Stewart spoke to him, there being no court that day, and his oft recurring gesture of drawing a begrimed and gnarled hand over his incipient beard, thus causing a most irritating rasping sound, caused some exasperation to arise in the normally untroubled breast of Stewart, particularly as it was now apparent, the conversation having drifted from one aspect of local folklore to another, that the J.P. not only did not know what a boswell was, but was trying, by methods inexpressibly clumsy, to rectify this defect without exposing his ignorance. Rather than let his contempt turn to frank anger, Stewart wished the gentleman good-day and proceeded to the doctor's house.

Here he encountered a different proposition: the doctor was a boswell enthusiast. He knew everything about boswells, the history of each one in England, and many of those abroad, especially in Vienna; he had read of Stewart's loss, seen the photographs of the man from Scotland, and heard the broadcast from London. But like those many football enthusiasts who are liable to assess with sound judgement the various merits of Association football teams but who are, forever it seems, denied the opportunity to enjoy the spectacle of a game, the doctor, though he knew all about the shape and size and weight of boswells, had never had the joy of seeing one, handling one, or owning one—and he explained hastily, so profound was his knowledge, that he was aware that seeing, handling, and owning were but one thing, for you could not do one without the other. And it was no fault of his own, he added, that this joy had not come to his life; had he known, for example, that Stewart owned one, he would have tried to persuade him long since to part with it. So the conversation went on. To the doctor, this experience of speaking with Stewart was like unto that of a man who, anxious to travel the globe and explore its little known ports but forever denied the chance, listens with rapt attention to each word that the passing sailor utters. The doctor's eyes were fixed on Stewart, his manner was transformed, his breathing seemed to cease like a Yogi's in an early exercise, so that Stewart, encouraged by his attention, told how he had acquired his boswell, how he tended it, and how he felt on that awful morning when he discovered he had lost it. Minutes became an hour, and an hour an evening, an evening which forever after transformed the doctor's life, for he had talked to a boswell owner, or rather, to an even rarer specimen of mankind, a man who had owned a boswell and then had lost it. Odd as it may seem to you, no thought of censure crossed the doctor's mind: the sadness underlying the tale did not escape his experienced ear, and knowing the reaction of a stupid world he neither blamed nor pitied Stewart, but gave the warmest sympathy which an understanding man could offer.

Stewart's next call was the vicar who listened with a professional sympathy, and when the story was finished he sighed. He rose to his feet and slowly walked to the opened French windows: there was quite a considerable silence. Then he spoke. 'You remind me of that woman who lost her mite, and who swept and cleaned everywhere until she found it. Your story makes me think,' continued the vicar, 'of the man who lost his sheep and didn't know where to find it.' He lapsed into silence again, then strode about the room. It was now quite apparent that Stewart had entranced him with his modern illustration of an old and familiar text and, certain that no help was forthcoming in his search, Stewart made a muttered excuse to get away, and the vicar shook him warmly by the hand, thanking him with the utmost sincerity for his interesting visit, and dashing off to his study as soon as Stewart was safely on the other side of the front door. Stewart, hoping to have received a hint as to where he might look for his boswell, and going empty away, had time to reflect gloomily on his life, a life whch was altering radically since he had become obsessed with his search for his boswell. And though he himself was conscious of the change he was not, even now, aware of those small and trifling, or those more important, defections which other people were forced to remark on.

Stewart was a bachelor, a writer of repute, and a famous journalist. His novels and articles were widely read and appreciated, not only in that narrow world where good work is valued, but in that wider sphere of ordinary dull humanity where, in spite of the innumerable obstacles, brilliant work cannot fail to stand out. As a result of this, Stewart's financial position was a happy one, and he would have been able to indulge any whims if he had had any. But while he did not live austerely he certainly lived plainly, and far from hoarding his money he disposed of it readily to all who called in their need.

He lived with an aged couple and a dog as his only companions—that is, when he was at home. The old couple who attended to his needs acted, on the female side, as housekeeper, and on the male side as gardener and general factotum, and having experienced all the tribulations of professional domestic life they did not hesitate to say to all who might ask, that Stewart was the most considerate gentleman they had ever worked for. That was before he lost his boswell, and when the change occurred they could not understand it.

Stewart had always treated them as old and respected friends rather than hired retainers, and often conversed with them on many subjects. In the old carefree days, if the thought of the possibility of boswell-loss had presented itself to him, he would undoubtedly have discussed it with them, but it had not, and he didn't. Nor had he even mentioned that he possessed one at any time. Even more curious was the fact that now that he had lost it he never thought to tell them, and they, able to read only the largest newspaper headlines and listening only to a weekly broadcast service, neither saw, nor heard of, reports of the loss.

For the loss had strange effects on their lives.

Stewart, previously so punctilious in the matter of their weekly wage, now forgot to pay them, and although this lapse was glossed over with a smile when they ventured to ask for their money two weeks later, it was even more embarrassing to approach him on the second occasion when the wages were four weeks overdue. Then there were those odd sixpences and shillings which accumulated during the week when, for example, old Saunders nipped out to get stamps while Stewart was hurrying to finish his article, or when cigarettes were obtained under similar circumstances; money which normally Stewart always remembered to add to the weekly wage, but now, when he was forgetting everything, these small amounts added up to cause a financial embarrassment to the old couple who were not even receiving their wage. Stewart's dog, although unable by nature to voice his bewilderment, showed in his eyes the question which everyone was commencing to ask: What in heck has happened?

Indeed, the editor of the illustrious newspaper to which Stewart contributed his articles had this question very much in mind, for, noting the marked deterioration in quality in his noted contemporary's work, he was forced to omit it from its usual place, making some trivial excuse both to Stewart and to that wide public which, hitherto, had waited from one week to the other for it. Although Stewart's literary friends knew of the loss of his boswell, none of them—not even those who knew what a boswell was—connected his sad deterioration with his loss. Men shook their heads as they beheld the mighty fallen, but the editor, oddly enough, kept his faith, the reason being—though it has nothing to do with this story—that he had recently acquired a boswell himself, and he knew what a loss does entail.

After two months' fruitless search Stewart happened to meet the Member of Parliament for his area. The M.P., though he was aware from current club gossip that Stewart's influence was on the wane, treated his well-known constituent with friendliness and respect, knowing from bitter experience that the man who is laughed at today may be the leader tomorrow.

Partly because of his continued setbacks, partly because of the amazing ignorance he had encountered in the matter of boswells,

Stewart had determined to say nothing again about his loss to anyone, but encouraged by a friendly smile he opened the flood-gates of silence and poured out his soul in a manner quite out of keeping with his recent resolve. Ending his speech with a request for help, and receiving only silence in return, he hastily inquired—so accustomed was he now to ignorance in high places—whether the M.P. knew what a boswell was. You can judge therefore the overwhelming relief he experienced when the M.P. clapped him on the shoulder and said, 'Of course I know what boswells are!' But then he started to laugh, and he continued to laugh until the pain and surprise showing so plainly on Stewart's face caused him to desist. He took his famous constituent by the arm and they both sat down by the village pump. When his hilarity was sufficiently under control, the M.P. commenced to speak: 'Listen,' he began, 'you are pained at my amusement, and amazed at my knowledge. You forget that in my job I must know these things, if only to know how to deal with boswell owners both inside and outside the House. Not that there are any,' he added with a smile, 'inside the House.' He paused, his manner now most serious, and then went on: 'That Scotsman, that broadcaster from Cornwall, that dramatic critic have hindered your search, rather than helped, for, as you know only too well, your true boswell owner does not parade his possession in the disgusting manner in which they have advertised theirs under the guise of helping you. I, as an M.P., have to be able to recognize a true boswell owner—as you undoubtedly were—even in the absence of the pomp and circumstances which surrounds some of them. Although small in numbers your influence in current affairs is not to be neglected, and, consequently, I do not neglect it. Otherwise I would not hold my job. But when I have the rare opportunity of speaking to a man who has lost his boswell, and the even rarer chance to give advice, I find there is only one word I can conscientiously give.' He paused, and Stewart waited eagerly. 'That word,' continued the M.P., 'that word is *Don't*! Don't try to find it! You are better off without it. I *know*. Good-bye!'—and he was gone before Stewart had time to rally from the shock of this wicked advice.

To be engaged on a search which others call worthless, to value something which men of affairs regard as trifling, to have the faith necessary to counteract ridicule, demands qualities which Stewart was fast beginning to suspect that he did not possess. He went to his garden and, in a mood of black despair, picked up a fork and began to turn over some ground on the patch nearest to him. Having dug once across the breadth of the patch he realized that he was digging up recently planted roots, and he hastily endeavoured to cover them again before Saunders returned to his duties. He was not successful, and his henchman stood there regarding him with that superciliousness which all gardeners reserve for all other members of the human race who cannot differentiate between a spade and a fork, contenting himself with saying—when Stewart had finally finished—'They ought to be safe in now, sir.' But he added, with no trace of gardeners' inhumanity to man: 'There's a patch down there needs digging, sir, if you really want something to do.' Stewart sighed, wiped his forehead and replied with a trace of bitterness: 'It's no use: nothing I do goes right these days.' The gardener replied in a voice of unusual gentleness, 'And why is that, sir?' Stewart was well aware that his habit—his vice—of confiding to all and sundry must be curbed, but remembering with surprise that he had not confided in Saunders he once again told of his loss, and the curious effects it had produced. He was more than surprised when Saunders took out his pipe, lit it, and said very gently: 'So that's what it was! You lost your boswell.' Stewart asked why he had spoken in that manner. 'Well, rightly, I don't know,' answered the old man. 'In the first place, I didn't know you had one—though perhaps I ought—and that makes you a proper boswell owner.' Stewart asked: 'Why?' 'Because a proper boswell owner never speaks of his possession,' said the old man, echoing the words of the M.P. Stewart, thinking that he had perhaps overheard his earlier conversation, asked rather sharply: 'What do you know about boswells?' The gardener looked around carefully before he whispered the reply: 'I've got a boswell myself!' Anticipating Stewart's thought that it was a very expensive thing for a man in his position to have, he added: 'It came down to me in the family, sort of heirloom.' Stewart remarked that he was lucky to have got it that way, but expressed the view that there might be a danger that he did not value it as those who had got theirs the hard way valued theirs. The old man smiled: 'No danger of that,' he answered, 'not if you'd been brought up in my family.' Stewart then made his customary request for help, which the old man appeared not to hear, for after a time he said: 'I've known four people lose their boswells, but none of them ever found them because none of them would take advice.' Stewart replied with a touch of indignation that he would do anything to find his. 'That's what they all said,' replied the old man sadly, 'but when it comes down to it they don't.' 'Just tell me how to start,' pleaded Stewart, like a camel clutching at the last straw. 'I'll have to think about it,' said the old man quietly, 'and when I'm thinking, perhaps you'd care to dig that patch down the bottom there, so that I can start planting next week.' With yet another plea for the old man's help, Stewart took up his fork and walked off to a patch of ground that was so thickly covered with weeds that the prospect of making it look like brown earth again might easily have made his heart falter. But he went to work with a joyous spirit, glad because at last he had found someone who understood. Some hours he worked on that plot of ground; it had been neglected for years and the work involved was considerable. The old man sat down on the terrace, his pipe well lit, his brow placid in gentle contemplation. It was not long before Stewart, for the first time in eight weeks, had completely forgotten about boswells, so occupied was he with the problem of how to get deep weeds uprooted, what best to do with the rapidly accumulating pile of rubbish, and how best to light a garden fire. Soon he took his coat off, then his tie and collar, and he had just experienced the freedom of having his shirt off when there, to his astonishment, he saw his boswell! He ceased work at once and looked at it with deep emotion. Holding it carefully in his hands, he rushed back to the old man, crying out: 'I've found it! I've found it! Look!' With eyes tear-dimmed with joy and hands a-shake with excitement he showed it to the gardener, and the old man looked at it tenderly. He took his pipe from his mouth and said: 'Yes; mine's just like that—only not quite so decorative.'

D. J. WILLIAMS

A Good Year

Translated from the Welsh by Wyn Griffith

The rent of Pant y Bril was fifty shillings a year, and as Rachel relied upon a calf to provide the money, the day the cow calved was one of the great days of her year: not the greatest of all, for that honour fell to the day of sale. Once only did the cow fail her, and it took the best part of her life to recover from that disaster.

She talked so much about the price she hoped to get that the neighbours—some of them owning many calves—could almost reckon their profit or loss for the year according to the price of Rachel's calf. If she got fifty-two and six, it would be a good year and everyone paid his way; fifty-five shillings meant a year of prosperity, and some unexpected weddings. But if the bargain were struck on Rachel's small hard hand at forty-seven and six, a lean year followed, and if the price fell as low as forty-five shillings, it was high time to hold a service of intercession.

Rachel pondered deeply upon these matters as she knit her stocking in the garden immediately after dinner, the fleeting warmth of an April day quickening her ruddy complexion. Her dog, Cora, with her tail curled into a small yellow ring on her back, sniffed here and there, finding more delight in this riot of smells than in the scraps of dinner she had just finished. Spring and its magic were in the air: wherever she looked, Rachel saw young growth, on currant bush, gooseberry, and the red rose climbing up the house. She looked at it all, this miracle of sudden birth, as if she saw it for the first time, unconsciously drawing it all into her own life. Could she hope for spring in herself, or must she dwell for ever in that long autumn that cut short the summer of her youth, fifteen years ago, when she was left a childless widow mourning the gentlest of husbands? Fifteen years of hard scraping for food, of sacrifice of body and of soul. She had made the best of it, in spite of lapses. But had not King David himself sinned and repented and found forgiveness, as the preacher said on Sunday? And now she felt so cheerful and contented, untroubled by her past, that she knew that her sins were forgiven her.

She glanced at her clothes: a short white shawl on her shoulders, a well-ironed check apron neatly pleated, and her brightly-shining shoes. Before coming out, she had looked into her mirror and found that the crowsfeet under her eyes were less noticeable than usual. In the gentle warmth of the day, with young life budding round her and permeating the world, she felt ten years younger.

A moment later her mind went back to the sermon, and she blushed a little, without knowing exactly why. And then came another impulse, equally inexplicable, to return to the house for her coarse apron and her clogs and to clean the pigsty. None too soon, as she had noticed in the morning when she fed the pig. But before she made up her mind, a gruff voice greeted her over the garden gate and startled her, and she turned cold and virtuous within.

'And how's my bonny today?' The words came thickly, with a beery richness. 'Here I am again.... I'll buy your calf from you.'

'I might have known that this lump of a fellow would turn up,' said Rachel to herself as she tried to hide behind a currant bush, and her eyes fell guiltily upon her neat black shoes.

'Ah-ha! Playing hide and seek, my pretty? Let's have a look at you ... aren't we grand today? Just look at her!' said Tim as he placed his elbows on the bar of the gate. He knew well enough that he commanded the garden, and he thought of the gold that lay snugly in the long grey purse in his trouser pocket. A cunning rogue, turning up each spring, long before the snowdrops, to inquire into the fate of the first-born calf.

'I'm not selling the calf this year, to you or anybody else,' said Rachel. She had been forced to leave the shelter of the currant bushes, and her anger had driven the blood to her cheeks. 'Clear off.... I'm finished with you!'

'Did you ever hear the like? Going to retire and live on your means like Griffiths Tŷ Sych, I suppose! But maybe you're going to rear him ... Rachel Ifans, Pant y Bril, Mark One X Bull!' Tim roared with laughter at his own joke.

'You fool! It isn't a bull calf, and as the cow's getting old, I'm going to rear it.'

'I don't know about the cow,' said Tim, his small black eyes twinkling dangerously. 'I know you're getting younger each year. Let's have a look at your new shoes ... let me see if they fit properly. And I want to see how you got those pleats in your apron,' he added as he tried clumsily to open the gate.

'If you come one step nearer, I'll set the dog on you!' shouted Rachel. But Cora was too intent upon her own business in the hedge even to protect her mistress.

'No use calling Cora ... she knows me well enough,' said Tim. 'Come, my beauty, let's have a squint at your calf. We'll strike a bargain soon enough.' He nodded his head towards the cowhouse.

Suddenly a clod of earth flew past him, followed by a second and a third.

'Just you dare to come here again until I send for you, you scoundrel,' shouted Rachel, ablaze with righteous indignation. And Tim, cunning as he was, saw that he was on the wrong tack this time. He retreated, mumbling to himself about the strange ways of women.

As soon as she saw that he had gone, Rachel went into the house, relieved at her success in casting Satan out of the garden, but weeping a little in her excitement. Sitting by the fire, she succeeded even in conquering that uneasy conscience which had pricked her ever since last Sunday's sermon. But in her joy she forgot that the devil is never so dangerous as in defeat; before the warmth of her gratitude had cooled, new thoughts began to stir. A vision of Tim, dark and ungainly, striding up the lane with the soil falling about his ears. She began to laugh riotously at the thought that a slip of a creature like herself had sent him flying. What would the neighbours say?

But after all, why should they know? Many worse than he, all said and done, although his tongue was as rough as his beard. But he had no right to comment on the fact that she was wearing her best shoes ... she wore them for her own pleasure, not for his. If he came back that night—as he might well do, for he never bought a beast without going away once or twice or even thrice, to screw down the price by a few coppers—if he returned, she'd salt him well in the matter of money.

The lamp was on the table, and Rachel sat meditating in the dusk. Perhaps she had been over-hasty and had missed her market: the rent was long overdue. Suddenly she was roused by noises in the cow-house. Walking along the passage from the kitchen to the stalls, she saw Tim feeling the calf's ribs. The calf arched his back in gratitude.

'Not a bad calf, Rachel, I must say,' said Tim as he came out, ignoring the events of the afternoon.

'He's all right, but his price is beyond you,' Rachel replied significantly.

'Come now, don't be awkward. Tell me your price and we'll make a deal of it. It's getting late, and I've a long way to go.'

'No need for you to have come back,' said Rachel briskly.

'Don't waste time. I know you're dying to get rid of the calf ... you wouldn't have slept tonight if I hadn't turned up. Seeing it's you, I'll give you fifty shillings.'

Rachel was surprised at his opening bid. 'I won't get forty for it,' he continued, 'not after I've dragged it twenty miles to Carmarthen fair next Saturday ... not a chance.'

'Fifty-five,' she answered stiffly.

'Tell you what I'll do ... we'll split. Give me half a crown and a cup of tea.... I've a great thirst on me.'

'Fifty-five,' said Rachel obstinately. 'And not a penny will I bate even if you stay the night.'

'No, no ... never mind the half-crown. A cup of tea is all I want.'

'You're talking nonsense,' she replied.

They haggled long over the remaining half-crown, although Rachel was anxious to close.

'Since you're so obstinate, you can have your half-crown,' said Tim, tired of it all. 'Give me your hand, and we'll close it on fifty-five.'

She snatched her hand away.

'You and your dirty tricks . . . fifty-five? I said sixty-five all along. Fifty-five, indeed!' She laughed into his face and ran back into the house.

'You fool,' she continued, holding the door half open. 'If you hadn't been so cheeky about my best shoes, you'd have had the calf for fifty shillings, and luck-money as well. Did you think I put my best clothes on because you were coming?'

'Heaven alone knows,' Tim replied.

'I know well enough, I'm telling you. And it's my turn now . . . you can have the calf for sixty, and maybe I'll throw in a cup of tea. Make up your mind quickly before I shut the door.'

'You can keep you calf till his horns grow through the roof,' said Tim.

She slammed the door.

Tim had not gone far before he was caught in a heavy shower. He turned up the collar of his coat and took shelter beneath a holly tree, his mind in a turmoil: angry with Rachel for fooling him, still more angry with himself. The sky darkened and the wet clouds raced. More rain to come. On his right, long miles of cross-country trudging over moor and marsh. On his left, an arm of lamplight reaching out towards him and the rain falling across it. There was Rachel in her clean apron and her bright new shoes that cost her so much, laying the table for tea. Pride, Avarice and Ambition struggled within him as the rain poured down upon his head.

Suddenly he heard the click of the door-latch, and a wide shaft of light penetrated through the rain. He saw Rachel peering into the dark, her hand shading her eyes.

'Three pounds is a terrible price to pay for a wee thing like that,' said Avarice.

They still talk of it as the most prosperous year the country ever knew.

GERAINT GOODWIN

The White Farm

He walked on to the little veranda and sniffed the morning breeze. It had become a rite now—on these days of holiday—the clear air off the sea, off the mountains, always seemed better in the early morning. But this morning it really was good, he thought. Inland, there was the clear-cut freshness of the mountainside, the fields all marked out and clear in their colours, and just a circle of mist, like a frill of steam, around the summits.

He took two or three deep breaths and heaved audibly. He was a big man, with a heavy aggressive jaw, his face very brown, and his brow, which reached up through the thin hair, blistered with sun and the salt water. His eyes were blue and sure, and faintly contemptuous, and his hands large and clumsy.

He stood there on the little veranda, leaning against the door and watching his wife, very small and trim, shaking her dark hair back as she busied herself with the oil cooker, a white apron about her, and the little waist tied with a large bow. The small delicate movements of her, the large anxious eyes for ever fearful, always moved him.

He went over to her and put his big hands on her shoulders.

'What about today?' he said briefly.

She did not look up at him: instead, she slipped free and went on with the cooking. They were up late and she was not quite herself.

'Where?' she asked over her shoulder.

'Pant what-you-call it,' he said, peeved. '*You* know.'

'If you like,' she said in the same matter-of-fact tone.

'If *you* like,' he went on. His heavy face went childish in his sulk. But he was going to humour her. He felt that he owed her something.

'But you've got the game!' she said turning to him.

'That can wait,' he replied in the same peremptory way. 'They're nobody, anyhow,' he explained.

'But you promised,' she insisted.

'Did I? I said that I *might* make up a foursome.'

'Oh,' she said. 'That's different.'

'After all,' he went on magnanimously, 'I've got a wife.'

She did not answer, but turned to the stove again with a little shrug.

'It's not much fun for you . . . I know,' he said. He caught her by the shoulders again. 'My pretty one!'

She bowed her head on her breasts like a drooping bird. He felt uncomfortable, the words muddling him.

'My little one,' he said again in the same tentative way. He squeezed her shoulders until she winced.

'Oh, leave me alone!' she cried out.

He went out on the veranda again. Perhaps, after all, it was his fault. But then, he told himself, they were on holiday, and after all a man was a man. But he was worried all the same. And yet things could be different. If only he had a square deal. That was the phrase always on his lips—a square deal. He wanted to know where he was—and where the other person was. Then they could get down to things. That had been the secret of his success—and he had been successful. He was hard, as he said, but always fair. Up North, he would explain, they were made like that.

But had he had a square deal, now, in the ever-present, from his wife? He wondered—he had begun to wonder more and more. He did not like to think that he had not—but he wondered. And now, at the end of a year of marriage, they were farther apart than at the beginning. They were not drifting apart so much, as they *were* apart. And was it his fault? It was not that they had ever been together—her little world was like herself, so small and tender and wisp-like: for ever proof against his loud and obvious heartiness. It was like hammering on a closed door and blustering on the step: and there, beyond, was the quiet and the mystery.

And yet she loved him—there was no doubt about that. He had swept her off her feet and she had never found them again: the heavy aggressive sense of him, the I-am-what-I-am triumphant had, at first, bewildered and then captivated her. He was not sure how it had all come about, but he guessed it. And he continued to play his trump card—his only card—in the hope that things would right themselves. But it was up to him to give the lead—he felt that it would always be up to him to give the lead.

'Feeling better?' he said, when he went in. He gathered her in his arms but she turned her head away. Then he lifted up her chin. He knew how to humour her in his clumsy way.

'We'll be off in no time,' he said unctuously.

He went out into the sand-swept garden, with its line of sea thistles tossing, and tore the tarpaulin off the big saloon car. Then he began to tinker about with the engine, and then went round with a duster like an old maid dusting.

Within an hour they had started. He knew that it had to be done sometimes—this journey to her father's people up in the mountains. The Welsh were funny people—they got something out of it, this journey to the old folks at home, even if the home were a hovel. And as they all had a home somewhere, they would all have to go back to it. Well—if it amused them! But the old man—he was a wealthy London-Welsh draper—was more Welsh than she was, and he seemed to care very little, for he spent his time at the bowling tournament at Eastbourne. A funny lot!

They had climbed beyond the little village but stopped once on the road to look back on it. In the summer sun it had come alight —just like a lot of broken china cups thrown on the shingle, and beyond it the blue fringe of sea running off into a haze. But that was the old village, with its one straight street and its white houses. Joined on it, like a fungus on an old bole, was the new part, with its modern red-tiled bungalows with their cream stucco sides. Beyond again, was the golf links which reached right down to the sand-hills, blown up in a bulwark against the tides, the clumps of rushes white in the sun like scrubbed hair. The moist sour-green earth spread down to the *morfa* (the marsh) which lay inland. The land was all green, with the light burnt crust of sand as a ridge, and the washed smudge of sea and sky stretching into the distance—the whole stretch of Cardigan Bay cupped within its two arms, far in the south, far in the north.

'There they go,' he said, tracing his finger through the window.

She had sat huddled in the front seat, her mind gone off.

'That's them,' he said again, breaking into the quiet. 'That's old Wilkie—over there on the fifth tee. There now—he's driving.'

He looked at his wife sideways, the little core of resentment in him hardening.

'You're not going to get all het up again?' he asked.

'Why—of course not.'

'I said, that's old Wilkie.'

'Well! I saw.'

'That's about all,' he said, slipping into gear. It was not worth troubling about. But his friends were her friends.

'A bit bleak,' he said, after a while. They had left the main road and the lane went off over the gently swelling mountain, two parallel ruts sluiced with storm water which lay around in pools. Sometimes the track was half cluttered up with shale, sometimes the surface was worn through to the bare rock. Around about, the mountains rolled up in a gentle sweep with the mist lifting above them. Now and again there was a house, with the few wind-blown firs about it as shelter, its white, wet sides shining in the sun, and the bare yard with a white-eyed dog skulking, and the waddling geese.

'Oh, John,' she begged. 'Do stop.'

He braked hard, with a faint smile of amusement at her urgency. He liked doing this for her. She got out of the car and ran off through the wet heather and stood up on a mound, her breast heaving.

'Better now,' she said, as she took her place. Her eyes were alight and dancing, and her lips wide open. He felt the load come off him. She excited him in the old way, so light and fresh in her young beauty, the poise and delight of her and the light in her face. She was something to be desired, as he first desired her—would always desire her. The rest was not there—had not happened.

He put his arm round her shoulder and crushed her to him.

'Not now,' she said, slipping free.

'Right,' he said, his mind reaching out at an infinite promise. 'A bargain!'

They had come to the brow of the last hill. Below them the road dropped into a *cwm*. A torrent tumbled over the mountain into it, swilling through the heather, leaping down into a spume of silver. And there, below them, was the house, standing out of the earth, with its upblown smoke curling up to them, and the pandemonium of barking dogs and the geese shrieking. It had all suddenly come to life.

A man was on the little trellis bridge, shouting. The dogs running up and down the track cowered down on their bellies and crawled back to him.

'*Uffern dân! Hei! Siân, Meg . . .*' he shouted.

'That's uncle,' she said, the words strung in her excitement. 'He won't know me: he won't know me. Now for fun!'

The old man came up to the car as it stopped. He had a round, full face, red with the weather, a grey fringe to it. It seemed hewn out in its angularity, and yet there was a light in it—a hardly distinguishable, distant gleam. And yet that was the face. The eyes were very blue and steadfast, and there seemed no end to them in their distance. He seemed always to be calling himself back as he spoke.

'The dogs will be barking,' he explained. 'Do not you mind them.'

He picked his words with great deliberation. But they were not sure whether he had seen them—his gently roving eyes had gone off again into the distance.

'*Dewch yma Sian!*' he shouted in a sudden roar. An old black sheepdog in the pack had gone slinking up for a furtive snap. Now she dropped on her paws and rolled her eyes up, her old head shaking in ecstacy. '*Beth sydd arno chi fach?*' he went on, sounding his voice as the old head rocked.

'She just come,' he went on. 'Her mister *wedi marw*—die, how you say? No teeth . . . see?' He opened her jaws.

'She obeys you?' said the husband.

'Oh, yess,' he explained. 'You know how? I tell you. You get a bit of cheese, see, and put it under your arm. Then after long time you give it her. Never go after! A bitch, see—a bitch like that.'

'Wants a master,' said the husband, helping him out.

'Oh—I won't say.' He put up his hands with mock horror. The laughter filled his face like a brimming jug.

'Don't tell lies,' the woman said in Welsh, laughing outright.

The old man never moved, but he turned his eyes on her, as though bringing them out of the distance.

'*Cymraes?*' (A little Welsh girl?) he said in the same even voice.

'A Japanese *really*!'

'Tut, tut!'

The young man stood and watched his wife in wonder. The tilted face, impenitent, and the laughing eyes. She went bubbling on like a spring. The two went on in their cross-talk, the old man, out of deference to him, still labouring in English.

'I'll be going,' he said. He got out his rod and flung his basket over his shoulders. 'I'll follow the brook up,' he added in parting. 'Don't worry.'

The old man watched him go, his face hardening. It was not polite. And yet his going had eased it as between them. It was as if a shadow had lifted.

'Softie! *Yr hen softie!* I'm Dilys,' she said.

'Dilys! Wili's Dilys?'

She burst out laughing.

'You are a funny one.' He caught her by the arm and led her in.

'Well, well.' He said no more, his face beaming.

Beside the old hearth he said casually: 'Take your seat.' She belonged. The hard-reached deference had gone out of his voice. He gave the peat fire a stir with the poker and moved the kettle across the spit.

'Well, well,' he said again. He spoke in Welsh now, his voice dropping to the homely familiar note.

'*Mam*,' he called. '*Mam*.'

The old woman came in, her thin spindle body bent across, an old shawl over her shoulders. Her eyes were very quick and bright in the old worn face—only her eyes, thin and bright, for ever hovering.

'Here she is,' he said.

The old woman shuffled across and peered at her. '*Fach*,' she said, putting her arms around her. 'Oh, the little dear.'

She reached her feet into the fender and leaned back into the old horsehair chair. The worn old house possessed her—the brass harness round about, the old dresser with its line on line of blue china plate, the rich earth smell of the peat. That fire had never been out for two hundred years, her father had always told her. And here it was! And all around, through the little tight shut windows, was the moist green of the mountain, reaching up like a shelf, and the distant rumble of the brook.

Pant-y-Pistyll—the Hollow of the Spring. Always the drifting mist, for ever lifting, and the noise of the water, the sharp high tinkle to the deep, harsh earth-flooded roar of the winter: the green earth, the smell of peat and the high blue crust of the mountain—that was her home, her father's home, and that was where she belonged. She let it all possess her, gave herself up to it, as to a lover. She had gone away from herself, far, far away. Now she was—only now she was: never before, perhaps never again, but now she was.

'Oh, *Nain*' (grandmother), she said. She threw her arms around the old woman and bent her head in the old shawl.

'There, there,' said the old woman, brushing back her hair with her old withered hands. She pressed her to her old breasts and crooned to her as to a child, taking the deep, breaking sobs to herself.

'The old *hiraeth*' (longing), she said to her son, standing beside them. The old mother waved him away. He went out into the yard.

When she came out again, her eyes red and fresh, he was standing there, just as she had first seen him. Beyond him, across the brook, was the little chapel, small and grey and silent, and around it was the little wall of piled stones, lurching up against the weather, a tiny yellow sprinkle of stonecrop spilt across it. Tied on the gate was a little tin offertory box that rattled in the wind. Beyond, the grey stone slabs stood up on end among the lank grass. That and the farm were the only buildings for miles: beyond the land ran off into the mountain.

'It's time your father came back,' he said.

She bowed her head.

'Never mind,' he said gaily. 'Plenty of time. You tell him we are still here.'

They had walked beyond the little graveyard to the lush hay-field. At the bottom was the river running down the valley in a brown fresh: the little brook leapt to meet it.

'Where is Morlais?' she asked.

He pointed over the sheep-walk on the mountain. 'He can't go far now,' he pointed to his hip. 'A horse kick him. Pity—ay, indeed. A strong chap too.'

He shook his head, destroying the memory of his son's hurt.

'You were only little things—last time,' he said. 'Hair down your back.'

'Fifteen years,' she said.

'Sure to be.' He looked into the distance and nodded.

'You made a house to play,' he said, 'out of the old wall.'

'Down there,' he went on, pointing.

She followed his finger. The old stones were still trailed about the field.

'Awful mess that house,' he said, wagging his head. 'So *serious*, you two.'

'Fun!' she said savagely. She could not see through the cloud of tears. She twisted and untwisted her glove and turned her head away.

'You'll be waiting for Morlais?' he asked.

'No!' she cried out.

'Pity. He'll be that sorry.'

'We must get back,' she said, a note of terror in her voice. She ran into the field in her anguish, the wet grass to her waist. The old man followed her.

'Take time: take time,' he called gently. 'No *great* hurry.'

He went on up the river calling, leaving her alone. She stood there beside the water. Years ago she and Morlais had gone off to look for its source. They never found it: they never would find it. It had no beginning as it had no end. She remembered and yet she could not remember. It was so long ago.

The water went by in a fresh, lightless and gleaming, and then beyond her through the gorge which led out to the sea; it went by her, strangely dark and gleaming, with the tufts of foam swilling down its centre in a long white line. And all above it were the hills, heavy and brooding, the little sheep clamped on to them, bleating forlornly, and the sky with no light to it. The ancient heavy sense of it possessed her again, the timeless glimpse of it. She stood there in the wonder of it, unmoving.

'Gone to sleep?' It was her husband behind her. She had not heard them return.

'Isn't she a funny one?' he said to her uncle, in a way of explanation. He was hot and excited with his sport by the brook-side.

'You *must* go?' asked her uncle, dropping his eyes to her, strangely still and steady.

'I must,' she said.

'Yes,' he said. 'Perhaps so. Tell your dad. Plenty of time...' He waved his hand upwards. He nodded in the old ancient way of his.

As they roared up the hill from the house, she saw him standing there, his dogs about him, his wide open face lifted.

PR8966.E5 C6 1992 CU-Main

Elis, Islwyn Ffowc./Classic Welsh short stories /

3 9371 00041 0670

PR 8966 .E5 C6 1992

Classic Welsh short stories

DATE DUE			
MAR 3 1 1997			

CONCORDIA UNIVERSITY LIBRARY
2811 NE Holman St.
Portland, OR 97211-6099